NOT YET

Liz looked ready to bolt. Without giving her any warning, John pulled her into his arms and lowered his lips to place a swift peck on hers. But what started out as a brief thank you turned into something more as he felt the soft contact and tasted the sweetness that was Liz.

So he tried for more. He ran the tip of his tongue against the seam of her mouth. Coaxing. Tempting. But she did not open for him.

She wasn't ready. He felt a tremble run through her body . . .

BOOK YOUR PLACE ON OUR WEBSITE AND MAKE THE READING CONNECTION!

We've created a customized website just for our very special readers, where you can get the inside scoop on everything that's going on with Zebra, Pinnacle and Kensington books.

When you come online, you'll have the exciting opportunity to:

- View covers of upcoming books
- Read sample chapters
- Learn about our future publishing schedule (listed by publication month *and author*)
- Find out when your favorite authors will be visiting a city near you
- Search for and order backlist books from our online catalog
- Check out author bios and background information
- Send e-mail to your favorite authors
- Meet the Kensington staff online
- Join us in weekly chats with authors, readers and other guests
- Get writing guidelines
- AND MUCH MORE!

**Visit our website at
http://www.kensingtonbooks.com**

Irene Peterson

Glory Days

ZEBRA BOOKS
KENSINGTON PUBLISHING CORP.
www.kensingtonbooks.com

ZEBRA BOOKS are published by

Kensington Publishing Corp.
850 Third Avenue
New York, NY 10022

All Kensington titles, imprints, and distributed lines are available at special quantity discounts for bulk purchases for sales promotion, premiums, fund-raising, educational, or institutional use.

Special book excerpts or customized printings can also be created to fit specific needs. For details, write or phone the office of the Kensington Special Sales Manager: Attn. Special Sales Department. Kensington Publishing Corp., 850 Third Avenue, New York, NY 10022. Phone: 1-800-221-2647.

Zebra and the Z logo Reg. U.S. Pat. & TM Off.

ISBN 0-8217-8010-7

First Printing: February 2006
10 9 8 7 6 5 4 3 2 1

Printed in the United States of America

To H. Roy, Elyse, and Karyn,
Mom and the real Bourbon John.

Chapter 1

"Too . . . early."

John slapped the alarm clock off the nightstand and pulled himself back onto the pillows. Still dark as pitch outside. The only light came from the red 6:00 of the damned clock. He used to have a big fish tank that glowed blue all night long. Great for sex, as he remembered, until some dimwit in the throes of passion tossed her stiletto heel at it. It hit just right and speared a hole directly in the intake tube, dislodging it. Fish water spewed throughout his apartment. End of fish—quiet, floaty little things that never did anyone any harm—and end of peaceful blue light. The only gurgling sounds he heard now were from his stomach.

Another loud buzz. Not the clock. The door? His or downstairs? The incessant off-key droning through his brain forced him awake. He cursed.

Three days of surveillance without more than a couple of catnaps and he'd managed three hours' sleep. And now some idiot couldn't keep his hand off the doorbell?

This was somebody's lucky day.

He'd locked up his Sig.

Raking his fingers through his hair, John eased

himself out of the bed and made his way naked through the office to the frosted glass door. With perverse pleasure, he flipped the lock and yanked it open.

Nobody there.

And he was awake.

A shower might help, but the thought of getting wet so early in the morning irritated his cat DNA. After coffee would be soon enough. He did take the time to pick a towel off the bathroom floor and wrap it around his waist before venturing downstairs for caffeine. He needed coffee.

Badly.

Zanetti's luncheonette didn't officially open until ten on Sunday. Old Mrs. Zanetti, his landlady, usually had a fresh batch of coffee steaming away in the huge commercial brewing machine . . . not one of those sissy cappuccino makers, but real, one hundred percent Brazilian coffee with enough caffeine to clear his brain. He was welcome downstairs at any time, she'd told him since he moved in. And today he needed about a quart of black coffee to get his brain functioning.

He opened the connecting door, inhaling the fragrance of liquid intelligence. Mrs. Zanetti slept late, sometimes, but always got the coffee brewing before six. He reckoned she was in her apartment getting dressed—not allowing his brain to venture any further—and would come out if she heard him moving around the spotless stainless steel kitchen, so he hitched up the towel, just to be sure. The stacked cups called to him. She'd left a spoon and sugar packets on the counter, as she did every day. Two little packages of dairy lightener . . . whatever the hell that was . . . next to the spoon. This was new.

John pulled the handle and watched the coffee fill his cup. He paused, letting the perfume fill his nostrils, then turned to find a woman with a huge kitchen knife in her hand, standing ten feet away.

Liz barely had time to toss her suitcase on the saggy bed when she heard odd noises coming from the kitchen. Her grandmother shouldn't be walking around, fussing over getting breakfast for her when she was perfectly capable of making something for herself. But Flo was Flo and nothing, not even gout, could stop her.

As she rounded the corner, Liz stopped dead. This wasn't her grandmother rummaging in the kitchen. It was a naked man. A big, nicely built naked man with his back to her. Great shoulders. Whoa! This wasn't good, was it?

Think quick.

Her eyes searched for a weapon. The kitchen knives lay on the counter, washed and ready to use. She snaked out her hand and grabbed one, hefting it defensively against her chest.

He turned and started.

"Ah, shit!" He flinched, spilling coffee over his hand, sending hot liquid to the floor and his bare feet. He danced in place for a few seconds.

Liz saw great humor in the situation but maintained her cool.

"What the hell do you think you're doing?" Just the right amount of calculated heartlessness to scare off a guy wearing a tattered towel that covered not much more territory than a Speedo.

"Getting coffee, like I always do. Jesus, you scared me." He stepped away from the puddle. "Where's Flo?"

"Never mind where she is," Liz snarled. "Who the hell are you?"

Suddenly his expression mellowed as if he thought the threat was gone. "I'm her tenant, John Preshin. I live upstairs."

Giving him the once over, Liz took in his height and thick, dark hair that looked straight off the pillow. Nice. She saw his blue eyes twinkle as he returned her gaze, but as her inspection went a little lower, she got a real surprise. Something was stuck to his chest. Duct tape?

She worked hard to hold in a laugh. "You always come down here naked?"

His smile widened, showing nice teeth and making it very hard for Liz to keep up the don't-mess-with-me demeanor.

"Only on Sundays. This must be your lucky day."

That got the snort it deserved. But Liz lowered the knife, her eyes going back to the ridiculous Z of duct tape across his well-muscled hairy chest.

"Had a visit from Zorro last night?" she asked offhandedly.

The man, nonchalant as all get out, leaned one hand back on the counter and sipped from the cup. His eyes closed in obvious appreciation, but when they opened, they blinked down at the duct tape. He resumed his pose as if he had the silvery stuff stuck on his chest every day of the week. Yeah, right.

"Let me get back to you on that," he grinned.

And totally disarmed her for a second.

"Anything else we can offer you?" Liz struggled to hold in the smirk that wanted to come out.

"Doughnuts aren't in yet?"

What nerve! "Not yet. Shall I call you when they are?"

"If you don't mind . . ." His voice was deep and husky and dangerous.

Liz stepped back, denying the tiny thrill that spiked through her. "What kind do you like? And are you gonna clean up that mess on the floor?"

He reached across the counter, grabbed a wad of paper towels and bent to wipe the spill, showing far more of his anatomy than Liz had been prepared to see. Yet she couldn't take her eyes off the sight.

With that audacious grin plastered on his lips, John Preshin from upstairs stood, tossed the wet mess into the garbage and slowly padded past Liz toward the back stairs.

"Jelly," he whispered as he passed her.

The heat of his breath played on her neck and a chill sizzled up her spine, leaving her speechless. All she could do was nod and put down the knife.

Perhaps this day wasn't going to be so bad after all, he mused as he swallowed the last of the coffee and headed for the bedroom. A redhead. Hmm. He liked redheads, but then, he liked good-looking females of any shape or style. This one was gutsy, he had to admit, and he'd seen the subtle approval in her eyes as she scoped him out. Never failed once he turned on the charm, unless it was with wise guys who didn't get his natural magnetism.

Or jerks with high-powered rifles.

He shut the thought away, crawled back into bed and felt sleep overtake him with gentle feminine hands.

The additional hour's sleep revived him enough to entertain thoughts of a shower. With a burp from pipes old enough to have voted for Roosevelt—Teddy, not Franklin—he waited for the water to heat. Cooler would be better, but John Preshin was no martyr. Not this morning.

As he stepped into the shower, the tepid water brought gooseflesh to his body and he shivered. At least something about him worked correctly this morning. Bit by bit as he scraped the soap across his skin, he remembered pieces of last night's drama after he'd located his quarry and tagged the guy for sure. Investigation over. So he'd allowed the bleached blonde to pick him up. She'd slithered against him and practically given him a handjob on the barstool after he'd bought her a martini.

There hadn't been enough caffeine in his Coke to keep him awake long enough to satisfy either of them but he'd left and gotten back to the office before crashing completely.

The tape puzzled him. After a one-night stand, had she marked him with her initial? What kind of crazy woman did a thing like that?

One best forgotten.

Not like that rash redhead downstairs. He knew she'd be something else.

As the water trickled down his body, he scrubbed at the puckered scar on his shoulder, gritting his teeth against the obscenely wrinkled flesh. From beyond the shower curtain, a different pounding began, not in the pipes this time. Somewhere outside, maybe in the street. Maybe a jackhammer trying to break through glass. It registered. His door.

"Keep your shirt on," he bellowed as he turned off the water, grabbed a towel and, soaking wet, wrapped it around his hips. These inappropriate interruptions were part of the trouble of living in his office.

He shook the water from his hair, took one quick, futile tug at the duct tape, stifled a scream and stomped through his inner office, bent on opening the door and giving major grief to whoever kept threatening to break the glass.

"What the hell do you want?" John threw open the door, startling the two people on the other side.

One he recognized. Cop named Stoffel, a sluggish ape of a man wearing a blue Asbury Park uniform jacket and all the rest. His swarthy face cracked into a smirk though his eyes moved quickly, scoping out the scene of John in all his near-naked glory. Just like any other cop. Behind him, a kid. A kid wearing an enormous nylon jacket emblazoned with some sort of logo, black watch cap and baggy jeans.

"What?"

Stoffel took a step back, eyeing John up and down with a malicious sneer that made John's returning good humor go sour all over again.

"This your kid?"

A negative stopped short of his teeth. Something required thought here. A kid. What was up?

"Dunno. Let me see."

The cop grabbed a handful of oversize jacket and pulled the kid from behind him so John could take a look.

"What makes you think it's mine?"

Stoffel snorted. "Caught him in the RexAll about to make off with some items. When I asked him for ID, he said he was Carl Preshin. Father was John Preshin, maybe I knew of you."

John kept his face and voice neutral. "And as luck would have it, you did."

The cop leaned closer, so close John could smell the coffee on his breath. A slight trace of powdered sugar dusted one corner of the cop's mouth. "I think this makes us even."

For what? John grunted. "Yeah."

"Now teach him it ain't polite to steal."

Reaching out, John caught the kid's shoulder and pulled him past the large man's blockade of his door. "I'll do that."

Stoffel tugged at the visor of his cop hat, gave a snicker as he once again eyed the duct tape and dripping wet private eye and left them. His control didn't last more than ten feet down the dingy hall. Doughnut-breath would have some tale for the boys back in Central.

Slamming the door didn't do wonders for John's brand new headache. He grabbed the kid and hustled him into the reception area.

"What gives?"

The kid looked up for the first time. Heavily lashed big blue eyes, wide with fear, looked back at John. "I didn't take anything."

"Jesus!" He snatched the cap off the kid's head, revealing short, spiky black hair with tips of blood red stuck against a pale face.

Panic made him reach for his ancient trench coat on the nearby coat tree. He fumbled to get it on, but he was wide awake now.

"You're a girl!"

Her eyelids lowered as she turned away slightly, and stepped back, out of reach. "No shit, Sherlock."

John raised his hand to scratch the hair on his chest, stopped it in midair.

"It says on the door that you do 'discreet investigations.'"

"That's right." He groped, one-handed without effect, at the buttons on the coat.

The girl dug into the pocket of her jacket. Holding out a crumpled bill, she said, "I'm hiring you to find my father."

He shook his head. "Nope."

Her challenging expression fell, replaced by one of weariness and defeat. "Why not?"

John scrubbed at his face again. "I can't enter into a contract with a minor. Especially a runaway. My advice—go home to your mother. She left him, probably for a good reason. Living with him won't be any better, believe me." He made to escort her to the door.

Hands on hips, fire in her eyes, the girl thrust the bill toward him again. "It's a hundred. A C-note. That's a lotta money." Her eyes scanned the dowdy office. "Looks like you could use the bucks."

"Go home to your mother, kid. Tell the new boyfriend to leave you alone, stay out of his way, and talk to the school guidance counselor. I can't help you."

Her chin went up and her eyes focused on him, daring him, wordlessly pushing. Then she turned her head and shot him a look that scorched his heart.

"I have no mother. I have no one in this world. What I do have, though, is a list of six names, any one of whom could be my father."

The words seeped into his brain, slowly, unaided by sufficient caffeine or aspirin. Without thought, his one eyebrow raised.

A tight smile curled the corner of her mouth.

"Your name, John Preshin, is at the top."

Chapter 2

"Wait here. Don't move. I gotta go downstairs for a minute, but I'll be right back." John pointed at the kid. "We'll discuss this as soon as I get back."

Without waiting for a response, John pulled the raincoat around him and tightened the belt. It was still early. Mrs. Zanetti probably wouldn't be in the kitchen to catch him in this bizarre attire, but he didn't want to risk scaring the old lady.

His bare feet made little noise on the rough wooden stairs, but a blast of cold air coming in through the space underneath the outside door made his nipples pucker against the damned duct tape. The tape tugged chest hairs out of his skin and he cursed. He needed more coffee.

Mrs. Zanetti's voice rang out from the back room. "Is that you, John?"

Relief came at the sound. "Yeah, Flo, it's me."

"Come on back."

John waited. No redhead in sight. Too bad.

Flo Zanetti had been a dancer in her early years. Her apartment overflowed with memorabilia from her glory days . . . head shots, faded feather head-dresses from costumes from long ago. A big old black piano stood against the far wall of her living room, covered with sheet music. The light straining through the flimsy curtains turned everything golden . . . even Flo herself, sitting in the faded chintz armchair by the window.

Her foot rested on a hassock, swathed in elastic bandages. Looked as if her regal ailment had flared up again. She motioned for him to come closer and shut the door.

"I see you had a bad night," she observed, the amusement flashing in her light blue eyes. "What's with the trench coat? You playing at being a spy?"

John looked down and saw the coat had come open. He pulled it over himself and felt the heat rise in his face. He was too old for this inquisition, but he liked Flo and knew she would burst out laughing if she saw that damned duct tape.

"Well, you know how it is," he drawled. And laughed.

She laughed along with him. "John, there's someone I want you to meet. Liz, come out here and let me introduce you to John Preshin. He lives and works on the top floor."

Liz appeared in the doorway of the smaller bedroom.

Flo patted the arm of the chair. "Over here, Liz. He doesn't bite. John, my granddaughter, Elizabeth Atwater."

Liz stayed where she was. "We've met. I found him wandering in the kitchen earlier."

The old lady shrugged. "So?"

Liz bristled. "Look at him, Grandma! He's naked under that ratty old coat!"

"So, what did you do, pull a knife on him?" Flo's eyebrow arched and John stifled a laugh at the picture she made.

"Yeah, I got the biggest knife I could find. I didn't know who the heck he was and I wasn't about to take chances."

Flo waved her off, dismissing her granddaughter's fears. "You two ought to get to know each other. You'll both be living under the same roof for awhile . . . so I suggest you unruffle your feathers, Liz, and make nice."

Another snort, this time pure scoff. "Not if I can help it."

John shot her a quick look, then turned his attention on Flo. "Hey, you okay? What's wrong? Anything I can do to help?"

Flo smiled and shook her head. "It's the gout again. This time the doctor told me I had to stay off my feet and gave me yet another diet. I hope this works. I took a chance and called Liz all the way in California and asked her to come stay with me until this spell is over."

John turned to face the younger woman, noting as he did that she was no kid, probably close to his own age, a little younger. Again that luscious red hair, pale skin, nice face, even with her less than welcome scowl. He knew she didn't really mean it.

"I gotta go, Flo. I'll just get another cup of coffee and get on back to the office. If you need anything, just let me know. Okay?" He patted her hand, this time noticing how frail it seemed, how thin. He turned his attention back to Liz and found her glowering at him.

"No mess."

He grinned at her, suddenly glad at this turn of events, then remembered his own surprise upstairs. Snagging a couple of jelly doughnuts and a carton of milk from the fridge, he juggled them up the steep steps, wondering how much worse his day could possibly get.

No kid.

Annoyance steamed through him . . . he'd gone through the trouble of getting her a doughnut and all. Then relief . . . what had he been thinking to even let her stay upstairs? She could have ripped him off . . . had there been anything worth taking that she could steal in the few minutes he'd been gone.

To his amazement, he felt a twinge of disappointment that passed almost instantaneously. What brought that on?

She was curled up on the office sofa. Asleep. Looking small and young with her hand near her mouth, thumb brushing her bottom lip like a baby. Sleep had smoothed the tension from her face and she looked all of twelve years old.

Ah, hell.

The paper with the six names on it had dropped to the floor. John put his doughnuts and coffee on the cluttered desk, snatched up the wrinkled list and sat in his desk chair, pulling the damned coat around him in case the kid woke up. His name, written on an old fashioned typewriter, really was at the top. Scanning the other names, he realized he knew every single one.

The summer of 1986. The beach house.

All six had spent the summer in a rental in Belmar.

They'd all been friends, some closer to him than others, but they'd all known each other and suffered one another's bad habits that summer. By the end of August, he'd been ready to kill two of them, but had been prevented from doing so by the need to return to school to finish his law degree.

And one of these guys was this kid's father?

He chuckled to himself.

He knew how to locate most of them. It wouldn't be too much of a strain—he could probably do it in half an hour over the Internet.

A soft sigh issued from the sleeper on the sofa, pulling his attention back to her. How old was she? Who the hell was her mother? Where did this list come from?

He thought about waking her and getting the answers, then realized she'd probably be in better shape with some sleep. He could use the time to get dressed himself, and maybe play around with the computer, come up with some addresses. Maybe he'd make a call or two, depending on the time it would take.

The kid. He knew that look of fear that had crossed her face. He'd worn it himself too many times.

Shit.

"You were awfully hard on John," Flo said as she hobbled painfully to the bedroom door.

Liz looked up from the edge of the bed, quickly changing her scowl to a small smile at the sight of her grandmother. "He's a man."

Flo entered the room looking at the big suitcase and still unopened bureau. "Need some help?"

"Maybe. Shouldn't you be sitting down, Gram?"

With a shake of her head, Flo refused assistance and settled into the lone chair in the small room. "Honey, I know it's been rough, but all men aren't like that S.O.B. you married. Maybe you shouldn't condemn them all. There are a few good ones left. John Preshin is one of them."

Liz flipped open the suitcase and examined the contents briefly, then stopped to look around again. She took a deep breath. As if stepping back in time, she could smell the musty salt scent of the Jersey shore in the bedding and curtains.

She'd come full circle. The Jersey girl had come home. Maybe it was true. You could take the girl out of Jersey but you couldn't take the Jersey out of the girl.

There were only precious memories in this place. The room looked exactly as she remembered it. Liz crossed the floor and tugged open the top drawer of the ancient bureau. It wasn't empty.

"Will you look at this?" She took out a faded bit of cloth and held it out to her grandmother. When the older woman's eyes squinted in question, Liz fluffed the gaudy red, white and blue rag until it fell into its halter shape.

"Oh, my Lord!" Flo fell to laughing. "That halter top! I'd forgotten that was in there."

Liz placed it against her chest and shook her head. "Lots of changes here, Grandma."

Flo shook with gentle chuckles and pulled out some more sedately colored tops from the suitcase. As she did, a small photograph slipped out and fell onto the bed. "What's this?"

Before she could grab it, Liz snatched it up and held it to her heart. Flo's face wrinkled as she leaned back. "I'm sorry, dear. Whatever. . . ."

"No, Gram. You—it's just—" Liz finally met her grandmother's eyes. "This is the only picture I have of Jesse. Everything else is gone."

Silence fell between them, so profound not even street noises seeped through until Flo, a bright smile wreathing her face, smacked her knee and struggled to get up. With a grunt, she sat again, but beckoned her granddaughter to her.

"Go in my room, honey. Top of my dresser. Go, now!"

What the? Liz left the old lady—Flo crowed with glee when her granddaughter exclaimed from the other room.

"Gram! Oh, Gram!" Liz cried as she rushed back, her arms laden with framed photographs and a small album. "It's Jesse! They're my baby—right here."

She hugged the photos to her chest. Tears she never thought she'd cry for joy rolled down her cheeks.

"Easy, baby," Flo crooned. "Easy, my sweet girl."

* * *

He tried gently tugging at the duct tape once again, this time pulling out at least ten hairs. At this rate, it would take him half a day to get it off and he'd be bald as a bodybuilder around the Z. He'd probably have to shave off the rest and look like a jerk . . . but who would see it?

A knock sounded at the bathroom door. He jumped and pulled out at least twenty more hairs with a small scream.

"It's just me, Mr. Preshin. I haveta use the facilities."

Oh, the kid.

"I'll be right out," he muttered and pulled his T-shirt on. The exposed end of the tape stuck to the thin fabric and pulled out a few more precious hairs.

She looked only slightly better than when she'd first appeared at his door. Her hair stuck up on one side and her eyes were puffy, but she had some color in her cheeks.

"Sorry," she whispered.

"No problem. Take your time. And after you're through in there, you and I are going to have a little talk."

Her muffled "okay" sounded from behind the bathroom door.

John waited, half expecting her to spend at least an hour in the can. She surprised him by taking only a few minutes.

The kid still had water dripping down her nose as she approached him at the desk.

Her face scrunched, but her eyes seemed focused on the front of his shirt. John sucked the jelly out of the hole in his doughnut, ignoring her stare.

"Still got that tape on ya?"

John felt heat in his cheeks. "My problem. Never mind that, let's get some things out in the open. Charles? What's your name?"

Her eyes strayed from his face to the container of milk and doughnuts.

"Go ahead. I brought them up for you."

The kid grabbed the milk first, took a slug and smiled. The doughnut oozed red jelly from the hole as she grabbed it.

"How long since you've had a good meal?"

With sticky fingers she pulled the spare chair up to the desk. Sitting, she turned the doughnut around and carefully licked away the jelly then sucked out the rest.

"Yesterday."

John felt something tighten in his chest and it wasn't the tape. "At home?"

After swallowing some milk, she said, "Truck stop."

John rose from his chair. "You ate at a truck stop?" Years of kidnapping cases and investigating bodies found in the woods flipped ugly pictures through his mind.

"Relax. I was with some friends. I knew what I was doing."

He felt his insides quake with fury. "Where did you come from?"

The girl licked more jelly off her fingers. He pushed a napkin across the expanse of old oak separating them. She nodded thanks.

"Okay. If I tell you, you have to promise not to call anyone. And you have to take my case. Otherwise, I don't tell you anything." A satisfied look crossed her face, as if she had managed to put one over on him. He disagreed, but figured he'd let her think she'd won.

"Are you in trouble with the law?"

"No."

"Are you a runaway? Are there people searching for you, wondering where you are, maybe even calling the cops?"

"Doubt it." She picked up bits of sugar on her fingertip.

"Why do you think that?"

"The nuns didn't exactly want me around any more."

He felt his eyebrows move. "Nuns?"

She leaned forward. "Deal?"

John tilted back in his chair. "Not on so little information. You're not over eighteen. I could get in a whole lot of trouble just talking to you here in my office."

The kid settled back in her chair, her face serious but comical for the dot of jelly on the corner of her mouth. "My name is Carly Anne Snow. This is the straight poop. That isn't my real last name . . . it's the name the nuns gave me when I was born. They told me my mother gave me my first name, but she left a few hours after delivering me. It was snowing outside, so the nuns called me 'Snow.'"

"Your mother left you . . . where?"

"The convent of St. Hedwig across the river in Philly runs what they call a residential treatment center. It's one of those places unmarried girls get sent by their parents to have their babies in secret . . . rich parents, that is. As far as I can tell, the sisters used to try to get the pregnant girls to repent and change their evil ways, but it's way different from the old days now. Still, when the babies are born, the mothers don't get more than a few minutes to look at the kids, then they're separated.

"From then on, the babies are cared for by the sisters and the mothers leave after signing papers to put the kids up for adoption. There's a waiting list a mile long for healthy babies and the sisters believe in being careful. The state gets involved somewhere along the line, most of the time. Sort of."

Her voice wavered a little as she reached the end of the sentence. John prepared for tears that did not come. He had questions.

"You didn't get adopted."

Carly shrugged. "I wasn't fostered and I wasn't allowed to be adopted. There was something weird about me. Mother Superior once told me that someone was paying my room and board."

"Your mother?"

Another shrug, this time not as casual. Her body tensed. "One of the nuns told me she was dead." A tear escaped and rolled down her cheek.

He waited.

"Last week, I turned sixteen. Mother Superior called me into her office to tell me that the money had stopped. She didn't know what to do. I could stay on at the convent as a novitiate or leave as an emancipated minor. Kind of like being in limbo, you know?"

John absorbed this information. It all sounded brutal. The kid clipped out the words, talking over the tears she tried to hold in. He'd put in a call to this Mother Superior as soon as he could.

"How did you get the note?"

Carly let out a laugh. "I see it as my birthday present from my mother. I took it from my file when Mother Superior left the office. And that night I split."

Brutal. John wished the dull ache in his head would stop, but her words reverberated through his brain and he absorbed some of the kid's tension by osmosis.

Carly moved to the edge of the seat. "I've been honest with you. I'm not a runaway. You have to have a home to run away from. I do not have one. I'm not even an orphan anymore because I'm sixteen. This emancipated minor thing . . . I read about some kid movie star declaring himself emancipated so his parents couldn't control his money. That's what it is. My mother left me with the nuns. The nuns didn't want me hanging around. I figured if I found my father, maybe he'd want me. It's a long shot, I know. Maybe he's been looking for me all along. Maybe he's been searching for his kid and now I can find *him* and he'll want *me* and take me with him and I'll . . . I'll be with . . . I'll. . . ."

The kid dissolved in tears.

John felt something wrench in his chest and restrict his breathing.

If she were his daughter, he'd want her around.

Chapter 3

The cold rain stung his face. He walked with purpose toward the oceanfront, hands shoved in pockets, head down. The street was February dead. No cars ventured out on the desolate streets of Asbury Park at this time of year, in this kind of weather.

The idiotic face of Tillie, with its fading black hair and hundreds of teeth, sneered at him as he passed by the old amusement building. Once a symbol of a thriving seaside resort, Tillie looked down at the world as the resort crumbled and slowly died. The building ought to be torn down. It made John feel old.

Rain pelted him as he stepped onto the street, not even bothering to look for oncoming vehicles. Maybe in summer, cars would come, full of parents pointing at the derelict buildings and telling their kids, "When grandma and grandpa were young, this was some place. They took me here a few times, but I was really little and don't remember all that much. That building used to have a really great carousel in it."

He kept on, needing to see the ocean. Wet sand made the broken sidewalk ooze as his footsteps melted through the gray slick. Wind whipped across the waves, sending flecks of foam toward the beach and remnants of the boardwalk. Grabbing the iron railing, he searched the surf. The waves pounded the shore, eroding the beach where in summer people still opened up umbrellas and gave some life to the shoreline. But now, the gray sky lingered over the crashing, restless ocean. The only one watching it was John.

He ought to turn the kid over to Social Services.

She needed help, the kind of help he couldn't give her. He could locate her father, maybe, and perhaps even identify her mother, but what good would that do?

He knew what she really needed. She needed a nice place to stay. She needed people to look after her. She needed to be in school and not alone in the world. She needed a family.

Man oh man. This newest blip could be a further complication in his already complicated life. He chose not to dwell on the kid right now, his thoughts turning to the lady downstairs. Her and that knife. Did she actually think a serrated bread knife would be sufficient to fend off a man who'd gone through the FBI Academy? He laughed into the sound of the surf. Flo had never mentioned a granddaughter. Or had she? The red hair. Flo's hair had been red in the head shots she had on display. He wondered whether this Miss Liz was half the fun her grandmother was.

A gull called out over the gray-green ocean, sounding like a child calling for its mother. Reminding him of the kid he'd left alone in his office. His newest complication.

He turned on his heel and made his way down the street, thinking all the while that he needed help on this one.

And he knew just where to turn.

The inside of the church was dark. A few candles flickered in their stands. He smelled the scent of hun-

dreds of bodies and wet wool, leftovers from the three
Sunday morning masses. The smoky, happy-birthday-
pleasant odor of extinguished candles lingered in the
air. A shadowy figure snuffed out the two large candles on the altar.

John gave a little grunt of satisfaction.

"How's it hangin', Father Mike?"

His footsteps echoed in the aisle as he approached
the altar. Out of habit, he genuflected and made the
sign of the cross.

"Altar boy knees," the priest frowned, but one
corner of his mouth twitched. "Arise, my son."

John grabbed onto the back of the front pew and
pulled himself up.

"Since when did you start this 'my son' business?
I'm older than you are."

The priest grinned and offered his hand. The men
clapped each other on the back. "What brings you to
St. Boniface's?"

"I need spiritual guidance," John replied.

The priest's eyebrow rose slightly. "Then follow
me," he said softly and led John out the side door.

John hated going into the rectory. The dark wood
and heavily curtained windows gave him the creeps.
Years of being Catholic brought with them the sense
that there was always something more about priests
than other men . . . something tied to the secrets and
mysteries that marked the Church and made things
holy.

Mike Ryan was far from holy. John had known him
since the early eighties. Nearly a lifetime ago, Mike
had been a hell raiser. The stiff white collar and black
clothing didn't seem to fit the man John knew wore
them, but then, Mike had made a brave choice in
giving up the world.

It had to be hard forsaking women and drinking
and smoking and . . . women.

Mike led him into the old kitchen, the one room in which John felt less oppressed. Clear glass windows, high, yellowed-white cabinets, old appliances and an ancient sink. At least it didn't have holy pictures all over the place. Here air was redolent with cooking smells, not incense.

Mike gestured to the cracked red vinyl chair with the chrome trim that probably dated back to the fifties. "Take a load off."

John eased into the chair, aware of the tug of the duct tape when he moved his arms to turn the seat backwards.

"Something to drink?" Mike quirked his eyebrow in question.

John looked at the teapot-shaped clock over the sink. "Nah, I'm still feeling last night." No lie, that. Every time he moved and the tape pulled a hair from his chest, he was reminded that he'd conked out in bed with some woman . . . slept in her bed and now he couldn't remember what she even looked like. She just hadn't mattered to him. He realized he could visualize the redhead downstairs vividly—the way her lower lip stuck out just begging to be tugged and teased, the nice curve of her hip—but the woman last night was pretty much a blank.

The priest grabbed a bottle of water then slammed the refrigerator door shut. John winced. "Damn thing keeps popping open. Probably needs new stripping around the edge. I'm afraid to touch it for fear it will disintegrate in my hand."

John moved back and held up his hand in mock horror. "Don't ask me to do it. You know I'm no good at that kind of stuff."

"Oh, yeah, I know. What I don't know is what brings you to St. Boniface's today. You have something on your mind? Need to confess something?"

John snorted. "Yeah, like I'd confess to you."

With a wicked twist, Mike took off the top of the water bottle. "Just thought I'd offer."

John shook his head. "If and when I ever need to confess anything, Mike, I'll go to another town, another church. I still can't quite adjust to you being a religious and all. Not after all we've been through together. He . . . heck no."

The priest laughed. "Is it so hard for you to believe I'm a priest?"

Looking at him, pinning him with his eyes, John answered, "Yeah. I guess it's something I just can't get used to. Not after some of the stuff we've done."

Mike shrugged. "That's in the past." He took another slug of water.

But John thought he saw a look of longing or sorrow in the priest's blue eyes. Maybe he wouldn't tell him about the kid just now.

"So, tell me, is this gig really permanent?"

The bottle slipped through Mike's fingers. He caught it deftly and replaced the cap. "Yeah, John. I'm a priest. I like being a priest. It's rewarding in so many ways. I think I really help my parishioners. Maybe all those years I was so wild lets me understand the things they're going through, especially the teenagers. I can say, 'I know where you're coming from' and I really do. I think they know it, too, despite this"—he touched his collar—"and seeing me at mass on Sunday."

John nodded slowly, picturing Mike smashing a beer can on his forehead. "So, do you ever think about some of the crazy things you did? Do you ever miss being able to . . . you know, do what you did before you signed up?"

The response took some time. Mike didn't speak right away.

"Sometimes, I look back at some of the crazy things I did and regret having done them. I don't think I'd care to relive those days. Oh, don't get me wrong. I'm not saying I'm sorry for being a screw-up. I never hurt anybody, that's for sure. When I think about those days at college, the frat parties and the drinking . . . I'm just glad they're over.

"I know I should have studied harder, gotten better grades, tried to please my parents more. But we were young. We were rebellious. Hell, I wasn't the one who always got into fights—that was DeAngelo and Georgie. The only person I really hurt, and I see that now, was me."

John spent the next few minutes in silence, remembering things he'd put out of his mind ages ago. Evidently Mike did too, because he remained silent, a thoughtful, disturbed expression on his broad Irish features.

Breaking the reverie, John asked, "You ever see any of the other guys?"

Mike paused as if collecting his thoughts. "I see Dutch every couple of months, but the others, no. You?"

This was definitely not the time to talk about the kid. A sharp pain passed through his shoulder. "I haven't seen any of them since the hospital."

John stood. Mike hung back, lost in thoughts, perhaps. "I'll let myself out, then. See ya, Father."

The priest gave an offhanded, distracted wave.

John suddenly wished he'd stayed on the boardwalk. This little chat disturbed him, but it seemed as if he wasn't the only one it disturbed.

How would Mike react to Carly?

Eventually, they'd both find out.

Dutch Van Horne lay in the hospital bed with the sides up. John scanned the room before entering. No sign of any other visitor or nurse. He slowly stepped inside.

"Hey, Dutch."

The man on the bed opened his eyes, blinked them and a trace of a smile shadowed his lips.

John moved closer, pulled up a chair and sat.

"No tubes today?"

Dutch gave a sigh. His head moved almost imperceptibly side to side.

"Can I get you anything?"

Again, the slight negative movement.

Leaning forward, John asked, "Do you remember that summer in Belmar?"

Dutch's lips curved upward. A distressful gurgle erupted from him. John smiled back at him. It had been a long time since he'd heard his friend laugh.

"Well, I was thinking about it this morning. I don't remember too much, except some of the poker games, and the afternoons on the beach, ya know? But I seem to remember there were some babes hanging around all the time. I don't remember who they were particular friends with or where they came from. Pretty, long legs—that's about all I remember. And . . . I remember them being there in the morning, so they both must have stayed the night lots of times."

He paused now, adding this to his memories. Seeing Dutch had keyed something in his brain. Blond hair, long tan legs. Their faces disappeared in a beery blur, though. And as for names, he'd probably never known them.

"Those were some times, eh, Dutch? I had that bartending job . . ."

"John Preshin, you sonovabitch, leave my husband alone!"

Shit. Dutch's wife stood in the doorway, tearing at the buttons on her raincoat, her face an unbecoming shade of purple.

"Get the hell away from him or I'll call security." Barbara Van Horne's voice rose to a screech, like fingernails on a blackboard that made the hair on the back of John's neck stand on end.

"Barbara, I just stopped by—"

She went to the bed, hovering over her husband's still form. "You were talking to him, getting him all worked up. I know you, John, you've upset him. I know by the look on his face. He's distressed, and it's because of you. Go away. Can't you see? He doesn't want you here. Leave him alone. Leave both of us alone!"

Dutch made a sound deep in his throat and his eyes were wild, all right, but John had a deep suspicion that it was his reaction to his wife's attitude rather than John's presence. Not wanting to upset either of them, he backed away from the bed.

"Look, Barbara, you know I'd never do anything—" he began, but she shut him up with a murderous look.

"You've done enough, John Preshin. You've ruined my life and you nearly killed Dutch. Leave us alone, for God's sake." Tears poured from her eyes as she hugged her husband's inert form. "Leave us alone."

He looked back, unable to see his former partner's eyes, to leave him with some kind of sign that he'd be back soon. He would be back when Barbara was at work, on his usual day. The subterfuge stunk, but he owed Dutch his time.

He owed Dutch his life.

Chapter 4

Liz placed the framed photos of Jesse carefully on the top of the worn dresser. The long flight from California and the cab from the airport in Newark were behind her and she thought this was a good thing.

She didn't feel like going over the past two years of pain and humiliation with her grandmother. Her divorce had shaken the old lady almost as much as the baby's death, probably as much as the accident that had taken her parents, but deep in her heart, Liz knew her grandmother was the one person in the world who loved her completely. Now that her parents were dead, Flo was the only relative left in Liz's pathetic family tree close enough to tickle her branch.

Maybe some day she'd tell her grandmother the whole awful story. But not today. She'd left California and all those fruitcakes and phonies behind. Let 'em stay there.

She looked at her reflection in the crackled mirror above the dresser and patted the wild curls that refused to be tamed now that her hair had grown so long. First chance she got, she'd do something about them. But for now, ah, what the heck. She plopped down on the bed and closed her eyes.

The laughing face of that man upstairs slid behind her eyelids. Instead of banishing him to the depths of nowhere, she allowed her thoughts to linger on what she'd seen, and despite everything she currently disliked about men in general and one arrogant, self-assured, grinning, gorgeous guy with a great bod who had duct tape plastered on his chest, she had to admit there was something about him that had attracted her instantly. Something animal. Something so primitive her body reacted before her brain had figured out just what it was that made her warm.

There was a touch of George Clooney about him, a bit of her favorite James Bond, Pierce Brosnan, and plenty of Hugh Jackman. Lots of Hugh. Lots and lots. All good guys, at least in the movies.

Her grandmother had said he was one of the good guys.

That remained to be seen.

But as her mind drifted, she realized she might not mind sticking around long enough to find out just how good he actually was.

Carly woke up hungry. Faint light came into the room from the one window on the side. She'd had her little chat with #1, John Preshin, and thought she'd convinced him to take her case. Where was he now? He'd left her sleeping once more on the lumpy couch.

Yawning, she got up and searched the room for a clock.

This office of his had three doors besides the frosted glass one she'd first come in. Time to explore.

She checked the bathroom, opened another door that revealed an unmade king sized bed and dresser. TV and DVD player on a junky stand in one corner. Clothes on the floor, overflowing from the hamper near a closet—yes—door. Peeking in there, she found things a bit neater. Hangers with plastic cleaner's bags full of shirts and sports jackets. One good suit, she discovered as she went through everything quickly.

John Preshin didn't appear to be doing all that well on the outside. That duct tape made her wonder about him, but he had nice clothes. Expensive ones. Maybe he needed them for work. In this case, they'd be an excellent disguise. No one seeing him the way she had would guess he had any class whatsoever.

"What other clues did you leave, Mr. Discreet Investigator?"

After making the bed, thinking it would be a nice surprise for him, she found the kitchenette with the small stove, definitely ancient refrigerator like something out of an old fifties' sitcom and sink. There were some cabinets with a few dishes and stuff and a drawer with cutlery and some knives and a wire cheese slicer. Very dull.

Junk food she recognized. The potato chips were slightly stale, but the cheesy puffs were reasonably fresh. Helping herself to a can of soda from the fridge, she sat at the small wooden table and munched on the puffs.

So, this was where guy #1 lived. So much for the mansion she'd envisioned. She'd wondered about him since reading his name on that stupid list a week ago. He was first. Naturally, he was most likely her father.

Well, he was tall enough. Way over six foot because he towered over her in his bare feet. Nice dark hair with a small wave to it—not geeky—just enough to not be flat and lifeless. Good teeth. Nice blue eyes . . . like hers.

Hairy. She'd never really seen a man without a shirt. Never had the opportunity, except at the city pool, and that had been a long time ago before the sisters found out where she'd been and forbidden her to go there again. The memory bothered her. She'd always tried to be good for them, not to disappoint them or earn their disapproval Without them, she knew she'd have been on the street.

But that was before She was free of them now, free of their restrictions. Ready or not, she was on her own until she found her father.

This Preshin guy, maybe he just looked fuzzy and out of sorts because of the way she'd been dumped on him. That cop . . . she'd seen the sparks between the two men. They didn't like each other much.

But she gave John Preshin credit for not turning her over to the police. He didn't exactly say she was his kid, but he didn't deny it, either. Just sort of slickly glossed over it so the cop didn't take her away.

That was pretty nice.

She cleaned up the little kitchen area, put the clip on the puff bag after tossing the stale potato chips into the garbage, and put the soda can in the recycling container by the stove. The blue bucket had three empty old green glass Coke bottles crowding the bottom. He recycled. He cared about the environment. Cool.

Dusting off her hands, she returned to the office area. She straightened out the cushions on the sofa, looked around for anything else to do and noticed the blinking light on the sleeping computer.

"You'd better not, Carly. That's private stuff." She went over to the desk, thought about sitting down, but didn't. Her fingers, itching to touch the keyboard, walked slowly around the mouse pad.

Closing her eyes, Carly thought she'd just extend one finger. If it touched something, well, so be it. The computer chimed to life immediately. She checked out the menu, found the icon for internet access and got online.

Fifteen minutes later, she got off, her conscience overriding her need to connect with someone, anyone out there who might care where she was. The

Daily Diary had accepted her password and she'd written down her thoughts about her journey. No one on her friends list had checked her entries in the last three days.

If her latest entry didn't garner any responses, she would keep on writing until someone noticed her.

She started when a knock sounded on the glass pane of the door.

"Mr. Preshin, it's me, Strap."

Cold knotted in her stomach. She hadn't counted on anybody showing up.

"Let me in, Bourbon. I got that info you wanted."

Carly held her breath.

The door handle rattled and Carly's mouth went dry. She heard some muffled curses outside followed by some scratching sounds, then watched as a paper appeared under the door. Waiting until she heard footsteps going down the stairs, she exhaled and quietly got up to retrieve the note.

"John, I was here but you wasn't. Got that stuff you needed. I'll be all over today, but you can get me on the phone. Very Truly Yours, Strap."

The guy had really bad handwriting.

Not long after the guy slid the note under the door, Carly heard footsteps coming up the stairs again. They were light, not masculine. She held her breath anyway.

After several taps on the glass, she heard steps away from the door, then a pause, and once again steps leading to the door.

"Mr. Preshin, it's Liz Atwater from downstairs. Are you in there?"

Carly breathed again. "Wait a minute, I'm coming," she called.

"Oh," a woman with red hair gasped as the door

opened. "I didn't think anyone was really here. I'm Mrs. Zanetti's granddaughter. I've come to ask for help with my grandmother. She'd like to change where's she's sitting and I can't seem to lift her out of the chair."

Her brows lifted in question. Carly realized she might need to do some explaining. "I . . . he's not here. Maybe I can help you." Mother Superior always told her to smile, that it put people at ease. She smiled.

The woman clasped her hands in front of her. "I don't know . . . miss."

Carly figured she'd better say something. "It's okay. I'd be glad to help."

With a small shrug, Liz seemed to resign herself. "Maybe between the two of us."

Carly stepped out into the hallway and pulled the door, not letting the lock latch in case she had to get back inside. "Let's go, okay?"

This woman really needed help, Carly figured, or else she wouldn't have come upstairs for it. She sensed that the woman had had to force herself to come up the stairs, although she couldn't say why. Something about the stiff set of her shoulders, her unsmiling face, her surprise at seeing Carly, not John Preshin, said a great deal without saying a word.

They entered Flo's apartment behind the luncheonette. The old woman looked at Carly and moved her shoulders with pain showing on her face.

"Grandma, he's not upstairs. This young lady was, though, and she offered to help get you out of there." Liz turned to Carly, her expression prompting.

"Hi, I—I'm Carly. I'm just visiting." She hesitated over the untruth.

Flo smiled brightly. "Oh, my. This is something. Isn't this something, Liz?"

The granddaughter looked Carly up and down, disbelief in her eyes. "Interesting," was all she said.

Carly thought fast. "He left early this morning on a case. I guess he didn't tell you about me coming, but it was a surprise and all."

This settled on the women slightly better.

She bent over the old woman. "Here, you want to move? Let me get on this side. We'll have you comfortable in no time." She motioned to Liz to take Flo's other arm and the two of them helped Flo make the painful trek into the bathroom and into the living room again.

John stepped into the vestibule and heard noise coming from Flo's place. Someone was playing the piano and he thought he heard Flo's voice and another going along with the tune.

One voice sounded awfully young and high.

Carly?

He knocked on the apartment door. "Flo, it's John. Can I come in?"

The music stopped dead.

"Sure, join the party!" Flo called out in a strong voice, more like her old self than when he'd seen her last.

He let himself in, surprised to find lights blazing, filling the room with bright cheeriness so different from the drizzle outside. Flo, sitting like a queen on her chintz-covered couch, had her foot raised on the cushions. The petulant Liz Atwater sat on the edge of the easy chair and Carly—Carly!—sat on the piano stool, hands poised over the keys, looking as if someone had just run over a puppy at his entrance.

John surveyed the scene. What was going on here?

Flo, apparently reading his mind, smiled and spoke. "Carly here has been entertaining us. She's quite the piano player, did you know that? Well, of course you did, John. She's been playing some of the old sheet music. The girl's got talent, sight-reading all those tunes. Brought back some memories of happy times." Her voice went quiet for a second.

"I hope she hasn't been a bother," he murmured, still trying to figure out what had happened to bring the kid downstairs.

"Oh, no! She's a dear!" protested Flo.

He turned to Liz, noting the pinched mouth was back.

"I needed help with Grandmother . . . she'd sunk so far back into the chair I couldn't move her. Gram sent me up to get you. Since you weren't there, Carly came down."

He nodded, then turned his attention to the kid. "So, everything all right?"

The brightness of her smile faded a bit. "I guess so. I didn't think you'd mind if I helped Mrs. Zanetti."

He ran his hand over his face. "No, of course not. I didn't want you making a pest of yourself."

His words slapped the smile off her face. "I . . . I didn't think I was. . . ."

"Oh, John, lighten up. Carly's been keeping me company. I don't often get to talk to people her age. Besides, she's a sweetie. Made me feel better hearing the way she tickled the keyboard. And since we're closed, she didn't keep us from anything." Her voice took on a chiding tone that made John bite down hard to keep from snapping at her that it was none of her business.

"It's nearly suppertime," Flo added. "You and Carly are welcome to join us, aren't they, Liz?"

Liz, starting at the request, took a few seconds to respond. "We're just having a light meal, but you're welcome, of course."

"Wow! I sure am hungry."

Carly's face lit and John couldn't help but say yes. He guessed the kid was plenty hungry. He knew he was. The thought of a hot meal held its appeal, especially when he saw the annoyed look on Liz's face. For some strange

reason, anything that pissed off Ms. Atwater, that got a
rise out of her, was fine with him.

"Let's eat!" he said. "I'm starving."

Flo sat in the booth, looking uncomfortable. Liz
made funny steam noises as she hefted the heavy stew-
pot from the burner. John watched her covertly. He
didn't want her to think he was interested in her, although her expressions of anger and resignation
intrigued him. Something about the fire in her eyes
drew him to her. And when he looked away, he saw
that Flo was watching him watch her granddaughter.

"It's just stew," Flo commented. "But Liz is a good
cook. She's going to be working in the store with me
until I'm able to be on my feet all day. This darn business slows me down too much for too long."

Carly huddled in the corner, her eyes alight. John
wondered why she was so excited, so intent.

"Your stew is great, Flo. Have you been giving out
your recipes?"

The older woman laughed, preening under the
praise. "John, only family gets my recipes. But thanks
for the compliment. No matter how old I may be, I
am not dead yet and I love getting compliments."

She turned to Carly. "You never told us where you
were from, Carly."

Carly flushed.

"I've lived in Philadelphia all my life. Well, on the
outskirts. But I know the city well enough. It's a cool
place."

Liz returned to the table and plunked the heavy pot
on the edge. "All right, let's have those plates."

John laughed. "Real home cooking."

Liz shot him an evil look. "If you want to eat, give
me your plate."

"Liz!" Flo's eyes sparked with impatience. "Just because

we're eating in the store, doesn't mean you have to be rude to our guests."

She tapped the ladle against the pot. "Grandmother, I'm sorry. I'm just . . . I'm just not myself today."

"Well, snap out of it, girl. The store opens up for breakfast at seven tomorrow. You'd better be ready with a smile or I'll lose my clientele. John here doesn't pay me enough rent to keep the building going without income from this place."

Liz pursed her full, rather luscious lips.

It amused John to watch Ms. Atwater hold back. She had come a long way to take care of her grandmother. If she hadn't wanted to be bothered, she'd have stayed in California. Something was up with her, something he ought not to think about. But he had never been good at controlling his curiosity. And it always got him into trouble.

"Here you go, Ms. Atwater. I like stew, so pile it on, if you don't mind."

He winked at her.

She wrinkled her nose at him.

He smiled, deliberately turning on the charm for which he was legendary.

She sniffed and plopped stew onto the thick white plate.

Carly hesitated before holding out her plate.

"If you show me where everything is, I'll wash up."

Flo brightened. "Why, dear, that's so sweet of you."

Liz looked at the kid, her expression softening. "That would be nice. I can use the help. It's been a long time since I worked the kitchen."

She sat after filling her grandmother's plate and her own. Noting the rise of her voluptuous chest, John watched her inhale the delicious aroma of the stew. *Down, boy!*

He'd waited for his hostess to start.

"Eat up," demanded Flo who seemed to be taking

some sort of delight in watching the goings on. "This is quite good, Liz. You haven't forgotten, that's for sure. Liz used to work with me summers when she was in school."

This bit of information added to her mysterious allure. "When was that?" he asked.

Liz chewed then swallowed. "Summers, late eighties, I guess. I got Grandmother to let me listen to Bon Jovi and Bruce on the radio. I like to think it brought in customers."

"Nah, it wasn't the music, kiddo. It was you that brought in the customers." Flo beamed at her granddaughter. "She used to wear shorts and halter tops when it was really hot, before we had the air conditioning installed. Fellas used to come from all the construction sites just to watch her."

"Grandma!"

John smiled again, directing it toward both women. "I would have come for lunch if I'd known you worked here."

Liz sniffed and kept on eating.

Carly's eyes went round and she ate quickly, but neatly. He intended to ask her some more questions after they left the luncheonette.

He had to know what to tell his parents when he took her there tomorrow.

Chapter 5

The kid sat so far forward in the seat she strained against the shoulder belt. He braved furtive glances at her, sometimes finding himself looking directly into those haunting blue eyes of hers. He'd looked away, but kept turning back to see if he could find anything of himself in her face.

Something other than blue eyes and the fact that she sucked the jelly end of the doughnut, just like he did.

Driving up the Garden State Parkway was a matter of routine. If he'd had a big car, not this old Jeep, he'd have turned on the cruise control device and settled back in the comfy seat. But he didn't have one, or the extravagance of cruise control. The Jeep was necessary for the four wheel drive and the small size. He could park it anywhere and not be afraid of someone stealing the hubcaps or anything else because it was so ordinary. He kept it dirty, something he'd learned in his previous life. Bureau cars were small and nondescript. Not that the bad guys didn't peg them as government cars—they just didn't attract too much attention.

He'd love to have more power under the hood, and cruise control, sure. Maybe a cassette player or CD player, but he settled for the AM/FM radio. He reached over to turn it on at the exact time Carly tried to do the same. She pulled her hand back as if she'd been scorched.

"Go ahead," he offered. "Just none of that rap crap."

Her hand shook slightly as she turned the knob. "I listen to the Philly stations sometimes."

She was awfully quiet. Did he scare her that much? She'd spent the night on the sofa, this time with a pillow and blankets. She said she didn't mind . . . what was he supposed to do? He had too much leg to try to fit on the couch and the bed was his and his alone. He'd never slept on the sofa without having passed out there first.

"So, I'm taking you to my parents' house. There's something there I have to look for. And I was thinking you might want to meet them. They love kids."

Carly touched his right arm. "Remember to ask for the WD-40 if you want to get that tape off."

He cracked a smile. She'd suggested he try the lubricant after looking on the Internet for how to remove duct tape adhesive. The kid knew how to get around on the computer, all right.

"So, how good are you with the computer?"

She shrugged. "I know the keyboard tricks and surf the Net."

"How?"

"Beg pardon?"

He slipped them into the toll booth, tossed coins into the basket and sped away. "I asked you how you learned to work the computer."

That seemed to pique her interest. She squinted a bit before speaking. "School."

"Ah," he said, dragging it out while he thought. "What grade are you in?"

Her body caved a little. "I was a junior."

John said nothing, absorbing the body language and the sigh she suppressed, wondering why. She must be sorry she left school. Her friends. Did she have friends?

"You like school?" Hell, what a lame question to ask a teenager. He didn't want to sound stupid and old, but he couldn't help it, not even to himself.

"Yeah. I liked it all right."

"Get good grades?"

She sat a little straighter. "Yeah. Real good."

He tapped the brake as they rounded a curve. "Like?"

"Good enough. My teachers were tough."

He tried to read behind her words, sense exactly what she meant. "Catholic school?"

She threw back her head and laughed. The sound tickled his heart in the oddest way. Like music he wanted to hear and never had.

"Oh, yeah. St. Aloysius. Ever heard of it?"

John shook his head with genuine regret. "Nope. Got a good football team?"

All he wanted to do was get along with the kid. He didn't want to sound as if he was trying to be cool. Yet he had some pride so he didn't want to sound completely lame either. Teenagers could spot lame a mile away. And lame was hopeless. No saving face after getting that label.

Carly laughed again.

"The worst! Probably the suckiest team in the world. They had a good quarterback year before, but he graduated. Most of the team graduated. . . ."

"Let me guess, what was left was pathetic."

She grinned back at him. "You got that right."

It had happened at his old school after he'd left. For some time afterwards, he'd deluded himself that it was because of him. "So, you like football?"

She sat back a little bit more. "I guess so. I got to see some of the home games and they were pretty good.

Interesting and all. And some of the guys were real hunks, but not usually."

Filing away this "hunks" information, he realized that this kid probably had more to her than he first thought.

"Do you have a boyfriend?"

Color rose on her cheeks and she turned to look out the window, but not before he saw her blush.

"Come on, you can tell me."

"Why? It's not like I'm ever going to see him again, or any of my friends. Or go to the prom. Or graduate." Her voice dropped into a low whisper. She kept staring out the window, but John could see her reflection in the glass as she waged a battle against her tears.

"Ma! Anybody home?" John entered the small brick Cape Cod house through the side door. Carly waited to be asked inside. He tugged on her hand. "Ma! Where are you?"

Rose Preshin, pleasantly plump and standing only about five feet tall, came into the kitchen and wrapped her arms around her son. He eyed the pink plastic rollers in her hair. Some things never changed.

"You could have called."

John gave her a squeeze and pulled her off her feet. She socked his arm until he put her down. "You always say that. I never think."

She smiled up at him, forgiveness wreathed in her welcome. "You know this is your home, Johnny."

Carly shifted her feet, drawing Rose's attention.

"Who's this?" she asked, stepping away and wiping her hands on her sweatpants.

"Mom, this is Carly Snow. She's a client."

Rose extended her hand to the girl. Carly took it and gave it a weak shake. "You're welcome in our house, Miss Snow."

"Uh, thanks . . . thank you. And it's just 'Carly'."

"Did you eat?" Rose looked first at John, then Carly.

John laughed. "Didn't I tell you she'd ask?" He gave Carly a wink. The kid looked confused and didn't answer.

"We could eat something, Ma. We've been on the road since before rush hour. Where's Dad? I have to ask him something."

Rose grunted. "Where do you expect him to be? He's in his shop."

He gave her a blank stare. "Huh?"

"In his shop. Where the old coal bin was. When your sisters moved back last month, he put up wallboard in there and that's where he disappears every day."

"My sisters moved in *here*? Last month?"

Firmly planting her hands on her hips, Rose seared him with a look. "Yes, both of them and your nieces and nephews, too."

John felt his plans for Carly sliding away. "Why?"

His mother made a noise of exasperation. "Why do you think? Their husbands, God protect them, have been deployed. I thought it would be better for them to come back here to live."

John heard the desperation in his own voice. "All of them? Where did you put them all? Where are they now?"

His mother stopped emptying the refrigerator and ticked off with her fingers, "Two upstairs in your old room. Two downstairs in the rec room. One sleeps in the small bedroom down here and Frankie sleeps on the sofa in the living room. And the kids are in school and your sisters are grocery shopping. I expect they'll be home soon."

"Oh, good." He nodded, not meaning it. There was no room for Carly here. Damn. "I'm going downstairs to talk to Dad for a second while . . . while you're whipping up lunch, Ma." He escaped down the stairs, leaving the kid to deal with—whatever.

Rose looked at Carly as she opened the refrigerator door. "I love feeding people. Don't even *think* you're putting me out. And I don't mind my family being here. There's always enough food, even if there isn't too much room around the table. Carly, that's your name, right?"

"Yes, ma'am. Carly."

She dealt out slices of white bread and slapped cold cuts onto them. "You like lettuce and mayo?"

Carly hesitated, looked toward the cellar door then back at John's mother. "Uh, yes. I do. Very much, thank you."

"Hmm, I haven't heard a 'thank you' around here in some time," Rose observed, talking under her breath. She looked up at Carly and smiled. "You're a polite child. My son called you his client. What is he doing for you, if I may ask?"

"He's . . . uh, going to find my father for me."

Rose turned her head slightly, catching the expression in the kid's face. "You lost him?"

Carly nodded slowly. "You might say that. I never knew him."

Rose's face crumpled. "Oh, you poor dear! I'm so sorry. I shouldn't have asked such nosy questions. But I know my Johnny will find him for you. He's got a real talent, that boy."

Carly accepted the sandwich plate Rose handed her. "I hope so."

Rose wiped her hands on a dishtowel, opened the cellar door and shouted, "John Preshin, get up here and eat. You, too, Stanley. If you're not up here in two seconds, I'm going to feed it to the dog."

"You better get up there, Johnny."

His father looked old. Standing there, wiping his hands on a greasy rag, he looked worn out and graying, with his tools behind him and his glasses halfway down his long nose.

"Come on, Pop. She called for you, too."

The older man turned, placed the rag on the workbench. "I'm not real hungry. She made me eat breakfast. I didn't want to eat breakfast, but she made me get up and eat. Hot cereal. Yatch! I hate hot cereal. I wanted bacon and eggs, but she said Frankie and Bill Junior finished them, so I had hot cereal."

John heard something in his father's voice he'd never heard before. "What's wrong, Dad?"

Stanley turned and raised his palms in front on him. "All these people in this little house! I can't turn around without somebody being there. A man can't even fart when he needs to without offending someone. I tell ya, Johnny, it's too much."

John put his hand on his father's shoulder. "Tell them all to go home."

Surprise washed over Stanley's face, replaced by sternness John had seen few times in his life. "I can't do that. They are home. This is their home, just like it's your home. They belong here . . . I can't ask your sisters to stay on the base all by themselves when their husbands are out doing who knows what.

"Besides, your mother told them to come home, and they came right away. I love them. All of them. But sometimes. . . ."

"Sometimes you wish there weren't quite so many of them underfoot?"

Stanley Preshin sagged then straightened when he heard another shout from the top of the stairs. "You got that right, boy. Maybe I'll take a little vacation. Maybe I'll go visit some of my buddies down in Florida."

John nodded and smiled, knowing full well the old man would never leave his wife for an hour much less a week or so. His pop had it good. He was well loved by a wonderful woman who never gave him a reason to want to be anywhere else but in this little house with her. It had been that way since they'd been married and would never change. That was the right thing for Stanley Preshin. A good life, a good wife and lots of kids around to keep him on his toes.

The image of the redhead from downstairs, her hair stuffed into pink plastic rollers, a flowered apron wrapped around her small waist, flashed in John's mind followed immediately by a streak of terror that slowly eased into a warm flicker before he pushed it away.

Even if he wanted all his old man had, he couldn't hope to have it. His future didn't allow for sharing anything with anyone for more than a few hours, tops. He'd drawn those cards seven years ago and his destiny lay in them. He had to be alone. Shaking the feeling away, he smiled gently at his father.

"Yeah, getting away might be just what you need, Pop. But come on upstairs. I've got someone I want you to meet up there."

The kid was quiet on the drive back. They'd left before all the others returned, but Rose had wrested a promise out of John to return on Sunday for a big family dinner. He'd found both things he'd been looking for in the cellar—the WD-40 was thrown in the back of the Jeep and the photograph was tucked in his jacket pocket.

"I like your parents."

The break in the silence startled him. "Yeah? They're something else."

"Your mother . . . she gave me a hug before I left and this." She held out a wad of aluminum foil.

John knew what it was without looking. "It's food. Probably enough to last you a couple of days. Did she say anything about you being skinny?"

"Yeah. She said I looked too thin and that I needed to eat more protein. Is she a dietician or something?"

"My mother?" John had never thought of that. Leave it to a kid. "No, she's not. She's just a good cook who loves to see people eat. Sorta like Flo. In fact, the two of them get along very well. Both of them could probably feed masses of people."

Carly looked pensive. "How many grandkids did you say she has?"

So, that's what she was thinking about. "There are four, two of each. The youngest is eleven."

"No babies?"

"Not any more. And if she's waiting for me. . . ."

Carly, her intense blue eyes shuttering, turned her face away quickly.

He watched her shoulders shake, wondering what to do to make up for his callous remark. Insensitive asshole! He berated himself the rest of the way back to Asbury Park.

Chapter 6

"You're a tough guy to reach." Strap eased himself back on the rickety chair in front of John's desk. A full grown man would have stressed it to the breaking point, but Strap could handle it without a problem. Carly had been in the office when the little man had let himself in. John had seen her eyes bug out, but her expression settled instantly into one of bland acknowledgement when he introduced the jockey to her.

"Gimme a second here, Strap, and I'll give you my undivided attention." John scanned the obituaries carefully, made a sound of disgust and folded the morning paper in half before tossing it into the circular file.

"I found him, all right. He's been holed up in one of the motels in Keansburg, for cryin' out loud. Why his wife wants him back, I could not guess. The fat slob had nothin' but pizza boxes and empty bottles of store brand orange soda all over the room."

Carly let loose a laugh, then put her hands over her mouth. John raised an eyebrow in her direction.

"Carly, why don't you go down and see if Flo needs any help."

Strap quirked down his eyebrows but said nothing.

Carly shrugged and lowered her chin, clearly not wanting to leave.

"Go ahead, kiddo. This is business and I have to get information from Strap that you might not want to hear, okay?"

"I promise I won't laugh or . . ." She gave a small huff and said, "Oh, okay."

She slouched out into the hall and shut the door quietly.

"Nice lookin' kid, Bourbon. Who is she?" Strap leaned forward, getting all four legs of the chair once more on the floor.

"A client. I'm helping the kid out, letting her stay here until I can locate her family."

"She looks a little young," Strap observed.

John took a deep breath. "Yeah, she's young. And the sooner I find her family, the better."

"She givin' you trouble? The great Bourbon John stymied by a little bit o'nothin' like her?"

"She's okay. I just wasn't expecting to take on another case right now. I've got four or five up in the air and very little time." He made motions to straighten up papers on his desk, avoiding eye contact with the jockey.

"So, what do you have for me I can tell Mrs. Jenkins?"

"What the heck is that inside your shirt?"

Carly stood outside the glass door, holding her breath. What was so important she couldn't stay in the room? She hadn't thought they'd talk about her, not for one second. So, the little man called John Preshin "Bourbon John". That sounded like something out of an old movie where everybody had weird nicknames. Gangster names.

She wished she had the nerve to ask him how he

got the name, but realized if she did, he'd know she'd been listening when she should have been downstairs.

He'd said she was "okay."

He'd taken her up to meet his family.

His mother liked her. His father had been funny and kind, but sad-looking. She'd wanted to stay and wait for John's sisters to come home, and the kids, but he'd rushed her out after they'd eaten.

Taking the steep steps as quietly as possible, she let herself into the kitchen of the luncheonette to find Liz cooking burgers and the air full of the wonderful smell of frying onions. Liz looked up, threw a wadded apron at her and said, "Can you turn these patties for me while I get out the fries?"

"Sure," Carly said and set to work.

She did what she was asked to do. Liz looked like she'd stuck her finger in an electric socket with her red hair springing out of the ponytail in corkscrews.

"This late rush," she explained while shaking the oil from the fries, "is because of the roadwork downtown, I think. Thanks for helping out, Carly. I appreciate it."

Carly looked around the kitchen. Grease dotted the stainless steel. Scattered papers from between the raw burgers decorated the floor. She picked them up, deposited them in the trash, then started washing down the backsplash.

Liz stopped schlepping plates, hands on hips, her head cocked to one side. "Hey, kiddo, where'd you learn to do that?"

"I'm used to helping in the kitchen," she said, not turning her head to face Liz.

"Want a job?"

Carly jerked her head and thought for a second. "I don't know. I never thought of it."

"Well, if you're going to stick around here for awhile, I sure could use the help and I bet you could use the money."

Yeah, but flipping burgers wasn't quite what I had in mind for the rest of my life. "I have to see what's going on before I commit. But if I'm around tomorrow, I'll be glad to help out. I just don't know what—" she shrugged. "Things aren't settled . . . I don't know what I'm doing yet."

Liz smiled and blew her hair out of her eyes with a sideways puff. "I know exactly what you mean. If you're around and you want to help, I'd be glad for it. My life isn't exactly going according to plan, either. But *if* you can, I'd appreciate you coming by."

Carly couldn't hold in the grin. A job! She couldn't wait to tell someone. Anyone.

She waited until she heard Strap's light tread on the stairs before going back up. Standing outside the door, she heard the horrendous sounds of a man in distress, moaning and groaning as if his guts were being ripped out.

Throwing open the door, Carly ran into the office.

"Dammit! Merciful mother! Yee-ow!"

The curses came from the bathroom. She had a pretty good idea what was going on, too.

"You all right in there?" she called, knowing pain when she heard it.

"Shit!"

Going closer to the closed door, she tapped on it. "Mr. Preshin? It's me, Carly. Are you all right?"

The door flew open. John stood, chest bared, his face red with tears running down the sides.

"Of course I'm not all right."

She noticed then that about two inches of silvery duct tape had been torn from him. It flapped as his chest heaved.

"Did you use the stuff?"

John winced and swore. "Yes. I sprayed it on."

Carly kept her eyes averted from the muscular chest and the bare patch where the tape had been pulled away. It was supposed to work.

"How long did you let it sit?"

Scowling harder if that were possible, John appeared to think over her question. "I sprayed it on then tried to peel away the tape."

Understanding dawned. She started to laugh but immediately coughed to cover it. "It has to stay on for a few minutes. On the website, they suggested at least ten to let the stuff work."

"Oh."

She coughed again at the outright stupid look on the man's face. "Yeah. Oh."

He looked at his watch. "I guess it's about that now."

Carly wanted to offer to help, but decided against it. He turned back into the bathroom and gingerly started peeling back the tape, cursing as hairs pulled away with it. Fewer, though, than before.

Standing outside the door, Carly asked, "How did you get that stuff on you in the first place?"

John didn't turn to face her, looking instead into the mirror. She knew he was looking at her, probably trying to read her mind.

"Dunno." He raked his hair with his fingers. "I can't do this sober."

"It would probably be better to use alcohol as an anesthetic. You could pour some on your skin," she observed, loath to see the man who might be her father swig from a whisky bottle.

Yes, she stepped back. She might be looking at her father. Wow! It might be him, this nice old guy with dark hair and blue eyes like hers. And the really nice family in the little brick house just a couple of hours away.

She should help.

"Maybe I can do something. My fingers are smaller, maybe I can peel it off easier."

John closed his eyelids. Teary fluid squeezed from the corners, yet he seemed to be debating whether he should allow her to help.

"No way," he muttered, then his expression changed to a sly smile. "Maybe you could ask Liz to come up. Yeah, you could go downstairs and . . . no. Not a good idea at all."

He tugged at the tape again.

"Look, you're in trouble here. Liz or Flo might be better at this than I could be. Lemme go get her so you can get that stuff off. It's got to chafe like heck. This offer will run out in a few seconds . . . one, two. . . ."

"All right! But no need to bother Flo, not with her leg bothering her. Liz. See if she'll come up."

He wondered if she'd dare come up. Liz had been the one to point it out, after all. And it would be fun to tease her, to see if she'd squirm or show any discomfort at touching him. Never mind how he'd react to her hands on his skin. So close. He'd get a look at her eyes, see if they were green or hazel today. Or maybe blue?

The dread of hellacious pain drifted away on a sea of anticipation.

Carly's thundering footfalls on the steps tore him from his pleasant reverie. He waited, unconsciously holding his breath, for other footsteps to follow and was rewarded by the soft hesitant tread of more mature feet.

"I got her, Mr. Preshin," Carly panted. "He's in the bathroom, Liz. Moaning and carrying on like a big baby."

John wrinkled his nose at the kid's reflection in the mirror and was rewarded by her merry giggle. She had a pretty good attitude for a kid who'd spent her life with a bunch of old ladies. Nuns. The thought made him shiver just as Liz stepped into the doorway. Her arms folded across her chest, her expression betrayed her amusement, though her lips did not break into a smile. He knew he could destroy her composure and he wanted to.

"Hi." He didn't turn to look at her, preferring the anonymity of facing the mirror where she couldn't read his face.

"Hi, yourself," she said, her voice even and slightly bored.

"Sorry to bother you, but I can't seem to grip this stupid tape with the WD-40 on it. If you could just . . . ?"

She shook her head and he half turned to catch it. "Let me see what I can do. But don't complain if it hurts."

"I'll try not to. Just don't rip it all out like some sadistic Nurse Rachet, okay?"

John shivered as Liz's hand neared his chest. He saw her pupils widen and satisfaction buoyed his spirits.

"I'll do my best. It might be easier if that stuff is working, anyway."

After several attempts at grabbing the end of the tape, she dropped her hands and blew out a frustrated breath. She motioned for him to step out of the bathroom. "If you sit on the edge of the desk in the office, I can probably reach it better. But you won't be able to scream in there . . . it's too close to the hall door. They might hear you downtown."

Grumbling for effect and sucking in his stomach, he walked to the desk and leaned against it. "This is no picnic for me, sweetheart."

He squared his shoulders. Now that the time had come, perhaps it wasn't such a good idea to have Liz help after all. The heat of her hand awakened lustful thoughts in him. Elevatingly lustful. The kid was standing there, her nose wrinkled, watching the show, and he felt a little uneasy with the audience.

Liz reached for the tape. He stopped her hand.

"Is Flo all right downstairs by herself? Maybe the kid

ought to go check on her, see if she needs a cup of tea or something."

Carly moved to the door. "Yeah, Flo might need some help. Call me when it's all over," she called back from the hallway.

He had Uptight Ms. Atwater all to himself. She raised her hands again and he did not stop her. *Go on, touch me, Red.*

"Who did this to you? Some kind of nutcase?"

He lifted his shoulders in a shrug.

"Lean forward just a bit," she suggested. "How long have you had this stuff on you?"

"Let's see. I noticed it for the first time the morning you came into my life."

She raised one eyebrow at him, as if trying to gauge his real meaning. "That's three days ago. What were you doing the night before that?"

The tip of her tongue appeared as she peeled away more tape with great care. Only a dozen or two hairs stuck in the adhesive.

She did not let her fingers touch his skin. While he wouldn't have minded at all, he got the impression that she would.

The next tug hurt like a bitch. Sweat trickled down his forehead but he didn't make a sound. Another rip and this time he shook despite his concentrated effort to remain still.

Liz stepped back. John saw her hands shake a little.

"I'm not enjoying this," she said. "I hope you aren't."

Her comment brought a rumbling laugh from him and she dropped her hands once again.

"Don't stop now," he said through clenched teeth.

Liz moved closer and tugged harder at the tape. This time a small smile turned up the corners of her mouth.

"So, you don't know who did this to you? What, were you unconscious?"

"Uh," he grunted. "I think I may have been asleep."

Surveying her unfinished handiwork, Liz muttered, "What, in some kind of kinky sex club or something?"

He leaned down, bringing his face closer to hers. "And what would you know about that?"

Liz slapped her hand on his chest. "Nothing. Nothing at all. But I thought you might."

John mulled this over, in between wishing she'd move her hand just a little bit lower. "As it happens, my line of work has brought me to a few of those places, but, no, this didn't happen in one of them. I don't really know where I was . . . I'd been awake for seventy-two straight hours and things tend to get a little blurry for me around then. I know I didn't *ask* for this, though."

"Who would be crazy enough to ask to have this gunk anywhere near all this . . . pelt?"

He couldn't help laughing again at her expression of disgust and wonderment. Mistake. Liz's careful, tentative touch became a quick, sharp rip.

"Ouch!" He rubbed his hand against some of the recently freed skin.

"Sorry!" Liz backed away, biting her lip.

John groaned, but not from the tape. Another kind of pain seared his senses.

Maybe this wasn't such a good idea after all. The subtle scent of her was driving him over the edge.

Liz dropped her hands to her sides.

"Don't stop now, kiddo," he said softly, putting more kindness into his tone than before. "You're doing a great job. I may get through this alive."

The top of the Z came away, covered in enough fur to make a small cat. Liz's eyes widened in horror.

Pain tamped down his desire somewhat. He gave her a lopsided smile. "Don't stop now. We're almost through."

The downward line of the Z left the furriest part.

The tape came away easily, though John jerked a few times at the sudden sharp sting of hair being yanked from his flesh. The bottom horizontal bar only crossed a thin line of hair a few inches above his navel.

Liz shook her head as her eyes surveyed the damage.

As much as he'd have liked her to carry on, he put his hand on hers and gently made her stop.

"I think I can handle this last bit myself." With a swift pull, he tore off the remaining tape. Tears sprang from his eyes and the denuded skin burned red, but the silver tape was gone. Rolling it up into a ball, he threw it into the wastebasket where it hit the morning's paper and bounced away.

"Aw, hell." He bent to retrieve it and tossed it directly into the can.

Liz looked ready to bolt. Without giving her any warning, John pulled her into his arms and lowered his lips to place a swift peck on hers. But what started out as a brief thank you turned into something more as he felt the soft contact and tasted the sweetness that was Liz.

So he tried for more. He ran the tip of his tongue against the seam of her mouth. Coaxing. Tempting. But she did not open for him.

She wasn't ready.

He did feel the tremble run through her body as he pulled her against him, squeezed, then set her away.

"Thanks."

Liz rocked a little on her heels. Her expression showed just a little shock, maybe, but not anger, which he half expected. More like deer-in-the-headlights.

"Yeah," she croaked, her voice just a whisper as she turned and left the room. He wondered whether she could possibly walk any faster without setting fire to the wooden floor.

The kid came back upstairs with a bottle of salad oil in her hand.

"Flo said to use this to get the adhesive gunk off."

He raised an eyebrow. "Flo? She let you call her by her first name?"

Carly stopped in her tracks. "Yeah, I kept calling her Mrs. Zanetti and she said it was all right to call her by her name. I still feel a little funny about it, on account of her being so old and all, but she wants it that way."

He shrugged. "If she said to call her Flo, call her Flo. What about the ferocious Ms. Atwater. What do you call her?"

"Liz."

Carly looked at him, her head cocked to one side. Women. They were meant to mother.

Rushing into her room, Liz shut the door quietly and stood with her back against it, letting the dark wood hold her up against the onslaught of feelings coursing through her body.

That insufferable man!

The nerve of him!

What did he think she was?

Easy?

Anger raged through her, swirling around in her stomach, tingling and taunting her as she pictured him, smug, so sure of himself with his chest sticking out. That hard, flat belly. That intent gaze directly into her eyes. His skin burning under her hand. For one brief moment, she'd actually enjoyed the way it felt against her palm.

Then the jerk had kissed her.

He'd taken what he wanted. No thought about whether *she* wanted his lips pressed against hers, invading her personal space. Taking. Taking from her.

Keith's image supplanted John's. Keith. The one who had taken the most from her. The one who had almost taken every single shred of her and flushed it down the toilet.

Old anger displaced the new as she relived every pain and heartache and humiliation suffered at her ex-husband's hand. She shook so hard she moved away from the door so her grandmother wouldn't hear the racket and wonder what was wrong.

Who was she really mad at?

The guy upstairs who didn't know anything about her at all? Or the man who had ruined everything she'd ever thought she wanted and needed?

This was a new start, in a place she loved and where she was loved back. So, the guy upstairs was a jerk. A good-looking jerk, but a jerk all the same. And it wasn't as if she hadn't wondered what it would be like to . . . oh, no. Stop it right there. So he'd kissed her. He hadn't torn out her heart and she knew she'd never let him get close enough to do so.

No one would.

John rubbed at the sticky outline of the tape on his chest, wincing at the hairless parts. He didn't want to look at the damage. He had work to do. He had to do something for Carly, get her someplace better. School. The kid liked school. How could he manage that? It didn't take him long to come up with an answer.

Picking up the phone, he punched in numbers he never realized he'd memorized.

Chapter 7

Dank's Tavern had been named not for its atmosphere, but its former owner twice removed. On a back street in the gray industrial part of Asbury Park, it made money by being open early and closing late, thereby catching shift workers and night owls and every oddball with money for a beer. No frills in this place, just knotty pine paneling on the walls with enough accumulated dust and grease to have aged them into near-respectability as fine antiques. Almost.

But it was seedy and dark and John liked it that way.

Beer signs from the past fifty or so years hung haphazardly from thumb tacks. Assorted Christmas decorations gathered grit in irregular festoons around the beer ads, lending the joint a look of extreme fatigue rather than former gaiety. The only thing that redeemed the place, in John's estimation, was the shiny brass foot rail that ran the length of the original chestnut-wood bar. That and the fact that no one asked anything about anyone as long as they kept drinking money out in the open.

The yeasty smell of beer permeated the air.

Dim lights cast a crusted amber haze over the bar itself, while the booths lining the opposite wall were dark and obscure. John made his way past the bartender, a former heavyweight boxer who wore his flattened nose and mis-shapen ear unselfconsciously, and signaled "the usual."

"Comin' up," Jake said. He slapped a clean glass under the club soda spigot, added a twist and pushed the finished soft drink toward John with a look of disdain on his permanently bruised lips.

He wasn't thirsty, but he knew that if he didn't order something, someone would be watching to see why. His business did not deserve speculation by the residents.

The back booth, dim in the shadows, swallowed him up while he kept his eyes on the door. He raised the glass to his lips, wet them and slowly savored the detergent taste of the mixer in his mouth. After all these years since he'd given up drinking hard stuff, it still tasted like crap.

But it would serve to keep his throat wet, and with all the talking he had to do, he'd need it before this meeting was over.

The door opened, creating a small vacuum that dragged dead leaves and debris from the sidewalk into the bar room.

From the heavy tread, he knew his guest had arrived.

"Afternoon, Father."

Mike, dressed in civvies, slid his glass of beer across the table and angled into the booth across from John.

"So what's so secret you have to meet me here? If there's something wrong, you could have come to the rectory." Mike's eyebrows were raised in that questioningly clueless way he had. John knew the man had a sharp mind but he could give the impression of empty-headedness when he wanted to.

John leaned back and toyed with the citrus peel.

"I don't think you want to hear this within the confines of the church, Mike."

All signs of good-natured affability fled from the priest's face. "What?"

"Take a sip of your beer first."

Mike raised the glass and took a long pull at it. "You've got me worried. Should I be worried?"

John shrugged and reached into his shirt pocket. "Depends."

Mike took the photograph. His relief told as the deep line between his brows vanished. "Hey, I remember this! Summer of 1986—that house in Belmar. That was one heck of a summer, wasn't it?"

John measured his words. "Yeah, it was. We had a good time, what I remember of it. I slept through the days and I wasn't around much at night. You were. You and the others had your nights free."

Mike reminisced, "We must have been drunk the whole time we weren't working the waves."

John nodded. "So I heard. You beach bums used to entertain while I was at work quite a bit, too, didn't you?"

Mike turned his full attention on John. "Yeah, I guess we did, pretty much. You know we did. You always used to complain about the beer cans."

Leaning forward, John asked, "Do you remember those two blondes in the picture?"

"Sure. Tammy and Bonnie. No, Bunny. Something like that. Maybe Bambi and Bunny?" Mike's face showed he had some fond memories of the young ladies, all right, until he slid back into priest mode. "Why . . . what's going on, Johnny?

He couldn't hold back the deep sigh; he didn't even try. "Did you sleep with either of them, Mike?"

Mike jerked away, knocking his head on the back of the booth. "John. . . ." His voice held a mixture of surprise and suspicion. And his face showed a sorrow deeper than hell.

"Just answer me, Mike. Did you?"

His friend wiped his big hand across his face, as if by doing it, he could wipe away regrets.

"Is this why you wanted to meet me here?"

John sipped at his soda. "Would you talk to me about this in the rectory? The church, maybe?" He raked his eyes over his friend, searching for something, anything, that would remove the priest from Carly's list.

Mike scrubbed the back of his neck, probably feeling the freedom from the collar, or wanting to hide safely behind it. John wouldn't let go.

Finally, after what seemed like a very long time, Mike answered. "Yes."

John lowered his voice to a faint murmur. "Which?" When Mike hesitated, he reached across the scarred table and gripped Mike's wrist. "Dammit, Mike, which one?"

Looking up briefly, the priest then hung his head before answering.

"Both. I slept with both of them."

He did the best for his client. For the kid, Carly.

After the shock wore off, Mike couldn't do anything for her other than get her into school again. He had enough clout to go through the cracks and enroll her in Mary Immaculate of the Grotto a few towns inland without tuition, and the two men figured out how to get around all sorts of other roadblocks. For a priest, Mike turned out to have retained a smattering of the cunning he'd displayed in his youth. For a priest, he still knew his way around, but John determined that, for a priest, he'd make Carly a lousy father.

"Look, Mike. I've got this list. All the guys who were at the house in Belmar that summer are on it," he said without raising his voice. "Even me. But I don't even remember these women, and the kid doesn't even know I have this photograph. She doesn't know which woman was her mother. I don't intend to show this to her until I find her father."

Mike's head was bowed. "I can't be her father."

John's anger flared. "Listen here, by your own words, you very well could be. I'm not going to do anything about it until I've spoken to all the others."

"And then what are you going to do?" Mike's words came out heavy and with a hint of anger.

"The kid needs a father. Hell, she needs some kind of relative. If I can't find a trace of her mother's family, if I can't find out her name for crying out loud, I have to find her old man. It's one of us. That's what the note says. Jesus, it's one of us."

The priest rubbed at his temples. "There are DNA tests now."

"Don't think I haven't thought of that. But maybe it won't come that far. Maybe I can."

"What, John? Get someone to admit to being her old man? That's a slim chance. For all I know, we all slept with the kid's mother. I remember those blondes. They went through the entire house, trading off, sleeping with anyone. Probably all of us."

He'd said no thanks. It came clearly to him out of nowhere. John Preshin had said "no thanks" to the blonde he found waiting up for him one night after work. He'd watched the goings on and hadn't liked it, but he'd said nothing. That was the point of being bachelors living down the shore. They'd all been in agreement there. Fresh out of college, they'd all wanted to get money fast and get laid even faster.

But he'd worked nights. By the time he'd gotten to the house, the sleeping arrangements had already been settled most of the time. His room was off limits to the others who all had their own rooms—the beauty of the big old house. And no one used it but him.

Except this one night when he'd come home dead on his feet and this blond babe was waiting for him, curled up on the sofa, wearing bikini underwear and a push-up bra. He'd gone straight to his room and crashed.

That night he remembered. He didn't remember which one it was, but he knew he'd kept his dick in his pants that night. Were there other nights when he'd accepted her offer?

He couldn't tell. He just couldn't remember.

They left the tavern together.

"I want to meet her, John."

Looking into the priest's face, John saw nothing of Carly there, not like he saw when he looked at himself in the mirror. But that didn't mean anything. Nothing at all. Heredity was a big crapshoot. The big Irishman . . . no, he wouldn't even entertain the thought.

"Okay, tonight. Or we can walk into bingo tomorrow and introduce her to your parishioners."

Mike's face flashed the fury for which he had once been famous, then regained control. "That's not quite what I had in mind. We could meet in my office tomorrow. We can tell her about Mary Immaculate and how great a school it is and how we've arranged for her to attend."

John held in a snort. "Now, there's a plan."

Mike shook his head slowly, his fists at his side. "I can't handle this, John."

He almost wished he could numb the pain he felt with a couple shots of bourbon, but those days of hiding in a bottle were long gone. Mike was taking this very hard and the two of them went way back. The priesthood really did mean everything to the big guy.

When they separated at the corner, John touched Mike's shoulder. "Maybe you won't have to. I'll see what I can do."

Good thing he'd walked to Dank's. The long run home would do him good.

After the luncheonette emptied out, it dawned on her that she'd been home for days and hadn't seen the ocean.

Liz stretched out the kinks in her back after tossing her soiled apron into the laundry basket. The lure of the water proved too much. It called to her, summoning the very salt water in her own body. If she didn't get down to the beach immediately, she'd explode. Or at least that's how it felt to her now.

How could she have stayed away this long?

Though the sun was nearing the horizon, Liz tramped down the deserted street, head bowed against a freezing gust. Over on the right she glimpsed the Art Deco entry towers that may have once been the gateway to the boardwalk. Mere shadows of their former glory, they stood against the wind and sand. If she squinted, they looked pretty good.

Same went for the wrought iron gingerbread of the Victorian-styled carousel building. As long as she squinted, it looked fine. She imagined some pipe organ music tootling across the stretch of ruined beach road that she had yet to cross.

Maybe some day soon, the buildings would be restored. Wouldn't that be lovely? Her thoughts wandered, passing through days gone by and the present. She had the entire lonely road to herself.

No. Not completely.

Off in the distance, beyond the Stone Pony, coming from the convention center building, some fool was out jogging.

A strong gust of wind buffeted her, making her turn her back to it, hoping her coat was thick enough to ward off the forty degree temperature. When she turned again, she saw that the jogger had made great progress with his long legs.

He approached the squat Stone Pony building. Liz noted his dark hair, his leather jacket and—oh, good Christ in heaven, it was John Preshin.

Her first thought was to hide. Unfortunately, there weren't any places nearby to offer more than cursory shelter. Even with her hood pulled up, if she could tell it was him at this range, he most certainly could tell the woman he was gaining on was her.

She hadn't really spoken to him since the incident of the kiss. Just thinking about it made her lips tingle. Oh, no, she scolded herself. Do not venture there, Liz Atwater. Stay cool. He's closing in. . . .

He stopped, some fifty feet away from her. Bent over, face red, he fought for breath with his hands on his knees and a hacking cough.

Real panic forced her to run to him.

"Are you all right?" rushed out of her as she put her hand on his shoulder.

John gasped in a long drink of air.

"Yeah." He panted like an old bulldog. "I'm okay."

Liz shook her head. "You don't look okay. You look like you're ready to pass out."

With a brave face she knew had to be forced, he straightened up and rocked a few times before standing still. "Been running for a couple miles. Good time for it. Nobody on the road." He sucked in more air and the ruddiness of his cheeks dissipated.

Liz assessed his general condition with a quick up and down. "There's never anybody on this road. But maybe you ought to walk around a little, cool down or whatever it is runners call it when they've had enough." For emphasis, she raised her eyes to look directly into his. That little glint of mischief was there again.

"Good idea," he wheezed, causing Liz to break into a smile.

"Well, I'm on my way home. See ya." She turned and started back toward the luncheonette.

"Wait! Liz, wait up!" He flexed his legs and dog-trotted up to her. "It's getting dark. This is no place to walk after the sun goes down."

"Humph," she grunted. "I'm not afraid of the dark."

John placed his arm around her waist in an all too proprietary way and Liz stepped out of it. He tugged her closer, but didn't grip her quite as hard this time.

"You may not be," he said, "but I am. Shall we go?"

Why not? Why not allow him to walk her home?

It wouldn't matter to either of them, not really, this physical contact. He was being a gentleman. Nothing to arouse the longing to be part of a pair she automatically blocked from her heart. But it felt good having his strong, secure arm around her.

Sure, why not?

The long day did catch up with her. The sight of the ocean had given her a second wind, but now Liz debated between going straight to bed and joining her grandmother and the kid for supper. The tantalizing aroma and hushed conversation coming from the kitchen decided for her.

She and Carly had been talking between rushes about an idea the kid had come up with and Liz wondered whether the kid had the guts to bring it up to Flo. As she stood in the kitchen doorway, she watched Carly push the meatball around on her plate, her head down as if she was avoiding Flo's intent stare. Or maybe she was getting up her nerve.

"So, you helped Liz again this afternoon? How was it?"

"Lots of customers. Liz and I took turns taking orders and making them up. More take-out today than yesterday, but the weather was better."

"Oh, yes," mused Flo. "Business picks up with better

weather. It's slow as all get out during the winter. Let's face it, Asbury Park just about dies in the cold. But it'll start picking up now."

What the heck. She wanted to hear what was going on.

Liz entered the room and sat with them. She'd changed her clothes, getting rid of the greasy apron and white blouse. At least now she felt cooler and didn't smell like hamburgers and fries.

"It was hectic for awhile, Grandma," she observed.

Flo chuckled, a warm, old-lady sound that came from somewhere in the depths of her soul. She put her hand on her knee and gave it a rub. "That's part of the fun."

Liz shot her a smile. "Did Carly tell you her idea?"

Flo looked first to Liz, then Carly. "No, is there something going on?"

Liz lifted her hand, indicating that Carly should follow through. Carly held back until Liz prompted her with a small nod.

"It's nothing, really, Flo. I was just thinking that, with summer coming on, maybe you might want to turn the luncheonette into an ice cream parlor."

Flo's eyebrow dipped then cleared. "Oh, so you found the fountain stuff."

Carly wriggled in her seat, so full of excitement Liz had to laugh. "I was putting a platter on the side, and I heard the counter, you know, on the left side over there, I heard it sounded hollow. So, after the rush, I looked around and saw the hinges. And then I sort of lifted the lid thing and there was all this stainless steel. Liz told me what it was, and I thought it would be great to, well, serve ice cream. Fancy stuff. Ice cream parlors are really hot now. Everybody loves ice cream. And this place could be so cool! All that old-fashioned stuff. A real ice cream parlor."

Liz checked out her grandmother's face as she seemed to consider the kid's proposal. "Nobody much wants ice cream in winter. Summers, yes, I could see opening up the fountain. But not in winter. Not here, anyway."

Carly's smile flagged, a little deflated by Flo's reaction. The kid really had had a good idea. Wanting to show her support, Liz turned to her grandmother and gave her a beseeching look.

"Grandma, Carly thought about that, too."

Flo eased back her shoulders and inhaled a deep breath. "So, what does she have in mind?"

Liz knew that look. The kid was nearly home free, but not knowing Flo as Liz did, she probably thought the piercing look was a dare to come up with something that hadn't already been tried. Something stupendous.

"Soup."

"Soup?"

"Not just open a can, pour it in a pot, but homemade soup. Like the kind the nuns made in a big steamer at the soup kitchen."

"Nuns?" Flo looked confused. Liz held in a laugh. Carly had already explained this to her earlier though she had to admit this bit of the kid's past had surprised her.

Carly pressed forward her case. "Nuns. I've lived with them and know all sorts of recipes for some really great soup. They taught me everything there is to know about cooking and baking."

Her enthusiasm overflowed. Carly was a natural saleswoman. Liz watched how she focused on Flo's reactions, as if trying to get a sense of whether she was reaching her. Her grandmother was a smart lady and an excellent businesswoman, but she might not like any of the ideas Carly had.

"And the two of you want to change the luncheonette into an ice cream parlor in the summer and a soup kitchen in winter? You like this idea, Liz?"

"Not soup kitchen. Soup *bar*. Very trendy stuff. *Big* difference," Carly explained.

Flo settled back in the booth. "I don't know. The luncheonette isn't doing too bad."

Liz stepped in with her two cents. The idea had grabbed her as soon as Carly had put it into words. "It isn't doing too bad at all, Grandma. It might do better, though. You'd make more money, probably, and with the resurgence of Asbury Park, you'd be in the forefront. You know the town is working on revitalizing the oceanfront. There will be plenty of business while the work is going on, and afterwards. We're only two blocks from the beach. We have parking and if we have something different to offer customers, we'll do fine."

"But what happens when the crowds move up to the beach in all those fancy restaurants and food stands?"

"Then," added Liz with a tight, emphatic smile, "we retire rich."

Chapter 8

John came out of the bathroom, cleanshaven and ready to face the day. He'd put on decent slacks and a shirt he'd had to take the cleaning tags off, just to bring her to Mike's. The kid scooted inside in a blur of teenage speed.

"I've been working on your case," John said as he waited for Carly to finish in the bathroom. Now she seemed to be dragging her feet, and they had an appointment to keep. He looked at his watch, checked the newspaper.

The door hit the side of the wall, carving a divot out of the cracked plaster.

"Did you find my father?"

Panic crossed her face which oddly pleased him.

The kid had on that huge jacket and baggy black pants with the watch cap snugged down over her hair.

"Good morning. And no, I haven't." He made sure he sounded pleasant. She turned her shoulder to him. Folding the newspaper after another quick scan of the page, he tossed it into the wastebasket.

"Ah, nothing to say this morning? Well, let's go downstairs and have a good breakfast, okay? No doughnuts and coffee, but eggs and bacon and toast with those little packets of jelly."

Still no response.

"Is that all you have to wear?"

She turned on him. "What's wrong with it? It's clean. And yeah, it is all I have to wear."

He gave a quick nod. "We'll have to get you some clothes after . . . I guess."

She muttered something under her breath that he didn't catch and was glad he hadn't from the look she gave him. Sullen. Oh, crap.

Grabbing his leather jacket from the coat tree, he held the door open for her. "Let's go downstairs, Carly."

She looked at him through her eyelashes, her head down, her feet not moving.

In two steps he was in front of her, hands at his side. "Don't pull this on me, Carly. I'm trying to help you. What I have to do to accomplish that is what has to be done."

"You came back late. I had all this stuff to tell you and you came back when I was asleep."

Ah, so there was more to it. "Yeah. I did. I was working. It happens. It happens to me frequently. I go and I come at all hours and I'm not used to reporting to anyone. It's my job. We have things to do today. Now, come downstairs so we can get breakfast."

She crossed her arms over her chest and jutted her chin. "What if I don't want to?"

"You'll like what's going on. I promise."

Enough cajoling. His father would have just given her a look. He didn't know how to give a sullen six-teen-year-old a look. Instead, he tugged off her cap.

Carly's natural blond hair tumbled out.

"Ho-ly Hannah!"

She grabbed at the cap. "What? Give it back."

He crushed the cap in his hand, his eyes fixed on her. "What . . . oh, that was just hair dye?"

She shivered. "Yeah. This is my real hair color."

"Uh, it looks . . . nice." That tore it. The blondes from the picture—it slid into place though he still had no idea which one had given birth to Carly. Another big, fat clue.

"Can I have my hat back now?"

He smiled, gentling now that the initial shock was over. "Nope. You don't need it."

Her eyes slitted. "Where are we going?"

He started out the door, turning back to make sure she followed. "You'll find out."

When they got downstairs, Liz was leaning over the counter reading the newspaper. If she was surprised by Carly's change in appearance, she gave no indication whatsoever.

John checked his watch, decided he didn't want to bother Liz for a real breakfast after all. He'd probably used up all his favors with her after the tape removal incident and he didn't want to push. And last night, up on the beach road . . . that didn't count for anything, but she had allowed him to get her home safely. Her actions and reactions to him were atypical, to say the least. A puzzle. He liked puzzles.

While the lady currently occupying his thoughts ignored him, she did, however, smile sweetly at Carly and offer to make her French toast, which the kid declined, snagging a doughnut instead.

"You guys off somewhere special?" she asked Carly.

Carly swallowed a chunk of doughnut before answering. "Some big secret thing. Ask him what we're doing, 'cause I sure don't know."

Liz pulled Carly close and said something directly into her ear. They both laughed and John felt his ears burn. A sure sign they were laughing about him.

Fascinated, he watched the two of them sharing

their little private conversation and the thought came to him that they were both good-lookin' babes. Hmm. Well, maybe the kid was a babe in training, but Liz sharing a secret with her face lit up and that great, mocking smile of hers was definitely a babe.

The kid. Some day she'd be a knockout. A heart-breaker.

Hell, she already was.

He almost felt sorry for the boys at Mary Immaculate.

John had already run through what he was going to say to Carly a thousand times. "Carly, this is Father Mike. He's found a way to get you back in school to finish out the year at least."

She'd be happy and excited and he'd be a hero for allowing her to complete her education. And Mike would get to see her and . . . well, whatever happened because of that, he hadn't a clue, but Mike would see the kid he possibly had fathered. In his own way, by getting her into Mary Immaculate on scholarship and eliminating hurdles, the priest would be doing all he could to help Carly. If it turned out that he was her father, at least he'd know he was doing right by her as much as he could.

And if he wasn't her father, she'd be in school instead of out on the streets. John would continue to look for her father. Once he found him, Carly could go live with whoever it turned out to be and she'd be out of his hair.

Funny thing was, and he hated to admit it to himself, he'd want to make sure she was happy and doing all right and that whichever son of a bitch claimed her, that bastard did right by her. Sixteen years changed a man. Those bums at the shore house had been all right to hang with on a limited basis, but some of them had been destined to be dirtbags. He knew it back then. Hell, Carly's very existence was proof of it. No real man would abandon his own child.

"Well, here we are."

The kid looked out the window at the imposing stone edifice of St. Boniface. Her expression fell. "A church? What's the big deal? I've been in church plenty of times. I'm Catholic, remember? Raised by nuns? All that?"

He chuckled. "Yeah, I remember. But this is important. I want you to meet somebody."

Her eyes lit for a nanosecond, then her lids lowered. "My father?"

He shook his head. "I'm good, but I'm not that good, Kiddo. Nah, Father Mike . . . he's a good guy. He and I—well, I'll let him tell you."

Sweat rolled down the back of his neck. He felt uncomfortable. Best to let Mike handle the situation his own way. They'd already decided to use his priest name, not his birth name. Carly was no fool. She'd memorized the names on that list. She'd know who he was and that would not be good.

Mike met them at the door after sending his housekeeper out shopping for the morning. John watched the priest's face as, with what had to be practiced care, Mike smiled beatifically at them both, giving nothing, absolutely nothing away. Priest greeting parishioners. Maybe there was an extra quarter inch to the wide smile.

"Father Mike, this is Carly Snow. Carly, this is Father Mike."

Mike stuck out his hand, grasping Carly's, then covering it with the other. Mike was a warmhearted type, came from a big Irish-Catholic family with eight siblings and about a million cousins. From personal experience, John knew they were huggers, but Mike did not bring Carly into an embrace.

He ushered them into his office, full of dark wood and pictures of Christ and His bleeding heart, and saints with bald heads and those with pious veils. A stained glass window of the Crucifixion let in dim light behind the priest's chair. John fought his sudden aversion to it all. It was his job to appear as normal as possible. For all their sakes.

Big Mike sat behind his enormous dark wood desk and bid them sit in two high-backed chairs he'd already set out. Carly, for all her usual noisiness, said nothing while he asked if they'd like coffee or soft drinks.

Tension rolled off her, though. John could feel it and hoped this thing would be over soon. She must be going crazy trying to figure out why she was talking to a priest.

"Well, Carly, this is a pleasure," Mike began. "John has told me a little about why you're visiting New Jersey and wondered whether I could get you enrolled in our local high school. I'm glad to say I called in some favors and you can start at Mary Immaculate of the Grotto on Monday." He smiled that priest smile of his.

Carly half turned to John. "School?"

John tried to gauge her mood. "If you want. It's not far, there's a bus that picks up the kids right outside the rectory every day."

Her lips thinned. "Catholic school costs money."

Mike offered an explanation. "We can take care of that. John here told me you were enrolled in St. Aloysius before you left Philadelphia. We can always arrange a tuition exchange."

She shifted uneasily in her chair. "I don't know." Looking to John, she lowered one eyebrow. Her eyes reminded him of an animal in a trap, ready to gnaw off its leg to escape.

"Er, Father, I'm kinda dry. I sure could use some of that coffee you offered before."

"What? Oh, sure. I'll go get you a cup. Carly?"

She shook her head.

Mike went to get it and as soon as he left the room, Carly leaped up and confronted John. "What's going on?" Her hands were balled into fists and her face flushed. "How could you do this? If they ask for my transcripts, they'll know where I am!"

John moved away from the back of the chair. "What difference does that make? You told me you got kicked out of your—out of the convent."

She swiped at her face with her palm. "Yeah, I got kicked out. But I don't want anybody to know, to be able to find me . . . not that they would. But how could you do this without asking me?"

He felt her anger, freshened after this morning's sullenness, and thought he understood. "So, Miss Snow, Mother Superior didn't exactly give you the list, did she?"

She backed away. "I told you I took it and left right away."

Even while sitting, his eyes were nearly at the same level as the kid's. He focused on them, willing her to tell him what else had happened, why she was so upset.

Carly went stone-faced, then tilted her head as if listening for something. "How long does it take to get coffee?"

She didn't want to talk about this to the priest, he realized. Catholic school—what a burden it placed on the young. He almost chuckled, but that wouldn't be appreciated, not at this crucial moment. So he asked, "What else do you want to tell me?"

Her chin went down to her chest. The blond hair tumbled forward, obscuring her face. "That money . . . that hundred dollars. It was in my file, in an envelope with my name on it. I took it. I stole it."

Ah. Now he understood. "So. What, you think Mother Superior has the cops out looking for you?"

She toed at a mark on the carpet. "Maybe."

He wanted to hug her. He wanted to brush the hair away from her face and tell her everything was all right, but he didn't. He didn't dare offer her comfort—he had no right.

"Do you want to finish out the year? Or at least, until I find your father? It would make it easier for transferring. You told me the other day that you liked school. Would it be hard to go to another school for awhile?"

She shook her head. "I guess I would want to finish. But, about the grades and all. Let me write and get them. They're mine, okay? I have a right to them. I know one of the ladies in the office . . . her daughter is a friend of mine. She'll send them via e-mail if I ask her. Probably."

"They'll need your transcript, that's for sure."

She looked at him once again, her blue eyes searching his, as if trying to decide how much she could really trust him. He watched as the doubt shadowed her expression then lifted. The relief he felt was nearly overwhelming.

"I'll get them by Monday. They're good. I wasn't lying about anything . . . well, not that. And I've never really lied. Not since we made our bargain, and not much before that, either."

If he said anything right then, he knew it would come out sounding funny, trying to get around the lump in his throat that had just appeared. So he nodded and, though he wanted to touch her, to reassure her, he didn't. He heard the doorknob twist and the swish of the door opening. Carly sat back down, her face giving away none of the angst he knew must be running through her.

"Here you go, John."

He accepted the cup of coffee. "Thanks, Father. Carly's decided she'd like to go to Mary Immaculate."

Mike's shoulders sagged as he sat back down. "Good. That's good. You know the bus will pick you and the other students up out front here, right? If it's cold or raining, most of the kids wait in the vestibule. I'm usually around then, so I can introduce you on Monday, if you want."

Carly seemed to consider this. "Yeah—I mean, yes, Father, I'd like that."

"Uh, Father, we'll have her records for the school by then . . . don't you worry."

"Everything is set, then. It's a good school, Carly. I think you'll really like it. The kids are good kids. . . ." He let his voice drift off and sat there, looking at Carly.

"Well," John put down the coffee cup, stood and indicated she should, too. "Thanks for your help, Father."

"Yes, thank you, Father Mike." Carly tilted her head as she looked his way. Color rose in Mike's face under her scrutiny.

"You're both welcome. Anything else I can help you with?"

Carly shrugged. "I don't think so."

John put his hand under her elbow and moved toward the door with the kid. "Thanks again, Father."

Mike gave him a tight smile. "See you at Mass, John."

John let out a laugh. "Yeah, someday soon."

The sun chose that moment to come out and shine through the window at the priest's back, giving him a rosy glow, an eerie aura that, if John were a superstitious man, he would have thought God had deliberately caused for some weird sign. What was it with all this religious stuff all of a sudden? He'd never believed in signs or miracles and wasn't about to start now.

He got Carly out of there as fast as he could.

She was awfully quiet on the walk back to the office. John wondered what was going on in her head but did not dare ask for more information than he already had. They walked the two blocks, huddled in their coats against a pre-spring breeze from the ocean. Along the way, John stopped at a newsstand and picked up a copy of the *Times*. The old man behind the counter gave the kid the once over, then asked John for an introduction.

"Carly, I'd like you to meet Curtis Cleveland. He's a fixture around Asbury Park. He also does a little work for me now and then. Curtis, this is Carly, my . . . client. She'll be around here for awhile. If I send her down for the *Times*, you'll know it's for me."

Curtis smiled at Carly. "Pleasure to meet you, Miss Carly. John, I got that other information for you. Wait here, I'll just be a second getting it." He disappeared toward the back of the newsstand and returned with a sand-colored envelope. "Here y'are. I think this will help with that thing from the other day."

He winked.

Carly laughed.

John took the envelope and was about to leave when he turned back to Curtis. "How's your oldest, Curtis?"

The black man smiled with warmth and pride in his eyes.

"Kind of you to ask. He was workin' hard at those midterm exams, I think he said last time he called home. His mother fair bust open when we got the grades. Straight As." His chest puffed out a little and he stood straighter.

"That's good. Real good, Curtis. Next time he's home, have him come 'round. I want to hear all about it—from *his* side."

"He'll be home around Easter time, he said. He promised his mother he'd take her to church Easter Sunday. I'll be sure and tell him."

John nodded good-bye and walked briskly back to the office. Carly called out to him to wait up.

He slowed down. "So, what do you think?"

"About what?"

He tried to appear nonchalant. "Oh, everything. A new school. Curtis. Father Mike."

"I'm cool with going back to school, but I'm maybe a little worried . . . about fitting in and all."

"You'll be fine."

"Yeah, I guess so." She paused, then continued. "I like Curtis. What's this about his son?"

They crossed the street in front of the office. "Oh, he got in a little trouble awhile back. Curtis sent him to me to . . . I don't know. Talk to him about stuff. I did. We've been friends since then and he always stops by when he can. He goes to school in Virginia and it isn't easy for him to come home much."

"Oh."

John stopped her from opening the door. "Look, Carly. I have to do some work. Will you be all right here alone?"

She gave him a small smile. "Sure. I'm going to help Liz with the lunch crowd."

"I don't know when I'll be back. You okay with that?"

"Sure, I can find something to do."

"Okay, then." He fished a few bills out of his wallet. "Take this. I talked to Liz and she said she'd help you buy some clothes later, after the luncheonette closes. I don't suppose you like shopping, though, do you?"

The look she gave him was worth a good laugh.

No one could be as dumb as she thought he was, not from the look on her face.

He laughed all the way to his Jeep.

Carly disappeared inside, went up the stairs, into the office and sat down at the computer.

She had work to do.

Chapter 9

"So, are you tired yet?"

Liz brought her hand to her brow with deliberate drama. "Not quite done in. But I don't think there are any more stores for us to scour." She smiled, but the kid had to realize her heart wasn't in it.

"Is there any money left?"

That made Liz chuckle. "A little."

"Enough for us to get a taco or something?" As if on cue Carly's stomach growled on empty. "But not a cheese-burger."

With a smirk of agreement, Liz nodded. She'd made enough burgers to last a lifetime already. "I think there just may be enough for a couple of tacos and something to drink. And when we passed the taco place before, that delicious smell got to me, too."

Carly and Liz juggled the packages then made their way toward the food court. Between them they balanced a tray covered with wrapped food and one with soft drinks. They both sighed as they sat down at an empty table.

"How do you do it?"

"Do what?" Liz asked.

Carly stretched, then settled the packages beneath

the table. "Shop like that. I mean, I've never spent three hours straight shopping. Without stopping."

"It's not easy, but haven't you ever done this before?"

Carly's expression turned wistful. "I always wanted to, though . . . shop until I dropped with lots of money at my disposal. I never had that before."

Intrigued and somewhat surprised, Liz leaned forward, her taco held tightly in her hand. "So, your Uncle John decided to treat you. That's great. Has he always been your favorite uncle?"

"Uh." The kid paused.

Was she trying to come up with a good story?

"I only just met him the same day you did."

The minute it was out of her mouth, she clamped her lips together.

Oh, ho, she must have realized she'd let loose too much information.

Liz choked slightly then sipped at her drink. "You never met him before?"

She had to hand it to the kid. Whatever else was going on, Carly was going to keep it to herself for now. Did it matter? What did she care about John Preshin? Even if it looked as if the kid wanted to say more, Liz wouldn't press. It was none of her business. *Don't get involved*, her little internal voice shouted.

Carly cleared her throat, apparently having made a decision. "My mother is dead. She knew John real well. I thought I'd look him up while I was in the area."

Liz didn't buy any of this.

"Look, Carly. My grandmother says John is a good guy. I'm sure your mother thought so, too. And I admit, I have no right to ask you so many questions other than the fact that I'm nosy. He's a strange man . . . oh, I don't mean bad strange, just difficult to read. You must have picked up on that already."

Carly giggled and sat closer to the table edge. "Have I ever! The first time I ever saw him, he opened the door, just wrapped in a towel with this huge strip of duct tape across his chest! Nearly freaked me out! But wait, there's more," she paused at Liz's guffaw. She joined in, then added, "He has this huge scar on his shoulder, right or left I can't remember just now, but it looks like he got shot. Can you imagine?"

Liz sobered. "Gram told me about that. He did get shot. You know he used to be with the FBI, right?"

Carly put her fist on her lips. "Uh, no, I didn't. We haven't had that much time to, you know, actually talk much."

Liz let that pass. "But that awful duct tape? I bet there's a good story behind that."

Sipping from her soda, Carly dithered then continued. "I'm not sure I really want to know about that. But I was the one who found out how to get it off."

This just kept getting better and better. Liz asked, "How did you do that?"

Carly chewed on her taco before answering. "I went online and found out that you need this stuff to spray on it. He said he knew where he could get some, so we went all the way to his parents' house and he brought it back here."

That tidbit made her eyebrows arch. It was too easy picturing John's chest. Broad and nicely muscled . . . *don't go there*, her inner voice warned, louder this time.

Liz wiped a napkin across her lips, noting she'd removed most of her lipstick as she did. "So, did you meet his parents? What are they like?"

Nodding, Carly's face brightened. "His mom's real nice. She fed me and gave me this huge package of food to bring home for later. John said she's like that to everyone she likes."

"I've never met them myself, but Gram likes them. She's met them a couple of times, she told me. What's his father like?"

"He's funny. He looks all sorrowful and sad. John's

sisters moved back home with their kids and he's crowded out of his house. He doesn't look like John, he's shorter. I think John looks more like his mother, only she's tiny and has gray hair already. But she sure can cook. I'm invited there on Sunday for dinner."

Liz bit into her taco precisely and chewed slowly. Thinking. He didn't act much like a family type guy. But according to Carly, he was. Hmm. She had lots more questions for Carly but didn't dare appear to be pumping the kid.

"It must be getting late. Maybe we'd better get a move on," Carly ventured.

Liz sipped at her drink and nodded. "Yes, it's after four. You'll want to get all this stuff unpacked and hung up. And we have to stop for some groceries, don't forget."

"Thanks for bringing me here, Liz. I've never shopped like this in my whole life."

"Anytime," Liz replied and found she meant it. She'd had fun shopping with the kid. Carly, not *the kid.*

Everything she'd tried on looked great on her, one of the incredible bonuses of being young and built just right and extremely pretty. Liz remembered she'd been that way, too, but it had all seemed so very long ago. This fact was brought home vividly when Carly had thrust a beautiful soft brown and blue outfit at her and insisted she try in on "for fun."

The skirt and top looked really good on the hangers, but to Liz's chagrin, when she'd reluctantly gone into the dressing room and actually put them on, she'd been shocked to see that the outfit looked better on the hanger than draped over her body.

Boutiques were not for thirty-somethings. God! Mutton dressed as lamb. Three different views of her backside and none of them looked properly . . . proper.

The low cut top showed way too much top. And any more leg and she'd be showing her panties. Maybe ten years ago, but not now. Maybe in California, but not in Jersey. People were allowed to get older in Jersey.

And her hair! Good Lord, when had she last had it cut? And tamed? She honestly couldn't remember. It needed help badly, but it wasn't beyond hope. Not yet.

She turned the steering wheel, stepped on the accelerator and let Carly chatter, trying to pay attention but failing. Thankfully, Carly didn't require more than one word answers. Not now.

Mutton dressed as lamb? Wild woman hair?

She'd gotten a good look at herself in that boutique. While she still had a relatively good body, her life on the left coast had taken its toll on her.

And it bothered her now that she'd seen what she'd allowed to happen to herself. She hadn't really cared about her appearance in a very long time. But she should. She still had some good years left. Plenty of 'em.

Maybe it was time to start over *for real*.

If she wanted to, could she attract a man? One like that arrogant idiot upstairs for instance? Hmm. She got a little rush at the thought, like the old days on the boardwalk, playing fifty-two pick-up.

Maybe she shouldn't be so negative.

Changes could be made.

Chapter 10

Georgie Hahn occupied the third barstool from the back of the shabby tavern, right where his wife said he'd be. His voice had a sharpness to it and he kept putting his hand on the arm of the guy sitting half off the stool to his right. The guy looked ready to book. John approached, gave him a knowing nod and the poor guy eased off his perch and left the bar after sliding some bills at the bartender.

Georgie looked blearily up at John. After a few seconds, his face broke into a watery grin.

"Bourbon John! You old sonovabitch! What brings you to Linden? You know, the place—"

"Where men and oil are crude?" John responded, unable to keep himself from laughing. The old joke was still funny. He waited for Georgie to finish the ritual.

Raising his glass of beer, he drained it, belched and continued, "No, lad, where men and oil are *refined.*"

John slapped him on the back. "Good to see you, George. Been a long time."

"That it has, old son. That it has." Looking John up and down, he added, "You're lookin' good, for a government employee."

John's shoulder throbbed in quiet response. "Not any more, I'm not."

Brows raised in surprise George turned from his attempt to get the bartender's attention. "What, you say? I don't believe it. You were always so set on being FBI. What the hell happened?"

Rolling his shoulder, John gave his stock answer. "I'm out on my own . . . have my own investigation business." Thus neatly avoiding awkward answers to bullshit personal questions.

His former friend, mollified and too inebriated to remember his initial question, let it go. Instead, he gestured for John to sit in the vacated stool and flicked his hand again to the bartender. This time, with new blood to serve, the man came over and took the order. "Another for me and a shot of Wild Turkey for my friend here."

John wanted to wave his hand to signal not to bother, but he couldn't risk offending Georgie. He had questions that needed answers.

"Just club soda with a twist, thanks. Long drive."

After watching Georgie down half a glass of Rolling Rock and sipping tentatively from the cloudy glass, John felt his body relax. The hassle of driving up the Parkway and into Route 1 to Linden forced old memories back on him, memories he wanted buried forever. Georgie . . . shit, his hair was going, his teeth were stained yellow from the Luckies he still smoked as evidenced by the open pack in the pocket of his faded shirt.

The vague taste of lime trickled down his throat, lubricating it enough for John to start on Georgie.

"Hey, Geo . . . do you remember that summer we all lived together in Belmar?"

A grin appeared, changing his friend's expression to one of bliss. "Oh, indeed I do. That was the summer I got laid every single night."

A shudder rattled down John's back. The taste of metal replaced the sweet citrus taste inside his mouth. Shit. He turned to face George Hahn, looked him in the eyes and tried to read the truth in them.

Georgie was probably too beered-up to lie.

John pulled the photograph from his breast pocket and handed it slowly to the other man.

"What's this?"

John turned his attention on the bottles lining the back of the bar. His own face looked mottled in the dirty, marbleized mirror behind them. Christ, he looked sick. But he kept his voice calm, professional.

"Recognize this?"

"Shit, yeah. That's all of us. Even your ugly mug." He ran his hand over his balding head. "God, I had so much hair!" He smirked and brought the photo closer. "Who the hell took the picture? We're all here. You, me, Dutch . . . Francis Xavier. Stuart and good ol' Pasquale."

"I think Dutch's sister or brother came down for the day and took the picture. His brother. Yeah. Goofy-lookin' kid who had just turned twenty one. Wanted to celebrate. He had his camera and took this just before I left for work."

Georgie seemed lost in another time as he stared at the picture. John let him look long and hard without saying anything . . . waiting. He'd been trained to wait, to let people do the talking instead of asking outright for what he needed to know. It would come soon.

"Those blondes. Wow, they were somethin', weren't they? I used to pop one or the other nearly every night."

"Spare me those gory details, Geo. I wasn't around most nights, remember? And as for your sex life—well, I bet you don't even remember their names, do you?"

Shoving the picture back at John, George wagged his finger, his face flushed with indignation and Rolling Rock.

"I most certainly do. This one," he stuck his finger at the blonde on the left, "was Tammy. Tammy Lundquist . . . yeah, that was her name. The two of 'em were sorority sisters somewhere. I can't think of it now, but give me some time . . . I have a mind like a steel trap."

John sipped at his drink. George waved to the bartender. This time John passed his hand over his glass; the bartender nodded but poured George another. After a chug, George brightened.

"University of Delaware. Both of 'em. Tammy and . . . Tammy and *Bunny*! That's her name. This one on the left—her name was Bunny. Bunny something. Bunny, Bunny something. Let me think. Historical. Why am I thinking president? Real WASP, that I know for sure. Give me some more time and I'll remember."

John fumbled for change, hiding his impatience. He'd gotten one name and a small lead and possibly part of another name. Not bad. Suddenly he wanted to get into the Jeep and get back to his computer.

"Thanks, Geo. I gotta get goin'. Say hi to Beth and thank her for me, okay?"

As John rose from the stool, George stopped him with a hand on his sleeve. "Beth, she doesn't know about that summer, you know, Bourbon? She's a good wife and I love her. She wouldn't understand about what went on that summer. Hell, she's given me three beautiful, smart daughters and the woman is a saint. Times have been rough over the years, and I've been in and out of work at the refinery, but she's always been there for me. God, I love her. She might not understand how wild I was, if you know what I mean."

John knew. "I didn't mention anything to her, Geo. The past is past. Look, I'm not even on a case. Just found this picture stuck in a book, can you believe it, and couldn't remember the names of those women. I had to come down from Newark and figured I'd stop by to see you. That's all. We have to get together . . . all of us. Maybe stop in and see Dutch some day soon."

Realization hit George at the mention of Dutch's name. He nodded vigorously. "How's he doin'? Anything?"

John shook his head. "I can't tell. It was never very good. Some days are better than others."

"Maybe I'll get down on a good day. Yeah, maybe I'll drive down this weekend and pay him a visit."

John rested his hand on his old friend's shoulder. "Yeah, he'd like that." Tossing a five on the bar, he nodded reassuringly at his drunken friend and left.

Jesus, please don't let him be Carly's father!

Chapter 11

Linden, New Jersey, has to be one of the ugliest towns in the state. No, John reconsidered, not just the state. Maybe the entire East Coast. What with the oil refineries and the trucks and the chemical plants and the turnpike and Route One. Man, everything looked decidedly dirty and worn out. Even the quickie motels along the highway looked drab despite their neon and thirty-year-old attempts to clean up.

He'd never understand why there were so many houses in the town.

He'd grown up less than twenty miles away, but he'd had clean air to breathe and green grass on the lawns in summer. The leaves on the trees stayed green, too, until mid September.

In Linden, even though the trees were bare now, when the leaves came out, they'd be gray in no time.

He pulled onto the parkway and headed south. The drive from Linden back to Asbury Park, past the huge steel tanks filled with refined gasoline that fed the East Coast with fuel, took just long enough for John to think, to put things in some sort of order. So far, he'd spoken with three of the five possibles on Carly's list. Discounting himself because he could, he'd spoken with a priest, an invalid and a drunk. Any one of them could have been the kid's old man.

The thought left a bad taste in John's mouth. A priest. What good would he do as a father? Mike took his vow of poverty very much to heart. Celibacy, too. As far as John knew, Mike didn't slip away without his collar. If he did, well, it would be easy to understand, but somehow, John didn't think it happened. Ever. As for how the man handled that situation, that essential drive, Jesus, he didn't want to think about that at all. A sacrifice of that magnitude ought to guarantee expiation of all mortal sins in a man's past, present and future. Not getting laid, ever again. The thought boggled the mind!

No. Mike would keep his vows. But what if he had a child? What would he be able to do for her? Would he be forced to quit being a priest?

As straight up as Mike was, he probably would. But how would he support a child? What kind of job would an ex-priest be able to get? Used car salesman? Telemarketer? Jesus! Did Mike know how to use a computer?

He didn't want it to be Mike. Mike was one of the good guys, after all. Never hurt a fly. Always did the right thing. Always.

Would he quit the priesthood for his own kid?

The Parkway stretched, rutted and black, ahead of him. He grumbled as he guided the Jeep over the Driscoll Bridge that spanned the mouth of the Raritan River. When were they ever going to finish the new lanes? He drove carefully in the middle, avoiding the potholes while also avoiding looking over the side at the murky water far below. He shuddered, hating this part of the trip.

Okay, okay. Dutch. He didn't like to think about Dutch too hard. Dutch and his wife had never had kids. In the beginning, his partner had worried that it might be his fault, wondering and afraid that he might be shooting blanks. Idiotic things you talked about and confessed while on surveillance cooped up in a car for hours at a time. But, no, it wasn't Dutch.

He stopped at the toll booth and handed the guy a single. The old guy smiled and placed his change directly into his hand. John nodded, wondering what the hell kind of life it was, standing in a booth not big enough to hold a chair and a human being, for eight hours a day, sucking in polluted air all that time. A gas chamber might be bigger. He stepped on the accelerator.

One night while observing the action coming and going from a small mom and pop store that sold bootleg videos, Dutch had told him that Barb didn't want children. After one scare, she'd had her tubes tied so she couldn't get pregnant.

He'd watched Dutch set his jaw and fight some internal battle but never brought up the subject of children again. Dutch liked kids, he knew that. Dutch was godfather to three nephews. It must have hurt him not to have kids of his own. And Barbara . . . shit. She was a witch. Maybe Dutch would have been better off marrying someone else. But Dutch didn't believe in divorce.

He leaned back against the headrest of the Jeep and thanked his own commitment to bachelorhood. Seeing what Dutch went through with his wife, and some of the other agents . . . John had seen enough to know that his life didn't need the complications of marriage. It was complicated enough with family. A wife would have ruined him.

Hah! Ruined what?

No. Look at George's wife. She was a bona fide doll. And to put up with George's drinking all these years? Three girls, probably grown up by now. And, even though George was a lush and he'd never even moved out of the house he'd inherited from his parents, she'd stuck with him. Maybe that was love. Maybe she loved him, despite his faults, and kept to her vows. Vows again.

They kept coming up.

Dutch had never strayed, or at least John didn't think so. Dutch was too straight-up to screw around. Wasn't he? He'd screwed around in college. He'd fucked everything he could back then. But he'd gotten married and, apparently, stopped seeking pleasure with different women.

Maybe. He'd see if he could get Dutch to wink at him next time he managed to sneak past Barbara's evil eye.

Two potential fathers left.

Stu Cooper up in Piscataway. He could maybe catch him on Sunday when he went to see his parents.

And Pat DeAngelo. Jesus Christ, not that bastard.

Traffic was murder and Liz concentrated on keeping the car and its contents from bumping and crashing into the concrete Jersey barriers that lined the highway. Her fingers clutched the steering wheel in a death grip.

At least Carly seemed to appreciate the situation and did not talk to distract her. Normally, she liked the gossipy chatter, or any friendly talk, but not now. Their lives were at stake.

The luncheonette. Her grandmother had okayed the changes last night. They'd talked about it until Flo's eyelids drooped and Liz helped get her into bed. She'd stretched out in her room, staring at the ceiling and thinking.

It was a good idea. No, a great idea. Asbury Park might not ever come back to its former glory, but there were going to be changes and they were going to be massive. Money could be made. Construction brought people into town. The curious would follow, and those who were willing to take a chance at being in on the ground floor of the renaissance. And people needed to eat.

A soup bar wouldn't require too big of an investment and she had her alimony and her trust fund money that was just sitting in the bank. She wouldn't let her grandmother get in too deep, anyway, though she didn't know much about her financial situation. Gram had always had sufficient money, but whether there were secure investments other than the building and the business, Liz just didn't know. But she'd make sure she found out.

It was a reason for her to stay, though. A project of her own. Something to occupy her mind, challenge it.

Get it out of the hell she'd been through . . . no, don't go there. It's over. You've done enough crying. The past is past and tomorrow is what counts. It has to count, she warned herself, or your life won't be worth anything.

She pushed away the rush of dark thoughts and bad memories and worries about the future when the car ahead of hers stopped abruptly. Liz slammed her foot down on the brake and let out a little squeak. Carly jerked forward, safe in her seatbelt.

"Wow! What a moron!"

Liz agreed. "Must be a man."

Around four o'clock, visitors would show up at the nursing home some days, so John made it a point to come directly after three. He'd cajoled the nurses into letting him visit with Dutch before hours, charming them with his boyish smile and sometimes bouquets picked up at the convenience store on his way over. They loved him and didn't mind his visits.

Barbara did.

She'd instructed them not to let him see her husband during visiting hours.

Evidently the nurses disliked Barbara as much as he did, so they did not follow her orders. That's why John was in the antiseptic-smelling corridor at three o'clock. Before he opened the door to Dutch's room, however, one of the nurses ran up to him and tugged on his arm, pulling him toward the nurses' station.

"Not today, Mr. Preshin." Her indignant tone set his nerves on edge. "What did you do to that woman? Mrs. Van Horne said she went to court to get a restraining order against you."

Nonplussed, he turned his smile on the young nurse. "That's a load of crap! She has no cause. And Barbara Van Horne never stopped me before."

"I can't let you go in there," she whispered, shaking her head. "I could lose my job."

He gently extricated himself from her now insistent grasp. "I'll look into this," he paused and checked out the woman's nametag, "Grace. But, since I can't see Dutch, will you tell him that John Preshin was here? And make sure everything's okay? Will you do that, please?"

She nodded, her eyes downcast. "I . . . I'll do that, sure. As soon as I can."

John left the nursing home wishing he had something to crush with his bare hands. Like a throat.

How dare she keep him from his partner, his friend?

The Jeep started up after he tromped hard on the gas pedal. Flooding it would do absolutely no good for anyone; neither would driving off with this fury raging inside him. His hands shook while he fought off the urge to snap the steering wheel in half. Taking steadying breaths, he thought to drive straight to the school where Barbara taught.

And decided against it. Not in this condition.

He wanted a drink.

Jesus, it was only 4:30 in the afternoon. Turning onto

the beach road, he followed it down to the break in the chain link fence that had once secured three derelict buildings, parked and turned off the engine. The opening in the fence allowed him to see the Atlantic.

Time to think.

Waves pounded the sand, foaming and grinding away at the beach then slurping back into the grayish green water. He stayed in the Jeep, hands still clutching the steering wheel. He'd never really liked Dutch's wife, disliking her more after his friend revealed what she had done to guarantee she never had any kids. Odd, that, a teacher not wanting kids of her own. And Dutch so keen to be a father.

He'd kept his mouth shut that night, and even more so after the shootings that had left him with a bum shoulder and Dutch gravely wounded. Kept alive with tubes and medicines, but out of it most of the time anyway. Not able to move much more than his eyelids and some facial muscles. What went on inside his brain? That hadn't been damaged. Did he think about the past? About him? About the day his life ended in such misery? Did he think about good times? Did he ever think about those blondes in the photograph? About making love to one of them?

Of making a baby?

Shit. John flexed his fingers to get blood back into them. Cold wind seeped into the Jeep and wrapped itself around his legs. The old desire for a drink burned in his brain but he denied it. Far better for him to go home and check his answering machine, get back to work, get this off his mind. Sober.

As he restarted the Jeep and backed out of the space by the yawning gap in the fence, his stomach rumbled. He'd only had an egg and pork roll sandwich he'd fixed for himself before going to Linden. That was hours ago. With nothing else in his stomach, hunger hit hard. Growling beneath his breath, he pulled into the lot of the Park and Shop, determined to pick up some thick, red meat to throw on the grill back home. It had to be thick and it had to be beef.

He hated this place almost as much as he hated hospitals and nursing homes. The dull interior colors depressed the hell out of him and, no matter how many times it changed hands, the store always looked dirty. Not that he was some kind of clean freak—but this place creeped him out. This was the best place in the immediate area to buy meat, though, and the butcher was still on duty.

"Give me a T-bone about this thick," he said to the man behind the overflowing glass display case. With his thumb and forefinger he indicated just how much steak he wanted. The butcher, swathed in bloody white apron and work coveralls, smirked.

"Gonna cost ya," he laughed.

Shrugging, John gave the man the go ahead. "Right now I could eat it raw."

The other man paused, knife in midair. "You sure you want this much? That's a hell of a cut of meat."

John gave a curt nod, his mind already wandering, contemplating whether he had the patience to wait for a potato to bake. He could always nuke one.

A girly laugh made him turn his head.

"Well, look who's here!" Liz Atwater, looking a little worn and harried but definitely sexy with her red hair tumbling around her shoulders, drawled to her companion—Carly.

The kid gave a little start, almost as if she'd been caught with her hand in the cookie jar.

"Hi!" Brilliant conversationalist that he was.

Liz looked him up and down, much as he'd looked over the meat in the display case. He hoped she liked what she saw.

"Are you planning on cooking that for yourself or cloning a new cow?" She watched with him as the butcher slapped the enormous steak onto the white paper and wrapped it.

"It is my intention to fire up the outdoor grill and burn this magnificent steak on the outside while keeping it mooing in the inside."

Carly gasped.

Liz laughed at his corny joke, her guard down for once, a light, healthy, genuine laugh coming out. Had she wrapped her arms around him and kissed him on the lips, he'd have felt it the same way. Straight to the groin.

He adjusted his stance, reaching up to accept the package from the butcher when he sensed someone else had joined their happy little group.

"Bourbon John." The brittle, cigarette-rough feminine voice grated against every nerve in his body.

He looked down to see a small, hard-looking woman, hair dyed a brassy blonde, dressed in tight jeans and a thick jacket, staring up into his eyes.

Hers were mean.

"Yes, I'm John Preshin. Do I know you?" Going through his mental Rolodex, he could not put together this woman's face with a name. He couldn't say he'd ever seen her before.

Her eyes surveyed the scene.

"Oh, isn't this just peachy?"

Her hand came up and slapped him on the left cheek so fast he didn't have time to move away.

Turning to Liz and Carly, the woman spat out, "If you can't keep a better hold on your man, at least try to keep him away from us decent women!"

The blonde spun on her heel and stormed off, leaving John to put his hand on his cheek and Liz and Carly open-mouthed.

Carly recovered first. "What was that all about?"

John rubbed his offended cheek. "I haven't the slightest idea."

Liz's brow furrowed and she looked at him with an expression of extreme pain on her face. "You don't know that woman? She sure seemed to know you."

He muttered, "Must be a case of mistaken identity. Happens to me all the time. Maybe I just have that kind of face. People see me around, think they know me. But they don't."

"Right," Liz demurred. But her expression did not lighten. Evidently she did not think too highly of his explanation. "She called you by name."

With one last quick rub at his cheek, he said slowly, "She called me by my nickname. Half the people on the East Coast know me by that name. She may have been introduced to me ages ago, but I swear, I don't know who she is."

Liz cleared her throat. "Carly, we'd better get the rest of the stuff on the list for Grandmother. Or would you prefer I finish up here and you ride home with your . . . guardian?"

"I'd rather you took her with you, Ms. Atwater. I have another stop to make before going home. If you don't mind, that is."

"Of course not. Carly is delightful company." She shot him a glare that tweaked his conscience just a little. "Go ahead and do what you have to do. We like having Carly around."

They started off in the direction of the cashiers, but John called them back. "I like having her around. Don't think I don't."

Liz glanced over her shoulder, chin up, lips set in a tight line. Her look told him she didn't believe one word he'd said.

Six-pack in hand, John stopped in front of the newsstand and plunked it down in front of Curtis. The black man snaked out his hand and slipped the beer behind the counter. Without a word, John raised an eyebrow in question and Curtis shook his head. John shrugged and walked away.

He opened the door to his office and, startled, nearly shut the door to check to see if his name was still stenciled outside. Bags and bags filled the space, all marked with names of shops he'd never step foot inside. Ah, he remembered.

He'd given Carly money to go shopping for clothes for herself.

Looked as if she'd bought out the mall.

"Shee-it." He waded through the piles, deposited his brown bag of groceries on the minute counter in the kitchen and put the pint bottle of bourbon in a cabinet over the sink.

Hunger pangs squished through his gut.

Nothing would blur what had happened in the nursing home, but food might put him in a better mood.

John stepped out of the apartment and onto the small porch that served as a fire escape and grill platform. Once the grill heated up, he'd throw on the steak, but in the meantime, he put a potato into the microwave and cut the recently purchased head of lettuce in quarters. The February air still had a chill to it, but before long the welcome heat of summer would bring him outside most evenings. Alone, looking over the back end of Asbury Park.

This was no life.

A commotion sounded below as he stepped back inside. Carly and Liz must have returned from the store. John looked at his bare feet and stepped back into his deck shoes, preparing himself for company. It didn't take long for footsteps to sound on the stairs. More than one set. Oh, man. Liz was coming up with the kid.

Selflessly, he tossed two more potatoes in the microwave.

Chapter 12

A guilty furrow marred her brow as she hurried to pick up the bags of clothing. Liz kept reassuring her that if he'd given her the money, he'd meant it was okay to spend. But the kid didn't lighten up.

From the recesses of the kitchen John watched her scramble around the office space that was also his living room and currently served as her bedroom. She moved efficiently and with a dancer's grace. Had the nuns provided her with ballet lessons? Another question to ask the Mother Superior.

He had to put Carly out of her misery.

"I hope you got enough clothing to last awhile." Strolling into the room, he tried to appear nonchalant and Cary Grantish.

Carly stopped moving, clutched five bags to her chest and looked frightened. Not the effect he was going for.

"It's my fault," said Liz.

"I'm sorry!" Carly blurted out at the same time.

John looked from one to the other. "Wait a minute. It's okay. I'm not angry and there's nothing for anyone to apologize for. You need clothes for school and hanging out. Liz helped you pick them out and

I'm sure she is a woman of good taste. Not one to waste money on frivolous things."

"We went a little overboard," Carly explained.

"I thought she needed plenty of everything, since she doesn't have much at all," continued Liz.

He put the barbeque tongs he'd been gesturing with down at his side. "Look, did you spend it all?"

Carly's head dipped, her eyes searching the floor. He noticed that Liz looked him straight in the eye.

"Yes."

Silence ensued. He let it drag on more than a few heartbeats before saying, "Good. That's good. A girl needs clothes."

The kid's head shot up. Her bright blue eyes shone with relief and . . . something else. Gratitude? He felt like such a shit for making her worry.

"Thank you." She looked as if she wanted to move but remained where she was, hands still clutching those bags.

"I'd like to see what you bought, though. I don't know much about fashion . . . but I don't want you going to Mary Immaculate's looking scroungy."

"Oh," Liz came around from the doorway to stand in front of him, "we got her the proper uniform, but we also got her some outfits for weekends and after school. Good enough for a date."

He hadn't thought about Carly dating.

He'd barely thought about her all day, but he certainly had not thought about the kid going out with a boy somewhere. Something around his chest squeezed air from his lungs, forcing him to inhale deeply.

"Oh. Good. That's good."

Liz's eyes narrowed.

John cleared his throat. "Liz, you were right about the size of that steak. There's plenty of meat for an army. I was just going to put it on the grill. Would you care to join Carly and me for some supper?"

He caught the bemused flicker in her eyes before she hid it. It didn't take her long to answer.

"Do you have anything to go with all that cow?"

He laughed. She never gave him an inch. He liked that about her.

"Yes, I'll have you know I have lettuce and baked potatoes."

"I . . . ," she glanced over to Carly who shot back a pleading look, "I'd love to."

What had he just done?

He couldn't remember ever cooking for a woman before. Liz was a great cook. For that matter, so was Carly. The only thing he knew how to cook that didn't come in a box was steak or pork chops. Baked potatoes? Did he even have butter? A quick mental inventory led to the refrigerator. The newly purchased sour cream would have to do. No butter. No salad dressing but tucked in the back he found a jar of mayonnaise.

The grill sizzled as he put the slab of beef on it. Instant gratification came as the smell reached his nostrils. He stood, tongs in hand, wondering what the hell had come over him . . . asking Liz to stay for dinner. And the clothes. He'd meant it; he wanted Carly to be dressed properly for Monday. How much money had he given them? Where the hell was she going to stash all those clothes?

There was a large closet he used for storage off the office. He'd filled it with crap when he moved in and hadn't opened the door since. Maybe there was room there. At one time, Flo had said that a few tenants had used the closet as a small bedroom. For an infant, maybe. He'd figure something out. Maybe the kid wouldn't be around long, anyway. This was temporary. Temporary, until he found out who her father was.

Two names left.
The two biggest assholes he'd ever met.
Yeah, right.

Something was bothering John. Liz didn't know him very well, but she could tell that something other than her presence was forcing him to behave the way he was. What was going on?

She saw Carly watching him, too, with the intent probing eye only a teenager could possess. The three of them walked around each other like cats on ice. He laughed, the deep sound resonating through his chest, but not quite coming out happy. Carly withdrew from conversation, leaving Liz to come up with idle words that had neither depth nor substance. Certainly not Virginia Woolf, but not what she'd come to expect from him. She'd watched him long enough, now, to figure out when he was being himself. And now was not one of those times.

Perhaps she shouldn't have accepted his invitation. Whatever was going on was making her testy. She kept moving around the tiny kitchen, watching John on the deck, watching how he moved, almost as if she were waiting for him to do something stupid.

Maybe she was.

He had a way of moving few big men were capable of exhibiting. His long, lean lines, the way he held himself told her he wasn't afraid of anything and nothing could hold him back if he really wanted to accomplish something. The set of his jaw as he played with the tongs . . . even that told her something of his determination. But tonight there was an emptiness in his eyes. That obnoxious little spark of the devil just wasn't there.

And Carly had withdrawn from the conversation,

limited as it was, to sit at the desk in the office, tapping the eraser end of a pencil against her thigh. Poor kid.

She tried so hard to be perfect.

"You okay?" Liz asked.

Carly yawned then put her hand over her mouth. "Oh, sorry! I'm so sorry!"

Liz laughed. "That's okay. You must be tired out from all that shopping."

The kid nodded. "I didn't really think we'd bought so much . . . spent so much money."

Liz bent closer and put her hand on Carly's shoulder. "Look, he said it was fine, and I believe him. Are you afraid he's angry? Is that why you're so quiet?"

With a heave of her shoulders, Carly paused, then said, "I don't know what to think. I think something's wrong, but maybe it's not me. Don't you think he's acting funny?"

"Eh. You can never really tell with guys. And I don't think you ought to waste any of your time worrying about it. If it isn't something you've done to bug him, it could be something totally unrelated to anything. Maybe he got a parking ticket. Maybe he's being audited by the IRS. Maybe he has a difficult case he's working on."

"Yeah," Carly whispered so softly Liz could barely make out the words. "Mine."

"Hey, ladies, are you hungry?"

John appeared before them, tongs waving, a wicked little smile playing about his lips.

"I think we're both pretty hungry. Is it ready?"

John stepped back out on the deck. She heard the clang of metal and a string of swear words.

Liz hurried to the deck door. John stood in front of the grill, cussing creatively.

Beside her, Carly tittered.

"Dammit! Dammit to hell! Sonovabitch!"

Liz tamped down laughter. "What's wrong?"

John slammed down the lid of the grill. The noise echoed from the building behind them.

"Ran out of propane. The f . . . darn steak isn't done."

Liz put her hand up to her mouth, coughed into it and lowered it to her side. "I'll start up the broiler in here."

He stopped, looking as if the idea had never occurred to him. Then he favored her with another of those beaming smiles of his.

"Excellent idea! What would we men do without you ladies?"

At least the banter was back. Liz went to the stove and checked the oven, then fired up the broiler.

"Where's the aluminum foil?"

Carly located it and placed it in his outstretched hand. John lined the broiling pan with the silvery stuff. She stepped aside while John placed the half-cooked steak on the pan and opened the door for him to put the pan inside.

Liz found it interesting that the three of them worked together. Almost in a kind of rhythm.

But the moment was brief.

"Hey, kid. Carly. Wake up. I have to talk to you. You can go right back to sleep."

He bent down and shook her shoulder.

The kid groaned and turned her face into the pillow.

John stood. "It won't work. Believe me, I know. My voice will ring in your brain for the next fifteen minutes, and you'll wake up all cranky and cuss me out. If you just listen to me now, you stand a good chance of going back to sleep."

The pillow sufficiently muffled Carly's words, but he was sure he wouldn't really have wanted to hear them anyway.

"I'm up." She propped herself up on one elbow.

Hair by Mixmaster. He remembered his sisters looking that way.

"I have to work. I'll probably be gone all day, maybe into the evening."

She yawned in his face, scrubbed her knuckles across her eyes. "Uh-huh. Okay."

A tinge of annoyance whispered through him. He was not used to explaining his movements to anyone.

"You might want to see if you can make some room in that closet over there. It's packed with my stuff, but I think if you straightened it up, there might be enough room to hang up all your new clothes."

She still didn't look fully awake. He knew how she felt. These early morning jobs never caught him at his best.

"Liz said she had some cleaning to do this morning. If you get hungry, you can go downstairs and mooch food off Flo. You hardly ate anything last night."

Anger flickered in Carly's eyes. He figured it was just teenaged reaction to feeling spied upon.

"Wasn't hungry."

"Well, if you get hungry, go downstairs. I gotta get going. And don't forget, tomorrow we're going to my parents' house."

She yawned again, this time covering her mouth with her free hand. "Yessir. I remember."

"Lock the door after me."

She nodded.

"Did you get notebooks and pencils and stuff?"

"Yeah. They're in one of the bags."

"I'll be back late, but I'll be back."

"Okay."

"Stay out of my room."

The anger flickered once again.

"You can use the computer, I took off the password this morning."

"Thanks."

"I gotta go."

"Go already!" she snapped.

He paused, about to snap back at her, then thought better of it. Teenage kid was entitled to have emotions.

"I'm going."

He nearly made it to the door when she called after him. "What did I do wrong last night?"

"Huh?"

He walked back to the fold out bed. "What?"

She sat up, pulling the sheet over her. "I asked you what I did last night that was wrong."

He sat on the edge of the mattress, ran his hand through his hair. What did she want him to say?

"Nothing. I just had a bad day yesterday." He looked at her eyes, trying to read in them the reason for her question.

"It wasn't me or the clothes?"

"No. I told you that was okay. Sheesh, you're so sen-si-tive. Liz knew it was all right. Why . . . did I say or do anything that made you think I was angry with you?"

Carly nodded. "Let's drop it."

"Did I?"

The kid looked him in the eye, piercing his very soul with her reply.

"Yes. Are you looking for my father?"

He stood, afraid the kid would read something in his eyes he didn't want her to see just yet. His voice came out harsher than he intended. "Look, kid, I don't have time for this. I have to work. And I don't have to explain myself to you or anybody else."

Her face fell, a look so hurt, so pained, it couldn't have been worse if he had struck her.

Chapter 13

John came down the stairs with a lightness in his step that definitely caught Liz's attention. The idiot. Peering around the corner into the kitchen, he beamed her a smile while she remained leaning against the counter, coffee mug gripped tightly in her hand.

"Morning!"

Liz screwed up her face in reply. *Likeable idiot.*

"You look cute early in the morning."

"Ugh."

He slid onto a stool and grabbed the sugar dispenser. She threw him a glare. "You usually get your own coffee," she noted. "And you're decidedly chipper. What gives?" Her hand automatically went to the coffee machine and poured him a cup. Pavlovian. At least she wasn't drooling, although John did look decidedly tasty in nice, neat casual clothes. He might clean up real nice if given the opportunity. Not that looks mattered all that much, she knew. But he sure had them. She sighed then realized what she'd done.

To cover it, she ventured, "Going to mass?"

He snorted a laugh. "Not me. I'm taking Carly to my parents' house for Sunday dinner and plan to do a little investigating while I'm there."

This caught her attention. She'd been dying to find out how the kid's case was coming along. "You're trying to find Carly's father? Following up a lead? That's sort of what I gathered from Carly."

John resettled himself on the stool. "Maybe. Kinda. I'm not really sure, but I'm trying. She doesn't think I'm working very hard, though, and I do have other cases."

"You knew her mother?"

"That's still not a fact, but I think so. Look, Carly doesn't know any of this, that's why she thinks I haven't been looking. And I don't think it's a good idea to tell her what I've already found out. Some of it isn't exactly glamorous. It isn't even nice. She's a good kid and she hasn't had it easy in her sixteen years on earth. It is my intention to find her father, or any relatives there might be, and get them together somehow. But I don't want to get her hopes up unnecessarily. There may not be any relatives. I haven't gotten that far."

She understood all too well. "I lost both my parents when I was in the ninth grade. That's when I came to live with my grandmother during the summer. The rest of the year I spent in boarding school, which was okay, but I would rather have been here with Gram. So I know how important it is to have family. Carly needs a nice family."

"I agree."

"If you find her father and he's a . . . I don't know . . . a creep. What will you do?"

John rubbed his hand over his face.

"Dunno. I suppose I have to hand her over to her father. It's only right."

The horror of his words seeped through Liz's entire body. Just when she was starting to think he might just be one of those good guys her grandmother claimed existed, he said something so stupid she wanted to kick him. Before she could get the angry reply out of her mouth, though, he backed off.

"Hey, wait. Don't go jumping on me! I haven't found her father, just some clues, some hints, some half remembered names. I haven't found *anything* for sure. And I like the kid. I wouldn't want her to go into something worse than she's already had, but I do not know what will happen. I do know she's got to go somewhere. She can't stay on my sofa forever."

"Why not?"

"You've got to be kidding. There are a million reasons why not. But I don't want to waste my time thinking about possibilities that may never arise. I'm going to find her father or some relatives and take it from there. Only blood relatives can have any claim on the kid . . . I know that much of the law."

Liz glared at him. "And in the meantime?"

John tapped his fingers on the counter as he appeared to give the matter more thought. "She can stay at my place, work for you and Flo, go to school, try to be happy. What's wrong with that?"

How could he be so callous? Didn't he care? Or was he just being true to his sex? A jerk.

"Enjoy your breakfast, John," she said as she left him at the counter. Under her breath, she added *if you can.*

John drove the Jeep with both hands on the steering wheel. He had a great deal on his mind.

"Did you find who you were looking for?"

He ran his hand over his face, keeping his eyes on the Parkway as they headed north. The sun was out, but the temperature was in the low twenties and great blasts of wind pushed and shoved the Jeep from all sides on the express lane of the toll road.

After an inordinate amount of time, he answered.

"Yeah. Only it was an old lady. She lives with her son in Delaware."

The kid perked right up. "So, you managed to track her down? How did you do it? Why did you do it?"

"It's boring. You don't have to act like you want to know."

"No, I'd like to know how you found this old lady. I really would."

He gave her a hard look, suspicious as hell whether her motive was purely one of interest.

"I work for lawyers, sometimes, locating people named in wills. Most of the time they're dead already. But sometimes I manage to find them when they're alive and then they can get the money or whatever they were left in the will. Sometimes, though, somebody wants to get money off of them, like for hospital or doctor bills. I don't do those cases. Not too often, at least. Sometimes when I need the money I'm forced to. But I don't like it."

"You must be good at finding people."

He allowed a tiny smile to quirk up the side of his mouth. "It's a gift."

Carly turned her face to the window. "Are you some kind of psychic or something?"

John chuckled. "What, you mean like old Madame Marie? Hell, no. Instinct. That's all I've got. And a trained investigator's knowledge."

The kid was like a dog with a bone. "Then how did you find her?"

"I searched records. I found her name in the town where she'd grown up. From there, I got lucky and found her married name. Then, from there, I located her children or at least two of them, and from there, I found where she'd moved."

"Was she glad to see you?"

He had to think about that. "Suspicious, at first. She'd never known her father. And he'd never even

seen her, but somehow, he'd kept an eye on her. I
don't know. Maybe he felt guilty and put her name on
an insurance policy. He's dead and I can't ask. But
she's going to get a few dollars to help her in her old
age. And from some old guy she never knew."

Carly ducked her head. "Her father," she whispered.

John looked over at her, then back to the road. "Yeah.
Her old man. He'd run off on her mother a long time
ago. Ida Mae told me that she'd seen a picture of him
once. But never seen him. She said her mother wouldn't
talk about him, just said he was a soldier."

The tension in her jaw relaxed and Carly slowly un-
curled her fingers. "So, he did some good after all,
right?"

"Right. The particulars are a mystery, though, and will
remain so. But she's happy. So that's good. Sometimes
these things make my day. This was one of those times."

"Did you ever think that maybe he loved her, maybe
that's why he named her on his insurance?"

No, he'd never given it any thought. "I have no way
of knowing. The mere fact that he named her meant
that he knew she'd been born, and knew what her
mother had called her. I don't know, maybe he had
contact with the mother and the mother never told
the girl. Things like that happen."

She pinned him with her eyes. "But maybe he loved
her. Maybe something awful happened to keep him
away. Maybe he was in a hospital. Or working over-
seas, somewhere he couldn't talk to her. Maybe her
mother was rotten and deliberately kept them apart."

"Look, kiddo, yes, any one of those scenarios is possible. I will never know. My guess is that he was in
prison, though I haven't checked it out. Or maybe the
mother chose to live a pretty bad life, on welfare, not
asking the guy for money, even though she knew
where he lived. It's possible. All of it is possible. We'll
just never know.

"But this story had a happy ending. So, you should be glad for Ida Mae and her family."

In a tiny voice, she said, "I am."

Mrs. Preshin kissed Carly on the cheek in welcome. Her hand went to touch the spot. She'd never had anyone kiss her hello before.

"We're not ready yet, dear. Why don't you go in the living room and meet my grandchildren? I think Jennifer and Lisa are there. The boys—maybe they're outside working on that old car. Frankie thinks he can get it running. Hah!"

Mrs. Preshin dismissed the idea with a wave of her hand then went back to the oven. Whatever she was cooking smelled wonderful to Carly. Pots and pans jammed the cramped kitchen and narrow stove. Dishes competed with glassware on the table. Carly straightened the flowered tablecloth, pulling it smooth while adjusting the stacked plates. Mrs. Preshin made a shooing motion.

"Go out and introduce yourself to the boys."

Carly stood, battling her fear of meeting new people, especially boys. Her inner struggle must have shown, because a tall, pretty lady appeared from the hallway and gently grabbed her arm.

"I'm Gloria, John's sister. You must be Carly."

She nodded.

"Good. I see my brother has deserted you. So typical. Let me introduce you around, sweetie. I can't believe he just dumped you here like this."

"Uh, he went to the bakery for your mother. He didn't . . . not exactly. . . ." Carly stumbled over the explanation.

"Hah! Yeah, right. He could have taken the time to show you around. My brother is an inconsiderate boor."

The sun shone with weak February light, but at least it wasn't raining. Carly heard the ringing bounce of a basketball coming from the driveway and the sound of male voices. Her heartbeat quickened.

Gloria pulled her along until they came upon the old car and the boys. Boys. About five of them. Carly wished she'd kept her hat on. Her pale blond hair always drew too many eyes in situations like this and she knew it. Why had she washed out the black rinse?

Gloria shouted, "Frankie, get over here. And bring your disreputable friends with you."

First one head shot up from the belly of the car, then another and another. The first one quickly covered his look of annoyance with a grin.

"Sure, Mom. Anything you say."

The boys made their way over to where Gloria stood, gripping Carly's arm, probably so she wouldn't run away.

A chorus of "Hey, Mrs. Barrett," sounded all around.

Gloria placed her hand on the shoulder of the young man nearest her. "This is Frankie. Carly Snow, Frankie. Carly's here with Uncle John."

Frankie, tall and dark-haired with greenish blue eyes, gave Carly the once over. His eyes sparkled when he finally greeted her.

"Hey, Carly."

"Hey," she managed to get out. She felt her face burn and knew it was red to the roots of her hair.

Gloria relaxed her grip on Carly's arm. "Well, you big goof. Don't just stand there. Introduce her to your friends."

He ducked his head and an embarrassed smile crept over his lips. "Mom—yeah, okay. This is Chuck. Jimmy. Choochie and Carl."

The boys nodded, giving the appearance that they did not care about her in the least, but she caught them checking her out just the same. Choochie smiled at her and Carly realized that he had the most endearing dimple. His light brown eyes danced merrily. The boys recovered from their embarrassment quickly and stood, arms dangling at their sides, looking down at Carly from their greater height.

They were all tall. Cute, too. Carly had never been the subject of this much checking out before, but that didn't mean she didn't like it. The boys vied for her attention, and Carly realized that control of the situation had passed to her. She could handle this now. She joked quietly, listened as they jostled for her approval with wild stories or put downs.

Oh, yeah.

This was a good thing.

John stared at the man he'd known as Stuart Cooper for the past twenty years or so. He'd never have recognized him if it weren't for the small gap between his two front teeth.

Everything else about the man had changed.

He had more metal on his person than John thought humanly possible. Ears, lips, scalp, eyebrows, nipples, running up his arm . . . silvery studs and rods poked out of ghastly white flesh all over the place. And what wasn't just plain skin was covered with tattoos. Big, garish, colorful tattoos.

John had difficulty keeping his eyes focused on the man's face.

Good thing he decided to visit him before eating some of his mother's good food. The man made him want to puke. But on to business.

"Stu. How goes it?"

Stuart walked over to John and extended his hand. "Bourbon John Preshin, as I live and breathe! How are you, you old sonovabitch?"

John returned the handshake. "Just up visiting my folks. On the way off the highway, I passed by the tavern and noticed the sign had been changed. What gives?"

Stuart Cooper eased himself behind the bar and started washing glasses. "It was time for a change. The old River-bottom wasn't attracting a very young crowd, so I . . . er, we decided to change some things around."

Looking around at the manacles and nooses dangling from the wall where there had once been deer antlers and examples of the taxidermist's art, John refrained from shaking his head at the abrupt changes to the décor.

"Interesting. So, has the clientele improved?"

Stu stopped wiping out the glass he held. Soap dripped down his riveted arm. "We're doing great. In fact, Leeandra is thinking of opening up another night, extending the weekend to Wednesday. We get our biggest crowds on the weekend, of course, but Wednesday will extend 'date night' a little."

John nodded knowingly, wondering what a date in The Marquis Club would be like. "Sounds good."

Stu looked around, a small twitch in his eyelid. "We're doing okay. It's a living."

"Good. That's good." John waved away his friend's offer of a shot of Wild Turkey.

"Who's Leeandra?"

Stuart started at the sound of the name. "My wife," he admitted, his voice so soft John had to lean forward to hear better.

Puzzled, John leaned forward also. "What happened to Bernice?"

Stuart confided, "She left me ages ago. Leeandra and I have only been married for a couple of years."

A tall, lean woman with loads of black hair appeared in the doorway behind the bar that used to lead to the kitchen. "Stuart! We're not open yet!"

The man shrank back a bit at the whip-crack sound of her voice. "This is an old buddy of mine, Leeandra. I've told you about him . . . John Preshin."

The name didn't register for her face went as blank

as possible under the loads of black mascara and contouring. She walked over to John, gave him the once-over, then cast him a withering look John supposed was aimed at being seductive.

Her voice, sultry now and almost purring, set John's teeth on edge. "So, big boy, where has Stuart Little been keeping you all this time?"

"John's with the FBI, Leeandra."

She backed off as if stung.

Not wanting to disillusion the woman, John explained, "Well, not any more. I'm a private investigator, actually."

She leaned over the bar, her breasts threatening to spill out of the leather bustier she had painted on her body. "Fascinating."

John held back a laugh. "Not really, but it puts food on the table."

His shoulder throbbed beneath his shirt. He wanted to get out of this sleazy S & M bar, but he had some questions for his old friend. That is, if the guy could even think through all that metal and the influence of his dominatrix.

Casting John a sidelong glance that promised all sorts of nasty things, Leeandra slid her hand down her husband's body and tugged at his balls. Stuart flushed. John ducked his head to avoid seeing the other man's discomfort.

When Leeandra disappeared around the corner into what had been the table area long ago, John decided he'd better press for answers quickly before he caused Stuart any of his wife's wrath.

"Stu, do you remember the summer at that house in Belmar?"

Wiping at the bar with a damp rag, Stuart appeared to think it over then replied. "Yeah, I remember it well." A small smile crept across his face, reaching his down turned eyes, bringing a glimmer of light to them.

John swiveled a bit on the stool. "Do you remember those two girls who used to stay at the house?"

Stuart positioned his back toward the doorway where his wife had exited. "Yes. I remember them. Jesus! I remember them."

Trying not to show his extreme interest, John tugged at the lapel of his leather jacket. "You wouldn't remember their names, would you?"

Stuart hunched over, dug out a glass and polished it with a clean cloth. His back still toward the door, he nodded. "Hell, yes. Bunny Adams was one. The other was Tammy . . . something. Scandinavian. Tornquist? No, that's the name of one of the regular guys who comes to the club. Let me think."

John waited. He couldn't let his excitement show. He had two names now. But the crucial question remained.

Slowly, he slid off the stool. "Do you remember, did you sleep with either of them?"

The amazing tattooed man flinched as if John had struck him. With a quick look around, he hesitated in answering. The room fell silent.

"Hell, yeah. I did. They were always asking for it, ya know? Insatiable, those two were. Once even both at the same time. Doggie dirty. They loved it that way. I gotta admit I enjoyed them both."

John's gut threatened to squeeze out his throat. He felt his whole body shake and tried to calm himself, just long enough to leave the premises without gagging.

"That all you needed to know?"

He twitched his mouth, gained control and said, "Yeah, thanks."

Stuart leaned both forearms on the bar. "That's what brought you here after all this time?"

"Yeah. You've been a big help, Stu. We ought to get together again, talk about old times."

Stuart laughed. "I'm not really allowed out of here

that much, but it sounds like a good idea." He paused, then snapped his fingers. "Lundquist. That was the name."

"Hey, thanks!" John shot over his shoulder as he neared the door to leave.

Stu called after him. "Hey, how's Dutch?

John stopped in his tracks. "He's alive."

Stu's head lowered to his chest. "Okay, man. See you around."

Not if I have anything to say about it, John thought. "Yeah, Stu. Good talkin' to ya."

As the door slowly swished shut behind him, John's stomach soured. For a second, he thought he might retch on the broken macadam of the parking lot.

He looked at his watch. Jesus, if he didn't hurry, he'd miss dinner with the family. After what he'd just seen, he needed the chaos he knew he'd find at his home. At least it was change he could tolerate. After all, it was family. They were stuck with him.

Chapter 14

Carly recounted the entire day's events to her captive audience, detailing the kind and amount of food, who had eaten and where they'd all fit. Flo listened with delight shining in her eyes.

"I know Rose. She's a good cook. I have that lasagna recipe, you know," Flo said when Carly paused for breath.

Liz cocked her head with unfeigned interest. "So, tell me about this Choochie character. That can't be his real name. What did he look like?"

Carly closed her eyes. "He's something else. He has dark hair and brown eyes, but a light brown, not dark or gray, just an unusual color. I don't think I've ever seen eyes that color . . . like dark honey with bits of gold. Nice teeth. Shortish hair, but with texture . . . not gelled up or anything."

Teenagers. "He sounds like a real hunk."

"Oh, yeah. His real name is Jason. He told me just before I left. Nice name. Real nice name."

"Contacts. He must have been wearing colored contacts."

After that announcement, Liz rose from the armchair and went into the kitchen area. She remembered being that crazy over a guy she'd just met. Lots of guys she'd just met. Being boy crazy was a prerogative of being sixteen. The whole time the popcorn blew itself to bits in the microwave, she indulged in some nostalgic thoughts of fifty-two pick-up on the boardwalk and the boys she'd loved and lost.

Sixteen had been a very good year for boys. She'd been in love every other week that year, so she knew what the kid was going through. Those feelings bubbling inside, that itch, that longing, that joy in the game. Wow. The game had been so much fun!

She returned with the popcorn and offered it around. Only her grandmother dug into the bowl.

Carly groaned. "Not for me, thank you. I'm still stuffed. I didn't even have dessert."

From her position on the sofa, Flo shook her head, her disappointment obvious from her expression. "Too bad."

"Aw, Mrs. Preshin gave me half the pie to take home. Want some?"

Liz broke the spell. "Hey, kiddo. Don't you have school tomorrow?"

"Oh . . . yeah, as a matter of fact, I do. I guess I'd better get going upstairs. My uniform is ready, but I don't know what else I may need. I put stuff in my backpack on Friday. They'll give me a little leeway, don't you think? First day and all? I hope. So, all in all, I guess I'm ready."

"Would you like me to go with you to the bus stop?" Liz offered, then rolled her eyes.

"Thanks, but no. It's just around the corner, practically, and Father Mike said he'd be there. Nothing can happen to me just going around the corner. I'll be fine."

Flo patted Carly's hand. "You'll fit right in. You're a sweet girl. They'll take to you right away, so don't you worry about it."

"Thanks, Flo. I appreciate you saying it."

"Good night, then, kiddo," Liz said. "In case you want breakfast tomorrow, I'll open up the grill for you at about six. Or maybe just a doughnut?"

"Jelly . . . and a carton of milk."

Jelly!

The way the kid said it, the tone of voice set psycho butterflies dancing in Liz's stomach.

It sounded so much like John.

Regaining control over her temporary madness, Liz reached out and squeezed Carly's hand. "Don't worry. Sleep tight."

Liz doubted she would.

Chapter 15

Mr. Preshin was awake. She had heard him walking around in his room, the slight thud of bureau drawers opening and shutting, but he had yet to show his face.

She didn't have much more time before she had to leave for the bus. Her uniform, rolled at the waist to an appropriate level above her knees, itched. So what else was new.

Why wasn't he coming out? Didn't he want to wish her good luck?

It was his idea to get her into school anyway. What was bugging him? Her eyes went to the clock once more.

The clock glared back at her. She had to go if she wanted to say good-bye to Liz and Flo and get that doughnut.

"I'm leaving, Mr. Preshin," she called out, trying not to sound too hopeful.

The bedroom door opened a crack.

"You all set?"

Why didn't he stick his head out?

"Yeah, I've got everything."

"Know what to do?"

"Yes. I'll go to the church and get the bus. How hard can it be?"

"Right." The door clicked shut.

Swell, she thought. Nice way to send a kid off to school. Have a good day, Carly! Be careful crossing the street, Carly! Do you have your lunch money, Carly?

Muttering, she made her way down the narrow stairs to the kitchen below. She spied the jelly doughnut and carton of milk on the back counter. At least someone had thought about her.

"Carly, take care now," Flo called from the luncheonette. Liz, busy at the cash register, gave her a hurried wave then turned her attention back to the customer before her who counted out change in his hand. Carly caught Liz's eyebrows going up in exasperation, her hands planted on her hips. She didn't blame Liz for not seeing her off.

John, she blamed.

He could have stuck his head out and looked her in the eye. He could have wished her good luck, or a good day.

Maybe he was still pissed at her from the other night.

Carly steamed off in the direction of St. Boniface's. Maybe Father Mike would have a kind word for her.

John groaned as he slid his sock over his foot. He hated having to leave his bed, but he had important work to do before leaving for the nursing home. Sleep had eluded him most of the night. Now he had to go through the day feeling like crap because he'd been thinking about the kid.

Carly.

She'd been a hit with his parents and the rest of the family. They'd taken her in as if she were one of their own. Telling her stupid things about him. Detailing family stories from way back. Talking about his great uncle blowing up a cow with a firecracker and how this same guy had been in jail for bootlegging. Great. Tell the kid about all their skeletons.

What would they have done differently if they'd thought she was his daughter?

Another Preshin.

Probably nothing. But there would have been lots of questions. And his family would not have stopped asking until they'd had answers.

Wouldn't do. Carly more than likely, absolutely could not be his kid.

He grunted as he tugged his jeans on and fastened his belt. Liz and Flo more than likely had given the kid breakfast. Yeah, he could even see Liz's early morning scowl change to a smile as she watched Carly leave through the kitchen. Yeah. Hmm. Good enough.

If he had a conscience, any left at all, he would have felt bad letting the kid go this morning the way he did. But he was getting too attached. She was like a stray puppy. If he allowed himself to really care, it would bother him when she went away with her father.

But, in reality, the chances of him finding the kid's father were getting slim. He'd ruled out all but the one remaining candidate. As he looked in the bathroom mirror, he decided that he didn't really need to shave, though the stubble was a couple days old. Gave him a more tough guy, hard as nails look. His hand rubbed against the dark growth and the scraping sound drew a harsh laugh from him.

He didn't have to be pretty for this day's work. It wouldn't help.

Mother Superior had had years to practice that look. With one narrow glance, she'd summed up John Preshin and found him wanting in every possible way. And she didn't have to say a word for John to know this. The pinched lips spoke volumes.

For this confrontation, he should have shaved and worn slacks, not jeans. But he was working and he worked in exactly what he was wearing now.

"I'm a busy woman, Mr. Preshin."

She fiddled with the business card in her fingers and kept her eyes lowered.

"I thought you might be interested to know that Carly Snow is staying with me until I can locate her father."

The woman slowly raised her head. He caught a tiny spark of interest in her eyes before she blinked it away.

"And what is it you want from me, Mr. Preshin? Carly Snow left St. Hedwig's of her own volition."

He cleared his throat. They both knew that wasn't exactly the truth.

"Carly was unable to tell me much about how she came to be at St. Hedwig's. From my understanding, this isn't an orphanage."

"It is part of a system, Mr. Preshin. We have rules we must follow."

John felt his impatience growing into anger but realized he could not display it in front of this rather fierce old woman. "So, you cannot tell me anything about Carly's mother? How the girl came to live in the convent when most kids go into foster care?"

"Carly was a special case. Arrangements had been made for her care."

"By whom?"

Mother Superior set the business card down on her desk and folded her hands in front of herself. "I am not at liberty to tell you anything about Carly, Mr. Preshin. She's out of my hands now. I don't even have her records any longer."

A pain shot through John's forehead. How convenient! Carly leaves and her file gets trashed. How had she been able to see it then if it was such a confidential thing? Something was definitely fishy about all this.

"Is that policy?"

The old nun, her gray hair short and cut close to her head, stood. She avoided looking at him now, though, and that was a tell all its own. "It's my policy. There are files relating to Carly somewhere in the state bureaucracy, I suppose, but I no longer have access to them since she turned sixteen and left us."

Feeling dismissal close, John took a stab at a guess, hoping to elicit a reaction from the nun.

"So, these confidential files just happened to contain a list written by Carly's mother, naming men who might be her father? And a bank deposit book? The kid told me she happened to see it on her birthday. Right here in your office. Monthly deposits to St. Hedwig's, yet in *her* file folder. The one with the list, and the hundred dollar bill in an envelope with her name on it.

"But *they're* gone? You don't know where they are?"

This time the woman looked him directly in the eye when she answered.

"It is unfortunate that Carly happened to see the folder. I will not deny what she saw, but I'm afraid I cannot tell you anything. This is all confidential, all our records are. For you to come in here, expecting to see them, well . . . Mr. Preshin, I can't help you."

"Can't or won't?"

His hand shook slightly until he clenched it into a fist at his side. Nuns. They were incredible. The government should use them as spies. No one would get any secrets from them, and the enemy would come away feeling guilty as all hell for having asked.

He stood and took a few steps toward the door. "You know what I think, Sister?" He turned to face her, wanting to see her expression as he delivered his little speech. "I think you know a lot more about Carly than you let on. I think you know her mother. I think you or St. Hedwig's was paid to take care of the little girl, probably by Carly's grandparents or their lawyer. Yeah, more than likely their lawyer. And I think that Carly shouldn't feel guilty about reading that file, or taking the list or the money. But she does. But you know what? I think it was her right to see it. And I think you left the folder there deliberately, but of course, you wouldn't admit to it."

The Mother Superior shrugged her shoulders. The weight of her omission must have been exceedingly heavy, he thought. If he could just get her to admit he was right. At least he could tell Carly not to feel bad about what she'd done.

"Carly is a headstrong young woman. She took it upon herself to leave St. Hedwig's and go in search of her father. When she stepped out of that front door, she ceased to be my concern."

He recognized a master of control when he heard one.

"In that case, I don't suppose you care, but Carly's in good hands and I *am* going to find her father. I am also going to find out who her mother was. You can take that to the bank, Sister."

Her lips pressed into a tight, thin line, the nun glared back at him and wished him good day.

Why, then, did he have the impression that she was not disturbed but pleased by his threat?

Lunch rush over, Liz leaned against the back counter and wiped her hand across her forehead. Did she have time to hit the bathroom or were there more customers lingering outside, finishing off their cigarettes before entering the luncheonette? Had she ever felt this wiped out?

She wondered how Carly was making out on her first day of school.

Flo poked her head around the opening to the kitchen. "Sweetie, the mail came. There's something for you, looks like it's from your lawyer. Want to read it out there?"

Liz shook her head. "I've got to take a break, Gram. I'll look at it out back."

Slowly she made her way through the crowded space between the service counter and the work counter, snagging a dirty plate as she did. Her lawyer? What could he have for her?

Nothing good. No additional settlement checks. Certainly nothing from her ex. *Nada* of real interest to her, she was positive. But she took the large envelope from her grandmother and walked into the apartment they shared. As her fingers touched the deep yellow packet, her sense of dread grew.

She carried it into the lavatory and tore it open.

Out came a smaller envelope, thick with something inside, the return address being that of her ex's lawyer. Hmm. The dread intensified.

Inside, a small, plain white envelope, addressed in the bastard's hand to her. Her fingers trembled as she peeled away the flap.

And stared with disbelief at the contents.

A birth announcement.

He'd had a baby boy.

Liz read the words, horror filling her to the point where she bent over the john and vomited so hard she found herself on her knees by the time she stopped.

He'd given his new son their baby's name.

Some of his favorite nurses were on duty this afternoon. He strode up to their station and leaned one elbow on the counter, flashing a rakish smile he knew made women melt.

One by one, the ladies looked at him. Their eyes

gave them away. Something was wrong. He'd never seen the normally cheerful women turn to stone.

"What gives, ladies? Are you going to keep me away today, or can I sneak by you?" From behind his back, he produced a bouquet of gaily tinted daisies.

Instead of showing their tolerant pleasure, they looked away.

Long seconds passed in awkward silence until one, the one he'd pestered the most from the time Dutch had been moved to the facility, stepped toward him and asked him to follow her.

They went in the opposite direction of Dutch's room. A nervous chill skittered up his spine. "What's up, Millie?"

She held open a thick door and asked him to go inside. After shutting the door carefully behind her, she bid him sit in one of the straight backed chairs of the nurses' break room.

He sat, hoping she would sit also.

Instead, she stood before him, hands clasped in front of her.

"Jesus, Millie . . . what's wrong? Why all this? What's . . . ." Slowly, her silence reached him through the walls of protective oblivion he had raised years ago.

"Dutch. What's happened to Dutch?"

Millie unclasped her hands and placed one on John's shoulder. "I'm sorry, Mr. Preshin, but your friend isn't with us any longer."

John started to rise. "Where did she put him? Is it because of me? What's going on . . . tell me!"

The nurse, her colorful scrub top unsuited for this moment, cleared her throat. "Mr. Van Horne passed away last Thursday."

John fell back in the chair. She might just as well have reached into his chest and pulled out his lungs and heart.

Dutch! Dutch, gone?

"Barbara . . . his wife. Di . . . Did she say anything about," he choked over the words, "funeral arrangements?"

Millie shook her head. "It all happened very quickly. Mrs. Van Horne had his body removed as soon as he was pronounced. She seemed to know exactly what she had to do and your friend was out of here within the hour."

Stunned, John tried to accept this news, tried to make sense of it. "Why wasn't I informed?"

"I'm sorry, Mr. Preshin. I wasn't on duty until after the body . . . Mr. Van Horne . . . was removed. Mrs. Van Horne and the gentleman with her left explicit instructions that no one was to inform anyone outside of the nursing home of Mr. Van Horne's demise."

John shook his head. "Let me guess . . . especially me."

"When I came on duty, I figured you'd already been notified by the family. I'm sorry."

John stood. "Where was he taken? Can you at least tell me that?"

"I'll have to look at the file, if you care to wait." Millie left the room. John stood there, every muscle in his body filled with rage and regret. He wanted to pick up a chair and smash it through the window, but somehow, his arms weren't cooperating. His hands, fisted so tightly he felt his nails digging into his palms, began to shake as the adrenaline coursed through him.

The nurse returned within seconds, stepping quietly into the room. "Mr. Van Horne's body was taken to McKaskie's."

"McKaskie's?" John didn't recognize his own voice as he whispered the name.

"The crematorium . . . in Neptune."

John turned away from the pity he saw in the nurse's eyes.

"We all liked Mr. Van Horne, Mr. Preshin. And you were a good friend, coming here all the time. None of us wanted to keep you away, you know. But we had to follow orders."

John snarled, "Following orders. Everybody is always just following orders."

Then, before he continued, he stopped, rubbed his hands over his eyes and apologized to Millie. "Sorry. I . . . I'm not angry with any of the nurses. I understand."

Millie's lips quivered. Her hand went out to touch John's sleeve, but he pulled away.

"Sorry, Mr. Preshin. I'm so sorry."

John stumbled out of the room.

Chapter Sixteen

"I think it's time you left."

John leaned toward the bartender. "Why?"

The man on the stool next to him muttered, "'Cause you're a white man making a fool outta himself in a black man's bar, peckerhead."

John found this remark uncalled for. "What's goin' on here? Can't a man have a refreshing drink in this place? Play a little pool?" He cracked his knuckles for emphasis.

The bartender's hands searched under the glistening wooden bar and clenched around the baseball bat kept there for emergencies just like this one. "I'm asking you nicely to leave. Look, you've proved your point, Mister. But I don't want any trouble, and you keep beatin' these boys at pool, there's gonna be trouble."

"What's the matter? Can't anybody here play pool good enough to knock me off the table?" He raised his voice in challenge over the murmurs of the guys nursing their beers at the bar.

"Anybody in here know this white guy?"

From further down the bar, an old man called out, "Yeah, I think I saw him talkin' to Curtis at the newsstand. Over on the main drag, you know the one I mean."

Behind him, John heard deep voices agreeing that Curtis was a good man. But the voices got louder and he found a distinct tone of disapproval in them. Especially from the younger men he'd already eliminated in an impromptu pool tournament who now formed a militant arc behind him. Their faces, reflected in the mirror behind the bar, were not welcoming.

He itched to punch one of them. He knew how good it would feel for his fist to make contact with flesh as he put everything he had into it. But, even if he wasn't seeing double, there had to be twenty men in the bar. And he stood out like a marshmallow in a coal mine. The odds of him coming out alive were not good.

Dutch. He needed Dutch at his back.

Dutch was dead.

He couldn't do it alone, even if that had been his plan in the first place. He had intended to have a drink, to get stinkin' drunk, but had opted for the pool table instead, beating one player after another with uncanny accuracy. It hadn't been enough to ease his soul-deep hurt.

"Okay. I know where I'm not wanted." Sliding off the stool, he glanced around the smoky room. Several sullen faces glared back at him. Not good, not in this part of town. He'd intruded and he knew it now. He'd won a great deal of money, too. Enough to get him jumped outside the door. So he dumped it on the bar.

"Drinks on the peckerhead," he called out as he left.

The young toughs went back to their beers and someone racked up the balls once more. The bartender spoke softly to one of the older patrons. The man nodded and followed John out the door.

Once on the main street, the man quickly turned back to get the drink he'd been promised for making sure the white guy made it safely out of the west side of town.

John filled his lungs with the cold February air. He

kept walking, automatically passing the shops and boarded up storefronts without looking at them or his reflection in the windows. He didn't want to see himself. He didn't want to see any trace of the man who should have been the one to die. Not Dutch. Dutch had pushed him out of the way after the first bullet had blown into his shoulder. It was Dutch who had taken the second shot in the neck. The one that had blown apart his spine.

John could have died then. Dutch shouldn't have been hit, but he was, and even if he'd stayed concealed, he could have been shot by any of the other wiseguys in the warehouse that night.

Maybe it would have been better all around if the bullet had hit just a little lower and he'd died right there. Stupid. He'd been stupid. He'd left his vest in the car. How stupid could he be?

But Dutch had worn his vest.

Dutch never screwed up, except when he married Barbara. That witch. God, he hated her. Almost as much as he hated himself.

Nearly three o'clock. He didn't feel the anger much after his long walk home. As he approached his apartment, he noticed that he'd parked the Jeep sorta cockeyed with one tire on the curb, the other three definitely not parallel to it. He'd only been angry then.

The ache in his chest hurt worse than his shoulder ever had. If he'd had a drink. . . . Hell, there'd been times he'd gone up the stairs on his ass, one step at a time very slowly. But that had never really changed anything and never would.

Dutch was dead.

Life wasn't too bad, Carly thought as she rushed down the cracked sidewalk toward the apartment. She wasn't that far behind at Mary Immaculate—she could easily make up for the two weeks or so. In some classes, she was only a few pages away from the rest of the kids. The kids had been cool but not stand-offish, except for that one girl, but then, wasn't there always one girl to spoil perfection?

She'd ignore her.

The kids at the bus stop had been nice. Father Mike had been there, his hand on her shoulder as he introduced her. Another junior, a girl, had been willing to help her get her bearings. She'd filled her in on most of the layout and which teachers to hope for and which people to be wary of and what she must never, ever do.

Carly laughed to herself. Bridget was sweet. Tall and athletic in appearance, she made the trip to school interesting. She was nice and full of gossip, but not catty. At least, not that Carly could tell from two conversations with the girl.

The ride home took nearly an hour. She'd have to figure out a way to do some homework on the bus if she didn't want to waste all that time. Darkness settled over Asbury Park making it appear even grimmer than it looked in daylight. The sidewalks were nearly empty, though. In deep winter, it would be pitch black by this time. One streetlight shone on the corner in front of the luncheonette, dark inside by now. As she made her way to the side door, she noticed the Jeep and John's bad parking job. She'd give him grief over it as soon as she got up there.

She flipped on the light switch at the bottom of the stairs and thundered up them, backpack banging into the walls with its weight of new books.

No light came through the frosted glass door. John must still be out. She dug into her pocket for the key he had given her a few days ago, but tried the knob first. To her surprise, it gave.

Creeped out by the darkened office, Carly sensed

that it wasn't empty. She could feel someone else in there as she stepped beyond the threshold.

"Don't turn on the light."

She started at the sound of John's voice.

"Why not?"

"Because I need to be in the dark." His words were slightly slurred as if it hurt to use them.

She refused to respond, fearing he'd kick her out into the night for good.

"Take your stuff and go stay with Flo and Liz."

"Why?"

He grunted, sounding more like a pig than a real pig. Carly gritted her teeth and stepped farther into the room. He sat at his desk. She could see him, covered in shadows, his dark hair fallen across his forehead, eyelids lowered. She could feel . . . something. Something was really wrong, but she dared not ask. Risking her precarious position now wouldn't be good. Things had been going too well. It had to come crashing down all around her like this.

Her luck sucked.

"Life is shit, kiddo."

With slow, deliberate movements, he folded up the laptop and wrenched the plug from the wall. "Here. Take this downstairs with you."

She stood, helpless and hopeless. As much as she wanted to ask him what had happened, she couldn't bring herself to do it.

With the thin laptop under one arm, she grabbed some clean underwear and socks from the bag inside the closet. She paused at the door, giving him one last chance to explain, to tell her what had gone so terribly wrong. As if to push her out the door, John covered his face with his hands. Carly left the room, closing the door softly behind her.

Tears stung her eyes as she knocked on Flo's door.

"It's me, Flo. Carly. Can I come in?"

Footsteps shuffled toward the door from the other side. "Sure, Carly. Come on . . . what's wrong, dear?" Flo stepped aside, allowing Carly to slip into the room.

Carly dropped her backpack, the clothes in her hand, flipped the precious laptop onto a chair and struggled against the tears. When Flo opened her arms to her, she stepped in and welcomed the warmth of the old woman's hug.

"There, there, child, what's wrong? Is it school? Were they awful to you? Did something happen?" Flo looked her up and down, a wrinkle of deep concern creasing her forehead.

Snuffling, Carly wiped the back of her hand over her eyes. "No, no, school . . . school was good. I liked it. But when I came home . . . John, Mr. Preshin . . . he's up there in the dark . . . and he kicked me out. His voice sounded all wrong. He's sitting at his desk and I don't know what's going on, but it isn't good. I'm scared. He told me to leave!"

Still holding Carly's arms, Flo shook her head. "Things like this happen sometimes, Carly. John hasn't had it too good for a lot of years, not since he got shot. Men aren't good at handling their emotions or talking about what's bothering them. Whatever is going on, he'll work it out. But he's used to being alone. It's best you stay here tonight.

"Probably by tomorrow morning, he'll be over it, but you can stay with me and do your homework and get ready for school in the morning. I'll send Liz up with some food for him later, but in the meantime, why don't you get changed and—do you have any homework?—do your homework down here and tell us all about the kids at school and what you did."

"Is he going to be all right in the morning?" She sniffled, reached for a tissue in her uniform pocket.

Flo shrugged. "I don't know. He's a man. Men do stupid things all the time we women can't understand

and wake up okay. My guess is he needs to sit in the dark and think long and hard about something and nobody can help him. But he's a smart man. He'll figure out whatever he has to and by tomorrow he'll be back to normal."

"Do you think so? I mean, he wouldn't kill himself or anything, would he?"

Flo stopped Carly from going any further on that line of thought. "Don't go there, kiddo. It's not John's style. Besides, he's too smart to do anything that stupid."

Carly looked at the older woman through tear-starred lashes. "You sure?"

"I'm sure," Flo said firmly. "Say, I was just going to have some cake. Chocolate. And a big glass of milk. Care to join me?"

Wondering if things would be back to normal ever, Carly followed the old woman into the kitchen. No use wringing her hands over this, but she couldn't push the worrying thought away.

The waves crashed and crumbled against the dingy sand as Liz watched through the distortion of her tears. Night came suddenly, enclosing the world in the relative safety of the dark. All good souls were on their way home, to the lights and brightness of their families.

Liz stood at the edge of the wire fence where the sand sifted against her boots. The wind off the ocean blew her hair into her teeth and eyes. Her hand kept going up to untangle it, merely out of habit. She'd been running on automatic since lunchtime. At long last, she felt the anger and loneliness drain from her, leaving her empty.

Nothing that bastard could have done could have hurt her more, she thought. His remarriage hadn't hurt. Hell, the divorce hadn't hurt this much. His accusations—now, they had hurt, and being hospitalized had hurt, but not as much as this blow.

But she was all cried out now. Reality seeped into the vacuum left by the lost emotions. Being a woman alone on the beach in Asbury Park in the dark was not exactly prudent. With any luck, though, someone would come along and murder her and all her heartache would be over. Now that was a bit rash! A casual glance told her that she was the only person on the oceanfront road. Too bad. *I guess it's even too shitty out here for murderers.*

Hugging her jacket closed, Liz began the short walk back to her grandmother's. As she passed the huge old houses that lined the street, she saw that most of them were dark, but some of the windows still framed patches of light. There were people inside. Not all of the old hotels and private homes that had been broken up into apartments were vacant. Some even showed signs of repair. There was that one huge skeleton of the old Oceana hotel, bare bones that must have once been something quite beautiful. She remembered it from when she was a kid. It had an elegance even now in its wreckage.

Your life is in the toilet.

She snorted a laugh. The voice in her head sounded exactly like Olympia Dukakis in *Moonstruck.*

Her grandmother was probably worrying by now and she hated making the sweetheart worry about her. She was supposed to be taking care of her grandmother, not causing her problems. Quickening her pace, she walked past St. Boniface's, not even daring to look at the stained glass windows to see if anyone was home. God was probably eating dinner.

The lights on the main street guided her home, but when she got to the parking lot behind the luncheonette, she slowed her pace. She didn't quite feel like going inside and facing her grandmother just yet. She checked out her grandmother's car, half hidden in the shadows of the Dumpster and recyclable containers, wary of anyone hidden in the dark. She'd found some kids playing back there one day and had to chase them away, fearing lawsuits. Adults could hide back there, too.

With a certain caution, she headed toward the small back porch. Overhead, the decking of the second floor porch formed a roof over this, making it almost enclosed and at least safe from rain. She huddled along the back wall of the building, trying to blot out bad memories and gather up courage to go inside and face Flo.

She noted the blur of something thrown from the top deck just before it hit the empty Dumpster and shattered with a horrendous bang. Shards of glass spewed onto the macadamized lot. Liz's heart squeezed up into her throat, but that didn't stop her from grabbing onto the railing and propelling herself upstairs.

Stopping at the top, she scanned the darkened porch, her eyes falling on the silhouette of John Preshin as he stood looking over the side, examining his handiwork.

"Jesus! What are you doing?" she panted, gulping in huge breaths to fill her lungs.

"Oh, hi, Liz," he drawled.

She took a step toward him. "You scared the hell out of me. What are you doing out here? It's miserably cold and damp."

John gestured expansively. She could see his white teeth as he grinned at her. "Welcome to my world." His arms included the whole of the backside of Asbury Park. Funny. She knew exactly what he meant.

"Are you drunk?" She knew she had no right to ask.

He produced a bottle of something. "Not yet, but I'm considering it. Care to join me?"

She walked slowly toward him. If he fell off the

porch, they could be in for a lawsuit for sure. "Maybe you ought to get inside."

He considered that briefly. "I might do that . . . but then I'd miss seeing the moon rise."

Figuring she'd better go along with him, she stepped close enough to see his expression. He didn't look wasted, just haggard and self-destructive. That was something she recognized readily enough. He probably saw the exact same thing in her face.

She averted her glance. "Okay, where's the moon?"

John indicated a point over the water to the east. "It'll come up over there, unless things cloud up. My guess is, however, that it will come up over there anyway, but we just won't be able to see it."

She smiled, despite herself. "I imagine that's true."

"Yep," he clipped out. "True."

They stood together, silent, for minutes, waiting for the moon to rise.

"There . . . there it is!" She gasped at its silver beauty in the black sky.

He moved close to whisper in her ear, "Told you so." While he was there, he inhaled deeply. Liz felt the air move against her skin and shivered, though not with the cold.

More minutes passed with the two of them, staring in awe at the rising moon. She could feel the length of his long body radiating heat along her own. Normally, she would have been repelled by the close contact of this stranger. Tonight, well, tonight she didn't move away.

"Here," he said, his voice low and rumbling. "Take a hit of this. It will warm you up some."

Reaching for the bottle, she asked, "What makes you think I need warming up?"

He moved away from her, coming to the wall of the building and folding his long body down until he was seated. "You can see the moon go higher from here," he pointed toward it, "and it's safer and more comfortable sitting than standing up."

For further emphasis, he patted the wooden deck beside him.

The seal on the cap ripped as she unscrewed it. After a quick wipe at the top, Liz lifted the bottle to her mouth and sipped at the contents. The bourbon seared all the way down, even though it tasted like burnt rubber. She took another sip in hopes of washing away the initial taste.

Headlights of a car coming down the road from the beach illuminated her face as she joined John.

"Hey, what's this? Tears?" he asked as she settled alongside him.

She jerked her face away from his hand. "Can't get anything past you, John."

Suddenly he had her chin and turned her to face him. "You've been crying?"

Liz tried to pull away. He tightened his grip, but used his other hand to dab at her cheek. His face softened and his eyes held hers. "Tell me."

His tone was compelling. Liz longed to get today's business off her chest, but it shouldn't be to a stranger. Not this one. Not *him*. She bit back words, knowing that if she opened her mouth, she'd tell him everything. She couldn't do that. Yet her heart needed its burden gone. Instead of speaking, she took a pull at the bourbon.

"Hey, that's supposed to be my outlet," he joked. "I'm the one famous for drowning his sorrows, not the pretty lady from Cal-i-for-ni-a. Shouldn't you be downing some granola or sprouts or something?"

She gave a short laugh and handed back the bottle. "I'm not much of a drinker."

"Hell you aren't," he said, screwing on the top. "Look at this! I could have sworn it was full when I gave it to you." Holding up the bottle, he indicated where he thought the level should be, right at the top. It was a good two fingers away from there.

They both laughed, then. Liz felt the whiskey easing the tightness surrounding her heart.

"I'm willing to bet I've had a shittier day than you," John said. His eyes flicked over Liz—bedroom eyes, turned down slightly at the outside corner, with heavy lids now and dark, curling lashes. No smile behind them, though his lips were curved a bit as if he wanted to smile but couldn't.

"You're on," she stated. "How's this for shitty? My ex-husband, the sonofabitch, remarried and just had a baby with his new wife."

John's hand moved sideways through the air. "Happens all the time. Unless you still have a thing for him, it shouldn't matter."

"Right. You're right," she said, "except for one little bitty thing."

John rubbed the side of his hand down her jawline. "And that being?"

Liz passed her hand over her lips. Yeah. One small thing. "We had a baby."

"You had a baby?" The awe, the astonished wonder in his voice surprised her. In the moonlight, she could see concern shrouding his eyes.

Taking a deep breath, she let it come out, said the words that had shattered her earlier. "We had a baby boy. He died from SIDS."

Her moon-watching partner said nothing but as she looked at him, his expression softened into something close to sorrow.

"That's pretty bad," he commented.

Liz squirmed against the wall, unconsciously brushing against John's big warm body.

When she settled, she continued. "So, what does the bastard do? He sends me a birth announcement and, guess what. He's named this baby after our son."

"No!"

"Y-e-s. I didn't think you could do that. I didn't think you could take a beautiful name and just give it to another child, not when the baby who had the name first died. I didn't think anyone could do that." Liz heard the way she sounded and tried to regain control.

All was quiet for a long time. The moon passed two fingers further across the sky. Liz and John sat shoulder to shoulder in stilted silence.

"So . . . why was your day shit?"

John, recovering from what he'd just heard, took a deep breath. He didn't think he could put it into words without the bourbon to loosen his tongue, and he had yet to take a sip from the bottle. But she'd shared with him; he owed it to her to share his miserable day with her. They deserved to share. They were two of a kind, really. Two miserable creatures sitting in the dark on a rickety covered porch, wasting time looking at the moon. Hell, they'd gotten so close in the past few minutes, it was as if they'd known each other forever.

"My best friend died last Thursday."

"Sorry."

"Yeah, you and me both."

She turned toward him, this time her breast brushing against his arm. "That's shitty."

"Yes, it is. And here's the best part. He got cremated and I didn't even know it. His bitch wife took him out of the nursing home and had him cremated without telling me . . . without telling anyone. He's dead and scattered all over some park, maybe, or worse yet, in a mayonnaise jar on her back porch, and I didn't get to say good-bye."

Liz nodded. He felt a little better. Sharing wasn't so bad, after all. Must be his feminine side doing the talking now.

"That's shit," she added, making him feel comfortable enough to say something more.

"For the past seven years he's been paralyzed because he took a bullet meant for me. I wasn't wearing a vest, Dutch . . . that's his name . . . Dutch was. I got hit in the shoulder and he pushed me out of the way and a second bullet came from another direction and got him in the neck."

"God!" she breathed.

Confession was indeed good for the soul. John felt the heavy lead weight lift from his guts. His chest loosened, too, and he took a deep breath of the cool night air. Liz's perfume mingled with the salty scent of the ocean. Smelled nice. He wondered, absently, how she would taste.

No, bad time. Here she was, mourning her child. He couldn't make a move on her. It just wasn't right.

But she looked up at him. One tear slid down her cheek and John's firm resolve melted. He reached for her and pulled her close. She didn't resist. She closed her eyes and he kissed her on the lips. Just once. He pulled away, half expecting her to slap him silly.

When she didn't, he felt a small smile tug at his lips.

"So, who won?"

Her eyebrows met and lowered. "Won what?"

"Our shittiest day contest."

She let out a laugh. "I don't know. It's pretty close."

John turned to her. "Yeah, it is pretty close, but . . . it's also getting really cold out here. Maybe you should go inside."

Liz returned his gaze. "Not without you."

Chapter 17

John pushed up against the wall until he stood. Reaching down a hand, he helped Liz to her feet. Did she mean what she'd said, or had he misinterpreted— damn, had she suggested she wanted to go inside with him?

As he stood there deliberating, Liz tugged at his hand and led him to the kitchen door.

He looked at her, not wanting to make a foolish mistake and ruin a potentially good moment. Her lips were set firmly, her eyes narrowed as she reached for the doorknob. He had his answer when she pushed open his door and dragged him inside.

Oh, yeah. John knew the signs and his luck was about to change.

"Which way?" The words were so breathless and soft, John had to lean down to hear them.

"To the right."

Liz hooked her finger through a loop on his jeans. "Hurry."

So he did.

They stumbled through the darkened office and into his bedroom. Making no excuses for its less than *House Beautiful* appearance, he shut the door firmly and paused. She took a few seconds to scan the room in the dark then pulled John toward her.

He felt the tips of her breasts as they rubbed against his chest. Her excitement caught him, rushed through him with a thrill he hadn't felt in a long, long time.

"What next?" he asked.

Liz stretched against him as she clasped her hands around his neck. Every inch of her burned through his clothes. He was about to suggest they get naked when he felt her tug his T-shirt from his jeans. Good start.

"Don't talk."

He helped a little as she pulled it over his head. She grabbed his hands and put them down at his sides. "Let me."

With one hand he went for her waist. "Can't I touch?"

Liz, feline smile at her lips, shook her head, sending the lush red curls bouncing.

He let go, after running his hand up to her breast. She batted it away. Her smile widened, becoming a Cheshire grin that sent a shiver coursing through him.

The belt went next, then the snap and, too slowly for the tension he felt building, she lowered the zipper. Her eyes lit as he sprang loose.

"Take 'em off," she ordered. John obeyed, helpless to control his laughter and protest at the same time. It seemed the logical thing to do, anyway. He stepped out of his deck shoes, ripped off his socks and peeled away the jeans before abandoning them at the foot of the bed.

A second of feeling foolish vanished as he watched her assess his body. While she said nothing, she ran her hands gently over his chest and biceps, marking with her fingertip the missing chest hair, down the flat of his stomach and stopped there. An eyebrow went up in question.

"Hmmm. Looks like someone ripped open a sofa."

Liz licked the tip of her tongue across her lips and John felt himself swell. He couldn't just stand there, but when he reached for her again, she placed her hand against his chest and pushed. He fell back onto his bed and wished she'd join him. Soon.

But Liz stopped him from reaching for her and stood, looking at him with a smile that made him ache. Slowly, she removed a thin bracelet from her right wrist, placing it on top of his dresser. She returned to the foot of the bed and raised the bottom of her sweater, exposing a lacy wisp of bra that barely held her breasts, her round, perfect breasts in place.

John fought the urge to grab himself. If she didn't move faster, he'd come anyway, but with exceptional control, he kept his hands at the back of his head and enjoyed the show.

With a flick, the sweater flew across the bed, but she kept her bra on. Next, she unfastened her slacks and let them pool at her feet, revealing the tiniest scrap of lace between her legs.

John's entire body bucked with want.

She was incredible. The woman teased him with subtle touches to her own body, first outlining her hips, tugging at the elastic that seemed unnecessary at best, then going up to release the fastening of her bra. He sucked in his breath when the lace fell away, revealing perfect, upturned nipples.

Then she stepped out of that other bit of lace and stood naked before him. The only light in the room came from outside. The moon, bright and strong, made it easy to see everything in black and white and gray. John didn't mind. He was nearly out of his.

Liz took a few steps over to the bed and put one knee on the end. John raised himself up on his elbows to enjoy the view as she began a sinuous climb toward him. A panther, grace and beauty and want—that was Liz.

A groan escaped him, making her stop in her tracks, her breasts just about even with his arousal. He didn't know how much longer he could just watch, watch and not touch. She slid the rest of the way up his body, flesh touching flesh, until her mouth descended on his and he lost any desire to fight.

"Condom?" she whispered in his ear.

He fumbled at the drawer of his nightstand, reaching and stretching beneath Liz's heat, finally producing a packet which she took from him and opened.

The condom and Liz's hands at last caressed him right where he wanted to feel her touch. Her heat. Her liquid satin.

Liz, her eyes shut, a glistening of sweat between her breasts, impaled herself on him. The exquisite shock lasted only seconds before she began to move, slowly at first, then faster and faster still.

In the fury of her ride, John at last clasped her around the waist, helping her, urging her, surrendering all thoughts but one.

She screamed out his name just before he shouted hers.

John eased out of the stupor of sated sleep. The weight of Liz's upper body on his chest made him grin into the darkness. Wow. Incredible. What an incredible woman.

He tried to check the time and couldn't find the clock. It must have fallen from the table when he'd opened the drawer. Damn. The room was darker than it had been before, so the moon had passed through the night sky beyond his window. Pity. He'd have liked to see Liz as she slept on his chest.

She'd had it rough in California. Losing a kid—he couldn't imaging how tough that would be. And the prick she'd been married to, what was his problem? That was a pretty sick thing to do, naming another kid the same name as a dead child. He had a feeling there was a lot more to the story, but he didn't want to hear it now. For now, he was content to stare into the darkness and enjoy the feel of a beautiful woman in his arms.

They'd become entangled in the covers and the room had chilled. As he reached for the blanket, Liz stirred, her breathing changing with a quick inhalation. She opened her eyes slowly, probably fighting through the alcoholic mist in her brain. Just how much *had* she had to drink? He wondered how she'd react when she realized where she was and who she was with. If she remembered what they'd done, he'd better protect himself.

She surprised him with a mocking smile and snuggled against him again. Carefully he pulled up the blanket to cover them both.

This was the time he normally left a woman. No matter how good they were in bed, how entertaining and inventive they were, he'd leave. Or they'd leave while he snored, picking their way through the debris of scattered clothing, frequently leaving important undergarments behind in their haste to get home to husbands or children or elderly parents.

He'd never really cared. Often, he'd wish they'd go and feigned sleep as they slipped out of the apartment.

He didn't mind the feel of Liz's body on his. In fact, he liked where she had her hand right now and felt his loins revive, readying for another round. Amazing thing, the male appendage. Especially his. He felt it rise, going along Liz's hip. Did she, or was she too deeply asleep?

Her hand tightened around him.

Oh, boy.

But this time, this time he wanted to be in charge. He'd followed, doing her bidding the first time. This time he wanted to touch her everywhere, taste her, suckle her breasts and explore every feminine part of her. He decided not to give her any choice.

A nuzzle on the back of the neck. A tiny lick on the earlobe. His hand slid over her silky skin to her breast and over the sensitive nipple and rested there. Her entire body quaked in response and she moved her hand up the shaft of his erection with a sleepy hesitancy until she reached the top. A quick, hard jerk made him growl low in his throat as he rolled her beneath him and proceeded to kiss her, devouring her lips, savoring the taste of woman and bourbon he found there.

She opened for him. He thrust into her, ignoring his original plan to be tender and gentle. If she were water, he was a man dying of thirst.

John needed to give her pleasure. The other time, she'd controlled the action. He'd let her because he enjoyed watching her seduce him. Animal sex—well, not quite, but close to it because he had done very little sharing. This time he wanted to give her the pleasure of a long, slow battle in which they both came away winners.

After the shit day they'd both endured, they both deserved to win.

Some time later, after he had once again made her scream his name and they had slept briefly, Liz awoke with a start so violent that John nearly reached for the weapon tucked under the mattress.

"What's wrong?"

Liz faced him, distress etched in her face and a look of horror in her eyes.

She pulled the blanket to her chest. Her eyes drilled into his and one finger scraped into his chest.

"This never happened, Preshin. Got it?"

Surprised, but not exactly sure why, he nodded.

She left the bed and with her back to him, put on her clothing. With one hand on the doorknob, she turned to face him.

"Good."

Chapter 18

Liz wasn't moving too well behind the counter. She moved as if she were treading water in a very thick sea. She knew that Carly watched her carefully, as if trying to decide what was wrong. So far, Liz hadn't pursued any conversation with the kid as she munched at the cereal that popped and crackled far too happily in front of her.

Gathering up her books, Carly looked ready to leave the steamy warmth of the luncheonette. She'd muttered "thanks" to Flo and Liz.

"Finish your juice, kiddo," Liz said softly because it hurt to talk.

Carly stopped, came back and gulped back the rest of her breakfast. "You okay, Liz?"

Liz squeezed her eyes shut. "I've got some kind of bug. I need coffee and aspirin in that order and I'll be all right."

"Sure?"

Liz pressed her fingers against her forehead for a second. "Yes, I'm sure. Don't worry about me."

Carly's face registered her doubts.

"And don't think that you had anything to do with my bad mood, either, kiddo. I know what you're thinking and I don't mind you staying with Flo. I had some stuff to work out last night and I did. Or at least I think I did. Don't worry, for Pete's sake."

"Okay. It's just that Mr. Preshin . . . he wasn't doin' too well last night. It was his idea for me to come down here. He sort of kicked me out."

Nodding slowly, Liz reassured her, "I'm sure you didn't do anything wrong, kiddo. Sometimes adults just do stupid things."

"You got that right." With a relieved smile, Carly left for the bus.

Liz watched the girl bounce down the street through the steamy windows of the luncheonette. The kid had too much energy. More energy than Liz could muster on a good day. Which this wasn't.

God! Her stomach flip-flopped when she poured out a black coffee to go. The young construction worker eyed her and asked if everything was all right.

She couldn't even fake a smile. Instead, she gave him a grimace meant to say it all.

It must have said enough because he handed her a five, patted her hand, and left with a swagger.

Obviously he'd slept well the night before.

Liz certainly hadn't.

She clamped her teeth around a groan. If her grandmother had any suspicion about where she'd been and what she'd done. . . .

Heat flamed her cheeks as the memories flowed unbidden through her brain. His long elegant fingers, his lips, his tongue. Liz retreated to the grill, scraping away grit and crusts of egg and an edge of pork roll.

John Preshin. That no account. That smirking, egotistical reprobate. As she dragged the spatula along the thick metal plate, the scene in the grocery store where that cheap-looking woman slapped his face played before her. It was obvious they'd slept together. Obvious to all but

John that there had been something between them and he'd totally forgotten the brassy blonde.

Her cheeks got hotter, probably because of the grill. Liz backed away from it, the spatula hanging limp in her hand.

Was she going to be just another notch on his bedpost?

"Did you see the signs about the prom?"

Bridget giggled and squirmed in her seat. Carly could feel the girl's impatience and knew something was up.

"Yeah, I saw 'em. What's so special about it?"

"Oh, nothing. Except this year, there's going to be a live band—rumor has it that Bruce Springsteen is going to show up. Can you believe it? Bruce Springsteen?"

Carly thought about it. "I know he's from around here, but he's . . . he's a big star. Why would he come to the junior prom at Mary Immaculate of the Grotto high school? Do you know how much money he gets paid to perform?"

Bridget winked. "Oh, yeah. He makes millions, all right. Except for one thing. Somebody told me he used to go with one of the teachers—before she was a teacher and he got married and all—and every once in awhile he comes home to visit and they get together. Five years ago he came and gave a concert in the auditorium. There are pictures of it in the showcase on the wall by the front office. Did you get a chance to look?"

Holy cow. Bruce Springsteen? *The* Bruce Springsteen? Here at her high school? At the prom? Oh, man!

She couldn't wait to e-mail Frankie and Jason with this news.

The halls were crowded. Carly didn't quite know

where all her classes were yet. She shouldered her way toward the computer lab, only dropping one book this time. Some guy swore, picked it up for her and waited for her to take it.

"Welcome to Mary Mac," he said kindly and went on his way.

When she finally found her class and took her seat, she was still dazed. Halfway through class, the kid behind her tapped her back and slipped her a folded piece of paper which she slid into the pocket of her blazer. On the bus going home, she remembered it and dug it out. With Bridget looking over her shoulder, she read the elaborate girly handwriting.

Hands off, jerkface.

"What's this for? Hands off who?" Bridget's eyes rounded.

"I don't know any guys. Some guy helped me pick up my book after I ran into him in the hall. I don't know who he is."

"Well," Bridget sounded serious, "looks like you ran into his girlfriend. If it's who I think it is, you don't want to mess with her. She can make your life miserable."

How could her life get much more miserable than it already was? But . . . new school. She'd be careful. "Who is she?"

"She's the one who gave you a load of garbage in gym yesterday."

"Her? What is she, the queen or something?"

Bridget stared straight ahead and spoke in a whisper. "You might say that. She hates anybody prettier than her. And she's nasty. Really, really nasty."

"So," Carly wondered aloud, "does this guy I didn't even look at belong to her?

Bridget's voice lowered. "She thinks so."

* * *

John stopped before the door, reading the name carefully to make sure. A "please do not smoke" sign filled the lower right corner. Though it had probably been there for a long time, the air in the old government office building still smelled like dead cigarettes.

Better that than urine, he figured.

Two quick raps on the glass got him a distracted "come in".

"Ms. Lundquist?"

The woman looked up, seemingly intent on returning to her work. Then recognition flashed across her eyes, but no smile of welcome. She went back to signing papers. He noticed that her hand trembled slightly as she guided the pen. He also saw the handles on the back of her chair before the gray of the wheels that were slightly tucked beneath the desk.

"Please take a seat," she said, "I'll be with you in a moment."

He was good at this game, he reminded himself, so he sat on the gray government issue chair and crossed one leg over the other.

Within seconds, she raised her eyes, dropped the pen and folded her hands on the desktop.

"John Preshin."

Her voice sounded barely controlled. He took in her situation and smiled acknowledgement. "It's been a long time since Belmar, Tammy."

She grimaced. "I didn't even know you knew my name."

"Oh, I knew your name, I just wasn't around much. I was tending bar when the other guys were guarding lives. I worked while they played." He allowed a chuckle to ease the tension of the moment, for it was there and thick enough to spoon up.

Tammy pushed slightly away from the desk, enabling John to see the wheelchair. "My fondest memories of the summer of '86 were of that beach house. But my pleasure was short-lived."

John knew his skills at consoling sucked. "What happened?" The words just slipped out without real thought and he wanted to kick himself for being so blunt.

Her turn to chuckle, but bitterness lay underneath it. "In late August of that year I was involved in an automobile accident. As you can see, it changed my life somewhat. But that was a long time ago and it cannot possibly be why you're here." She paused, looking directly into his eyes. He thought he heard her sigh. "Why *are* you here?"

He sobered, forcing the smile to disappear. "I need some information from you about your friend, Bunny."

Her tense smile vanished and her eyes narrowed. "Bunny who?"

John could barely contain his spurt of anger. "You know who I'm talking about. Bunny Adams. Your inseparable party animal friend from that summer. Your college roommate."

"Oh," she said and pushed her chair away from the desk a bit further. "That Bunny Adams."

He knew there couldn't be more than one. How the hell many Bunny Adamses could there be in the world? "Suppose you stop the games right here, Ms. Lundquist. I don't want to take up too much of your time and all I need are some simple answers. She used to be your friend. I hoped you could tell me something about her."

She gave him a hard stare, probably assessing his intentions, seeing if she could detect a lie. A line appeared between her eyebrows. With a small shake of her head, she seemed to come to a decision. "I'll tell you what I can, Mr. Preshin. It isn't much."

Some of the tension eased out of him. Tammy

Lundquist, wheelchairbound, still had good looks and what appeared to be no ax to grind. But one could never tell. She could be an expert at hiding the truth. After all, she worked for the government.

"What happened to her?"

Tammy put both hands on the wheels of her chair. "I lost track of her after the accident."

"Did you have a falling out?"

A small smile, hard and terse, appeared on her lips while the wrinkle in her forehead eased away. "You might say that."

John leaned forward to hear her better for her voice had gotten softer and she avoided looking directly at him.

"Tell me about it."

"I don't see why that is important."

"Just go on, Tammy. Talk to me about her."

"Your card says you are a private investigator. Are you on a case?"

He nodded. "A very important one. I represent a sixteen-year-old girl who is looking for her father. She believes that he met her mother in the summer of 1986 in Belmar. I'm following leads and they got me here."

Tammy rested her back against the chair. She wasn't buying his story, he could tell. He needed to add something to bring it home to her.

"The kid has lived with nuns in Philadelphia all her life. She was let loose a couple of weeks ago, left on the streets. But she's a smart kid and took some things out of her file when the Mother Superior wasn't looking. She has a list of names and they all have Belmar in '86 in common."

"What about the girl's mother?" Tammy's eyes narrowed again.

"Oh, didn't I mention that? They told the kid that her mother was dead."

Her fingers drummed out a little math, but if she

reached any conclusions, she kept her figuring to herself. "You asked me about Bunny Adams and if we had had a falling out. Well, Mr. Preshin, remember that little Morgan convertible she drove?"

Something niggled at his mind. He remembered every cool car he had ever seen. Yes, he'd seen a British racing green Morgan outside the house in Belmar but had never gotten a ride in it. It had belonged to Bunny Adams?

He shrugged the question away. "Sort of."

Tammy rolled back the wheel, readjusting her position behind her desk. "That belonged to my good friend Bunny Adams. She and I were going to Atlantic City when we got hit by a jerk in a pick-up truck. I spent three months in the hospital and after that more months in physical therapy." The bitterness oozed through the words. He sensed the pain it caused the woman to recall this and wished he could get her to talk faster, to finish so the pain would stop. For her sake, and his own.

"That must have sucked." *Good going, Preshin. Mr. Blunt and thoughtless.*

"You're damn straight it sucked. No more fun and games for me, that's for sure. But Bunny was driving."

John uncrossed his legs. "She got the worst of it?" That wouldn't fit the theory. She couldn't have died that day.

Tammy's face became a mask, though he detected tears forming in her eyes. She kept them out of her voice. "Actually, Mr. Preshin, Bunny Adams walked away from the accident with a small cut on her right forefinger."

"Damn."

Tammy's lips drew away from her teeth. "Her parents were very good about my injuries, though. They actually paid for my hospitalization and therapy. Out of pocket, but then, they had mighty deep pockets.

They even paid my tuition once I was able to return to U of D."

"That was generous of them."

His comment didn't go over well with the lady because she snorted. "Generous, sure. Considering their daughter was trying to kill herself playing chicken with a trucker and ended up ruining my life while she walked away with a cut on her finger."

"She wanted to kill herself?"

"Yes. She told me so."

"Do you know why?"

"I haven't a clue. Depressed, maybe. That's why we were going to AC. She wanted some action, to do something crazy. I thought she'd calm down with a roadtrip." Tammy remained still and the tears never did leave her brimming eyes.

John rose from his chair slowly. "Tell me, did she eventually succeed in killing herself?"

Tammy rested her hands on the desk, stared at her fingernails a few seconds and finally looked up at John. "Of course not. Although I haven't seen her since the accident, she sort of disappeared after that, I've seen her photograph in the *Inquirer*. She's alive and well and married to the junior senator from Pennsylvania."

And I'm stuck in this wheelchair for the rest of my life, John added to himself.

"I've taken up a great deal of your time. Thanks, Tammy. Take care, okay?"

"Yes, I'll take care, John. Have a nice day."

John sat in his Jeep, thinking over every word of his chat with Tammy Lundquist.

The short list of mothers had gotten even shorter.

Carly's mother was alive.

She lived in Philly, maybe just a few blocks away

from where her daughter had lived for the past sixteen years.

Christ. He knew the name of Carly's mother.

He knew he would have to make an attempt to reunite mother with daughter, but his gut told him it wasn't going to happen. Anyone who would dump a kid with nuns and see to it she was unadoptable—why would she do something like that? Did she know about it? Had she some motive, some reason for doing it? Or was there something behind it that no one could understand?

Some sort of conspiracy?

Christ, now he was starting to think like some kind of wacko. No conspiracy. But there had to be some sort of reasoning behind paying the kid's way all those years. And now, all of a sudden, why stop?

The kid. Her welfare was at the bottom of all this. He debated the options. If he told her, would she be better off? Should he say anything at all?

He'd taken on the job of finding her father. She believed her mother was dead.

Maybe it would be better to just let sleeping dogs lie.

Enough wrestling with moral dilemmas. He had more work to do, something that would bring in some money to make up for what he'd spent on the kid's wardrobe. But since he was already in Philly, he thought he'd do a little drive by and check out how the kid's mother was making out.

Tammy hadn't been uncooperative in the least. Reluctant. With good reason. She didn't owe him anything. They hadn't even known one another except by sight. He felt a twinge of regret for the woman. Strange the way things turned out for her.

Parts of Philly were about as bad as Asbury Park while other parts were downright magnificent. Outside the city was where the old money still lived. The Main Line—a string of mansions lined old Route 30, wrought iron gates keeping out the hoi polloi. Well, after he finished dealing with the riffraff downtown, he'd tool on out there and check out the digs of Carly's people.

The phrase stuck in his brain, refusing to leave him alone. Carly's people.

Not really. Not at all.

Chapter 19

Liz and Flo stepped out of their shoes and plopped into the welcoming chairs in Flo's living room. Liz fanned herself with the sheaf of papers they'd spent the last three hours obtaining at the borough hall. Her grandmother groaned softly.

"Well, that's over." Liz tossed the papers onto the ottoman, hoping they would stay together because if they slid off, she didn't have the strength or desire to pick them up just yet.

Flo exhaled with stage drama. "Who knew there would be such a fuss over changing a luncheonette into an ice cream parlor and soup bar? I mean, I thought they were the same thing. We're not changing anything, we're just uncovering things. Not one piece of equipment will actually be moved anywhere and we're not putting in new windows. I thought maybe some plants or something, but nothing like making the outside any different."

Liz laughed at her grandmother's pursed lips and peeved expression. "You'd think since we were doing something to improve Asbury Park, they'd give us a break. But permits are revenue and this city needs revenue."

"Not worth all the mazooma we had to put out," Flo fumed. "Why, when your grandfather bought this place, it didn't cost as much as we shelled out today for lousy permits."

Going over to sit on the edge of Flo's hassock, Liz picked up one of her grandmother's stockinged feet and began rubbing it. "This is a good idea, though, Gram. It's going to do well. We'll still have sandwiches, but it won't be as frantic. We can make the soup overnight. We can even freeze it and it will be ready in minutes. Our work will be easier and we'll attract the business people who are trying to make a go of revitalizing the town. In the summer," she continued, rubbing the other foot now, "we'll have parents bringing in their kids for ice cream. We'll get cute high school girls to work the front and we'll make a mint."

Flo nodded, her frizzed curls dancing. "Low overhead. I own this dump, so I don't pay rent. Just taxes. They're bad enough, sure, but we ought to do all right."

For the first time since leaving the town hall, Flo smiled. Liz hugged the old woman. She'd been surprised at her grandmother's decision to change her life. It meant trying something different after all the years of working the luncheonette. But she knew now that Flo looked forward to the experiment. She'd gone from dancer to showgirl to wife to mother and eventually to short order cook in her lifetime. The flexibility of the woman struck a chord in her own mind.

If her grandmother could change at this late date, perhaps it was okay for Liz herself to do some changing.

Starting with letting go of the past.

She wanted to do something symbolic. Something to signify her change in attitude.

What?

"Gram, do you have a hammer?"

Flo's eyebrow lowered. "What the heck do you need a hammer for?"

"You'll see." Liz made puppy-dog eyes at the old lady.

Flo shook her head. "In the basement somewhere. Probably on the old workbench. I can contain myself, dearie. I'll wait up here while you go search for the dang thing."

After rummaging through what she estimated as at least fifty years' worth of debris, Liz returned with a claw hammer. She went into the luncheonette, dim now in the late February sun and whacked at the plywood covering the soda fountain equipment her grandfather had boarded up so many years ago.

Flo hobbled in at the first squeal of nail being pulled from wood. She stood watching as her granddaughter ripped away so many years to reveal something glorious. That dull nickel plated brass, irreplaceable at today's costs, jutted up from the front counter defiantly.

"Look at it, Gram. It's beautiful. A little cleaning, a little polishing—we'll have to check all the gaskets and mechanicals—but it's going to be a real thing of beauty. Just you wait. Hiding there all these years, it's about time all this elegance saw the light of day."

"Yep," observed Flo. "That's just what I was thinking."

"Wow!"

Both women looked up to find Carly standing in the doorway.

She scurried into the luncheonette. "I heard the racket and had to see what was going on."

Flo beamed at her. "Here it is, little girl. See for yourself. All the fountain equipment . . . of course, it's going to need some work . . . I guess I could find somebody to clean it up. . . ."

Carly lit up. "No need. I'm right here! I'd love to help with this work."

Flo shot a look at her granddaughter then turned back to Carly. "I was hoping you'd say that, seeing as how it was your idea to start this whole enterprise."

"You know I want to help!" She fairly danced with

excitement. Flo put her hand on Carly's arm to hold her down.

"Kiddo, you have to do your schoolwork first, and then you can help down here. That comes first."

Carly put her hand on the smooth metal of one of the syrup pumps. "I can handle it. Believe me, I can handle it."

Liz, buoyed by the enthusiasm of her grandmother and Carly, suggested supper. "I don't know about you two, but I'm hungry and it's getting late. Carly, feel like making up some burgers and fries?"

"Me, by myself?"

Liz put her hand on the girl's shoulder. "Sure. You're part of this now. It's a team effort. You get to make the burgers and clean the grill. Part of the profits means part of the work."

Carly stammered. "Part of the profits?" Her eyes widened and she shook herself.

"That's what I said. You don't get paid for suggesting it, but you'll get paid for helping out. Deal?"

With a little jump, Carly did a few quick steps that got Flo dancing too. "Deal, girlie?"

"Deal!"

People are assholes.

He'd spent most of the day searching records in Chester, PA, only to find that the individual he was looking for happened to work for the town garage. He'd never have found the man if one of the secretaries hadn't looked over his shoulder and read the name out loud. No secrets in this town, he realized.

The man was delighted to learn that he was about to come into money from an insurance policy he never knew existed. A friend of his mother's, childless, had named him beneficiary when he was born and the guy never had a clue.

So here he stood to make a cool ten grand and he started getting jumpy. Asking questions about taxes and if it was some kind of scam. John had given him the appropriate papers and told him what he had to do to claim his small fortune and the guy started getting all defensive and weird on him.

John couldn't be bothered. He did what he had to do and walked away with the guy yelling after him.

Absurd. Why did money or the prospect of money turn people into complete assholes?

He wanted a drink.

He'd driven past the address where Carly's mother lived. Too posh for words. Huge wrought iron gates, not any of that plastic crap or even aluminum, but iron, with stone walls surrounding the mansion. There was real money involved, John knew, and if he could land the kid inside for a happy reunion, she'd live happily ever after for sure.

Maybe. But his gut burned when he thought about it. The woman had given up the kid sixteen years ago. Carly thought she was dead. Should he even tell the kid he'd found her mother?

In his sordid past, he'd always felt that moral dilemmas were best faced after a few shots of Wild Turkey. This situation was going to be sticky for sure. Especially for a man not used to facing too many moral dilemmas head on. Not any more, at least.

Maybe he could stick this on Father Mike.

As he drove the Jeep through the crowded rush hour streets of Asbury Park, John considered stopping at Dank's to waste some time, listen to the jukebox. Pool was definitely out. Besides, Dank's was a hole. And the kid would be home from school by now. Instead, he pulled up in front of St. Boniface's. A beat up old Chevy edged out of a space right in front and John maneuvered the Jeep against the curb.

Mike wasn't in the rectory. Tuesday. What the hell

did he do on Tuesdays at six o'clock? The lights were on in the church basement. Peering through the iron grates, John saw his old friend setting up chairs while several old men struggled with tables.

Bingo.

More accurately, bingo night at St. Boniface's. Thousand dollar top prize. Early bird games began at six. John checked his watch. He had a few minutes.

Walking around the south side of the church, he stepped onto the sidewalk and found himself face to face with an animated female.

"John Preshin! What are you doing at church?"

He felt his forehead wrinkle as he looked at the woman, trying desperately to think of how and when he knew her and drawing a complete blank.

"Uh, hi." Brilliant. Not a chance she might think he remembered who she was. His cheek warmed in warning.

The well-endowed brunette stepped closer until her breasts were mere inches away from his chest. She looked up at him, warm brown eyes heavily lined and shadowed and batted her eyelashes. The caked mascara flaked off leaving two dots on her right cheek.

"Did you get religion? Is that why you haven't called me?" She pressed against him, her hand running down his chest, heading south. He grabbed for it and held it.

"I'm working. Investigating. Uh, you know that's what I do."

Her smile broadened, the ruby lips pulling away from a definite overbite. "Oh, I remember, Johnny. You investigated me real well."

He fought the urge to gulp. "Uh, heh heh . . . right."

One of her meticulously painted eyebrows arched up. Then the eyes slanted accusingly. "You don't remember me, do you?"

He sought refuge in honesty. "No, ma'am, I'm afraid I don't."

With her free hand, she made contact with his right

cheek, sending him reeling three steps backwards. "You pig!" she screeched. "You bullshitting lowlife pig!"

She stalked off, her thin high heels clicking against the old slate sidewalk. John could see the heat radiating from her anger as she swore into the evening air. Throngs of veteran bingo players trooped by, heading for the basement. John waited, hoping no one had actually heard her mouthing off. Had anyone seen her slap him, well, that story would spread quickly enough at the tables. He faced public opinion if he went into the basement.

He knew he'd be vilified by the old ladies and applauded by the old men, but there were more old gals than guys. He'd be toast if they saw his face.

So he waited.

Fifteen minutes later, he descended the stairs into the gaming catacombs of Rome.

Chapter 20

"B-17," Father Mike's voice rang out over the noise of serious bingo players placing small plastic chips on rows of cards. "B-17. Anybody?"

Mike looked out over his ancient flock. The "early bird bingo" had been his latest idea. Since most of the elderly couldn't keep their eyes open much after eight in the evening, he figured he'd make the start time earlier so they could enjoy themselves and still make it home under their own steam.

Besides, he didn't care to see them droop over their cards. It made him think too much about death.

As soon as he spotted Bourbon at the back of the hall, he knew something was wrong. This was the absolute last place he expected to see the man. He jerked back his head to signify that he'd spotted his buddy and motioned to one of his helpers to take over reading the numbers.

Raul the sexton, obviously proud to be asked to do the honors, cranked the handle of the ancient ball machine and called out, "Ene-diez y siete!"

One of the elderly ladies shouted back, "In English, Raul! In English! How many times . . . ?" and her words were cut off by the grumble and buzz of the other early birds. Mike smothered a laugh with a cough.

Eyes followed his path as he made his way to John through the crowded tables. He felt his collar tighten. When he reached Bourbon, he grabbed him by the arm and propelled him up the stairs and outside. It was so cold he tucked his bare hands across his chest and under his armpits. John, leather jacket open with only a t-shirt showing, seemed unaffected by the cold.

"What's up?"

John scowled. "Bless me, Father."

"Cut the crap. Something's happened. Is it Carly?" Mike felt his stomach drop and his face start to heat.

John shook his head. "No. Yeah. Sort of."

"Don't yank me around, John. Out with it."

John shuffled his feet. If this were the old days, Mike would have expected his friend to have a beer in his hand. "I found Carly's mother. She's alive."

Mike's heart skipped a few beats then thundered in his chest. He turned away but immediately came back and looked his friend in the eye. "Where? Are you sure? Did you talk to her?"

Shaking his head, John jingled the change in his pocket. "I talked with her friend, Tammy, who has her own sad story, Mikey, but she told me how to locate Bunny Adams. Seems our Bunny did rather well for herself. She's married to Roland Evans."

Mike's hands moved automatically, splaying in front of his chest in recognition. "*The* Roland Evans, senator from Pennsylvania?"

John sent him a grim smirk. "The very one. The one everybody thinks is presidential material."

"Are you sure she's Carly's mother?" He didn't want to form any conclusions in his own mind without the truth.

John turned away, his hand going up to scrub at his face. "Well, it can't be Tammy. The kid's in a wheelchair and has been since the end of that summer. A real shame. She still has looks, but the chair . . . she was in an accident with guess who and guess who walked away unscathed?"

"No need. But are you sure?"

"Yeah, I'm sure. All the facts fit. But only a blood test would prove it completely."

Mike shook his head. "You'd have to get her permission."

John snorted. "Do you actually think she'd submit to a blood test? Would you?"

Mike felt anger surge through him. "Don't ask me that. John, do not ask that of me. I . . . I can't be Carly's father."

Again John turned away from the priest. "Yeah. I know. But I'm going to try to get to talk with her. And if she admits to being Carly's mother, then what?"

Mike rubbed his face and walked in a circle. He felt his shoulders hunch forward with the weight of revelation.

"Don't tell Carly. Not just yet. We have a duty to protect her. She's more important that a senator's wife. John, find out what you can, then we'll figure out what's best for Carly. We have to think of her first."

John thought it over and with a brief nod, walked toward his Jeep.

"Yeah. We have to protect Carly."

Mike watched him drive off, then plastered on a beatific smile and re-entered the church. He heard Raul calling out the numbers in Spanish and someone interpreting them for the others.

When the early birds saw him at the back of the room, they let out a collective sigh of relief.

Too bad he didn't feel it himself.

"Bruce Springsteen is going to be at Mary Immaculate of the Grotto's prom." After typing in the words,

Carly waited for a response. Frankie just had to be online—he said he usually got on right before he slogged through his physics homework. She smiled as she remembered him writing her about the lab with the huge Slinky toys.

That boy had a gift for writing. He was cute, too, but something about him, something about the way he had taken to her like some kind of big brother, was weird. She knew the effect she could have on guys and she didn't have it on him.

But he was great online. He knew most of her favorite online haunts. They liked the same bands and the same movies and that was cool, too. Although his face rivaled Brad Pitt's and he had a great bod, Carly just couldn't get over the big brother thing.

The computer screen shifted with an answer. "No way."

She cracked her knuckles and punched in, "Would I lie? He's been there before, rumor has it he used to date one of the teachers."

"Cool. I went to the prom last year. Cost me a wad of money and the girl dumped me the next day because I had to see my father off and couldn't take her to the shore."

"What a skank!" she typed in and waited for something more.

"It was lame, anyway. The DJ liked to play stupid games and give out prizes. Like maybe his last gig was a Bar Mitzvah or kid party. My tuxedo looked good, though. Like James Bond."

Oh, I bet, she thought. "Scan me a picture."

"Later. Gotta go meet Choochie. He has my calculus homework because he borrowed my book third period."

Carly pushed away from the desk. Time to do her own work. An hour later, she heard John's heavy footsteps on the stairs. She cleared off his desk. They hadn't really seen much of each other in the last three days or so. Not since he'd given her grief. She didn't want to do anything to bring that up again. As the footsteps approached, her stomach clenched. He could be such a grouch!

He stepped into the office and tossed his jacket on the coat rack. His face looked sort of gray and his beard turned the lower half nearly blue. His dark hair never looked combed, but this little lock fell over his forehead, sort of like Superman's. Same blue and black color. Weird, she decided.

"Hey," she said, tentative about his mood.

His brows unknit and a small smile played about his lips. "Hey, kiddo."

This was going nowhere.

"Did you eat anything?"

He flipped through his mail, dumping all but one envelope into the circular file. "Nah. I was kinda hoping there might be something downstairs. You eat yet?"

Carly shook her head. Liz and Flo had been so busy taking apart the soda fountain, they'd forgotten to invite her. "You don't have any food up here. I don't know if there's anything to eat downstairs, either."

John looked up, suddenly hearing her maybe. "What's up with downstairs? There's always food downstairs."

"Liz and Flo started taking apart the front of the luncheonette."

He paused. "Oh, where the fountain is? Are they really going through with that plan?"

Carly shrugged. "Looks like."

He stashed the one envelope into the side drawer of the desk. "What say you and I go mooch some food under the pretense of scoping out the soda fountain?"

Carly made a show of considering the suggestion. "Hmm, there are always burgers in the freezer. I think Flo made some kind of onion soup yesterday, before they started in on the stuff they had to do with permits. I saw some of the destruction before, but they hadn't finished wrecking things yet. We could go check things out and get invited."

"That sounds like a plan," he winked as he said it, making her feel included . . . part of something. She decided she liked it.

"Let's mooch. There's a fine art to mooching, you know. It's usually all in the eyes and body language. Do you think you could act like a puppy? All cute and desperately hungry?"

"I watch *Animal Planet*. I think I can do puppy eyes."

"Good," he chuckled under his breath. "You just may be a natural."

She couldn't figure him out. He flashed hot and cold. Sometimes he was human, other times he was bearlike and crotchety. Sometimes he made her angry and sometimes he made her want to cry. It must just be because he was a man and she wasn't used to them. She knew she had a lot to learn.

When they got downstairs, Liz ignored them. In jeans and a sweatshirt, she had her hair drawn up in some kind of topknot and strands of red corkscrewed around her face. Broken boards stacked by the front door as Flo pushed the broom across the floor tiles.

"Good evening, ladies," John said, drawing out the words in a kind of silky, sexy way. Sometimes he looked like Ashton Kutcher only beefier, Carly decided. This was one of those times. How could Liz ignore somebody who looked like Ashton Kutcher?

Liz put her hand on her hip. "We're closed."

John's head tilted as he eyed her. Carly watched, fascinated, as he plied his charm. He had his little subtle tricks, she'd seen him with Liz and Flo before, and knew he could usually get around Flo at least.

"Are we too late to help?"

Liz snorted. Flo held the broom with both hands near the top. "You're just in time. If you take that stack of boards out to the Dumpster, I'll feed both of you."

Liz's chin dropped to her chest. Carly heard her muttering under her breath but couldn't make out the words. To take away some of the sting of their intrusion, she offered, "I could start heating up that big pot of soup, Flo, and you and Liz could go wash your hands while Mr. Preshin gets rid of those boards. By the time I get cheese grated and all that, everybody should be ready to eat a little."

Starting toward the back, Flo passed by Carly and patted her on the arm. "You're such a good girl. There's toast for the top in the bread bin and grated cheese in the big fridge. I'm going to find that 'closed' sign and put it in the window before we eat. I don't think I have the energy to cook, kiddo. You're a lifesaver."

With a wink and a smile, Flo left. Liz stood around for a few seconds, watched Carly head on back to the big kitchen and apparently gave up protesting because she followed her grandmother out of the luncheonette.

Fifteen minutes later, the four of them sat in the biggest booth, quietly slurping hot onion soup smothered in melted cheese.

"I knew this person," John ventured between spoonfuls, "who grew up in Iowa or someplace like that. She came East one year on vacation and had onion soup for the very first time. When she got home, she tried to make it for her parents one night. They didn't have any Gruyere cheese, so she substituted Velveeta."

"That's impossible," Liz scoffed.

He waggled his brows at Carly then smiled at Liz. "Truth," he proclaimed, his hand over his heart.

To Carly, it looked as if Liz was really pissed off. Her eyebrows met in the middle, her frown gave her a rather uncomplimentary look which, considering the weirdness of her hair, kinda looked cartoony.

"Nobody is that backward."

To his credit, John did not snap back his answer.

"Honest. If I'm lyin', I'm dyin'. She used Velveeta on French onion soup."

"Could have whipped up a batch of Lipton's, you know," Flo added. "It's not that bad."

Liz gurgled, causing John to laugh out loud.

"Not as good as this, Flo. You are a soup genius. The soup bar is going to be a big hit."

Liz rolled her eyes as Flo preened.

There was something going on between Liz and John. Carly sensed it, but couldn't tell what it was. They'd always been sort of at each other, but this time was way different. It looked as if Liz wasn't comfortable having him sit at the table across from her. She kept shifting in her seat and avoided looking into his face when he spoke, even when he asked how things were going with the permits and all.

Mostly she kept quiet. Carly didn't know too much about Liz, but she'd heard from Flo about the dead baby and how Liz was having trouble getting over it. She imagined that if she had a baby and it died, she'd be hurt inside and very, very angry at God.

Mentally crossing herself, she gave up and finished her soup.

Liz sipped at the onion-filled liquid, wishing she could just finish it and get away from the table. John kept staring at her, making her feel self-conscious, making her heart beat faster and wish she'd at least put on decent jeans and a top that wasn't baggy. No, that wasn't right. She wished he'd just go upstairs and leave her alone.

Every time she glanced at him, he was looking directly at her. A smile, maybe a little smug, teased his lips. Soft lips, she remembered, then immediately dashed away the thought. Who cared about his lips?

It was that stupid dippy curl over his forehead that really made her crazy.

He blathered on, making Carly and her grandmother laugh over stories about strange things people he knew enjoyed eating. The guy in search of the perfect hot fudge sundae. The woman who drank raw eggs in beer in an attempt to increase her bust size. That was stupid. He said it worked, though. Surreptitiously, Liz cast a glance down at her own chest. John had mentioned the other night that there wasn't a thing to complain about there.

She agreed.

Oh, God! What was she doing?

Pushing off the bench, Liz intended to go back into the kitchen and dig out some ice cream. Before she could step away from the table, John grabbed her hand and held it. A tiny electric sizzle blitzed through her arm.

"Liz, is there any of that pie you had a couple of days ago?"

He gave her a goofy grin—so childish—and kept a tight grip on her hand.

She'd like to smack that grin off his face, then kiss it to make it better.

Oh, Sweet Jesus in Heaven! Where did that come from?

Her face heating, Liz tried to reply but stuttered her answer. "N . . . no, it's all g . . . gone, but there is ice cream."

Flo stepped in, adding, "There's fudge sauce in our kitchen. Carly, would you like some on ice cream?"

John and Carly nodded vigorously. "Oh, yeah!" they said at the same time, with the exact same emphasis. Liz stared at them, noticing for the first time how their eyes were the same shade and they both possessed a small dimple at the corner of their mouths. Their lips were shaped differently, but that dimple, winking out like that, was kinda cute.

She'd get the fudge sauce for Carly and let him put it on his own ice cream.

Oh, being bitchy didn't solve anything. He was there, he wasn't going to go away any time soon. One mistake had been made and would never be repeated. She could be nice to him if she felt the need. For her grandmother's sake and Carly's, she wouldn't bite his head off.

Heat raced up her cheeks as she remembered biting other parts of his body. To her horror, the phantom tingle of memory started down below her belly and warmed its way up her chest. *Oh, God, no!* She left the ice cream on the counter, gestured to Carly to come get it and left to take a long, cool shower.

Chapter 21

John woke up stiff after dreaming about a certain redhead. He groaned softly, smiling into the darkness and willing his body to cooperate. Today was going to be hard enough.

His knee creaked as he pushed himself to the side of the bed and tried to lever himself upright. Dull pain pinched his cheek. He moved his jaw back and forth, slowly, determining that he might have cracked a tooth somehow.

Damn it to hell, how did that happen?

Not today. He had no time for a cracked tooth today. So he slid into a clean pair of boxer shorts, socks and dress slacks and quietly crept through the office toward the bathroom.

The kid slept curled in a little ball on the sofa bed. Enough light from the street came through the windows and he paused to take a look at her.

Her thumb pressed against her lower lip.

She looked like a two-year-old with her shock of blond hair and that thumb.

Aw, hell.

Something heavy lurched in his gut. He recognized it for what it was, dismissed it out of hand and continued on to the bathroom. He needed to look reputable for a change.

This morning he would shave.

John waited for the entourage to leave the mansion office then followed the Navigator at a discreet distance. A phone call had established her schedule easily enough. All he had to do was find an opportune time to ambush her. The Ladies' Club luncheon looked good, but the hospital gig looked even better.

He'd try both.

She traveled with a secretary and a bodyguard. Why the hell would the wife of a senator need one of those? Hell, he didn't have to think. The world was a dangerous place. Anyone in any power position, even the wife of a senator, could be snatched and held for ransom. He'd ID'ed the guard as former law enforcement. The crew cut was a dead giveaway. Dress 'em up in suits and ties, they still looked like they were in-between doughnut shops. This one must have some brains, though. He'd been on the job for a couple of years, alternating between the senator himself and Bunny.

Ahh, there they were. He put away the binos and started up the Jeep, pulling around the corner just as the Navigator left the gates. Jeeps. Wonderful in their innocuousness.

One of the least glamorous things about being a private investigator was the waiting. It drove him crazy having to sit in his vehicle keeping an eye on doorways or motel rooms or parking lots for long periods of time, so he'd packed a kit of things to do while keeping one eye trained on his prey and the other mindlessly doing something.

Today it was word search. He had a knack for ferreting out backwards words and diagonal words and bottom to top words, but one could only take so much of this. He switched to his personal CD player, hated the fact that he had forgotten to replace the CDs with new ones and had to listen to the same '80s tunes he'd heard on the last stakeout.

Disgusted, he tossed the player and CD into the back seat. A glint of light winked through the birches, like a reflection of sunlight on glass . . . like a door opening or the mirror catching some stray rays. So he sat up and had his hand on the key, ready to roll.

The bodyguard came out first. He had a habit of rolling his tie and stretching his neck to relieve pressure from a too-tight collar, so John ID'ed him without any trouble. Dead giveaway. Next came the scanning of the immediate area and readjusting the shoulder holster. Cripes, how bloody obvious could the man get?

John laughed.

Next came some secretary type followed shortly thereafter by Bunny herself. Looking prim and proper with her hair in a French twist and a suit that boxed her attributes in sedately. Nice tits, as he remembered, but if she'd had any kids, they might be down to her belt line by now. You could never tell with big breasted women. At least he thought she had big breasts.

She paused at the door to wave to a throng of Ladies' Clubbers or whatever at the restaurant door before sliding into the back seat and disappearing from his view. The big-ass SUV rolled away slowly from the restaurant and pulled onto the highway.

John followed. He had checked out the hospital where she would be doing some sort of fund-raising thing, going up the elevator with her entourage.

He'd get her there.

What he hadn't counted on in advance was the lack of parking spaces. Of course Bunny managed to leave the Navigator at the front door, but John ended up coiling the Jeep up to the third level of the parking deck before finding a space. He cursed as he ran to the deck elevator for entry to the hospital itself. His chest squeezed and he fought for breath . . . Jesus! How long since he'd worked out at all? How out of shape was he?

A little b-ball, some weights, maybe. Soon. Yeah, real soon.

But he managed to get through the security in time to see Bunny step into the elevator. He slipped unnoticed around the huge columns of the entry, thanking the architect for providing him with such good cover.

The bodyguard, sunglasses still in place, checked out the elevator while Bunny's aide held the door.

John elbowed a potted palm off its stand, sending it rolling and crashing while Bunny's entourage froze in place. The guard reached for his piece, turning away from the door while hospital personnel gathered around the mess. John casually stepped inside the elevator and palmed the door shut.

Slick. Very slick, Preshin.

Behind him, Bunny Evans gasped.

John turned to her, flashing his killer grin.

Bunny's hand went to her throat. Her eyes widened. John knew the exact moment she recognized him.

"Hiya, Bunny."

Chapter 22

Flo fingered the envelope with nervous hands. Addressed to her granddaughter, it had come to New Jersey from California, receipt requested. The old lady had signed for it, hoping she'd done the right thing. In her heart, she doubted it.

Last time something had come from the lawyer, Liz had left the luncheonette and walked the streets of Asbury Park for hours, at least that was what she'd told Flo. Then she'd disappeared altogether for nearly the rest of the night. She'd come back the next morning looking like a beaten dog with red-rimmed eyes and splotchy skin and what appeared to be a rash on her neck and face. When asked what had happened, she said nothing.

They'd always had a better relationship than that. They'd always talked things out before, but not this time.

Throwing away the letter might be the right thing to do for both of them. Liz had been through enough hell in her lifetime. Flo knew some of it and still couldn't believe what that rat bastard husband of hers had done to nearly destroy Liz.

She never talked about the details and as much as Flo wanted to know what had happened, she hadn't the heart to ask. Bringing up pain never helped someone get over it. And Liz needed to get over it in order to get on with her life.

Flo tucked the envelope into her apron pocket and went back to work.

"Who was that, Grandma?" Liz stopped polishing the chrome on the soda dispenser. Her hair peeked out of the kerchief in damp coils and the rosiness in her face came from all the hard work she'd been doing readying the fountain.

"Huh?" Flo came out of her deep thoughts with a start. "Who was . . . oh, that? Just the mail. Something for John that had to be signed for."

Liz shook her head slowly. "You do so much for that man, you treat him as if he were your grandson. And what does he do for you?"

Flo's temper flared. "John Preshin has saved my life on two occasions, I'll have you know. Twice he found me when I'd fallen and he called the ambulance after picking me up and carrying me into the apartment. Twice! He treats me with respect, he pays his rent exactly on time and he isn't a pain in the ass most of the time. Knowing he's upstairs is a relief to me, and it should be to you, too, because this is a rough neighborhood. Nobody, and I mean nobody, messes with John Preshin. Everybody around here knows him, knows about the FBI, knows he's a man of his word. If they don't like him, they respect him. Or fear him."

With her hands on her hips, Flo faced down her granddaughter and knew she'd won when Liz apologized.

"Grandma, I didn't mean to get you aggravated."

"I'm not aggravated. I just wanted to set you straight about John. He's a good man, through and through. Sure he's got his secrets and quirks. But there's a reason for that." Knowing she'd said a little too much, Flo set to work stacking the glassware, the sundae glasses, sherbet sets, and the banana split boats into the glass cabinets behind the counter.

Liz tested the syrup containers, squirting a bit from each into a cup.

Going to the freezer, she grabbed the frozen fruit toppings and stocked the refrigerated containers then wiped down the counter.

"So, tell me, Grandma," she said with no special emphasis, "just what do you know about his secrets?"

Carly's day progressed steadily downhill. On the way to her next class, she bumped into the same guy she'd bumped into once before. He laughed, she blushed and ended up sitting at her desk just as the bell rang.

Sister Mary Ella's eyebrows nearly touched as she watched Carly walk to her desk and sit down, but said nothing. The whole room buzzed until Sister cleared her throat and started the lesson. Soon she lost herself in the tapping of the keys and the occasional question from a raised hand. Carly let go of her breath, relaxing to the rhythm of the keys.

The kid behind her poked her shoulder. She turned halfway around and removed the folded paper from the guy's outstretched hand.

Carly slipped the note into her blazer pocket to read later. Sister would read it to the entire class if she got her hands on it.

Class over, Carly followed the other students into the hall and opened the note.

Hands off him or you'll die.

She looked around, saw hundreds of uniform-clad students hurrying through the halls, but saw no one watching to see her reaction to the note. She stuffed it back in her pocket and took off for her next class, wondering as she went who had just threatened her life.

At lunch, she confided in her friend Bridget, showing her the note with its threat.

"Geez, Carly. This is pretty bad. You know all about
the zero tolerance thing at our school, don't you?
This could get somebody kicked out permanently."
For emphasis, she rolled her eyes.

"So you have no idea what's going on?"

"None whatsoever."

Carly turned her face to the window, still thinking.

To break the silence, Bridget asked, "Hey, want to
come over after school?"

Carly wished she could. "I promised to help finish
up the sandwich shop today. It's opening real soon.
Liz asked me if you'd like to sign up to work weekends
and over the summer, maybe."

Bridget's face lit. "We'd work together? That would
be great!"

Carly shook her head. "I'd really like that, but I may
be with my father by then. I can't promise anybody
anything, you know that, Bridgey, even though we'd
have a great time. I know it."

The other girl looked disappointed but nodded her
head. "I know how important that is to you, Carly. It's
your reason to live."

It was more than that, she thought. *Way more.*
Maybe more than anyone could ever know.

Chapter 23

Her eyes gave her away . . . they widened as she recognized him, then went dull as soon as it clicked in that he knew who she was and he'd hijacked the elevator. He watched closely as a pink flush crept up her elegant, pale neck.

She still had white blond hair, only now it didn't bear the streaks of a summer in the Jersey shore sun. Now it definitely came from a bottle, but caught up in the French twist as it was, John couldn't tell if it was soft or coarse. The color matched Carly's, but then any blonde would match Carly's hair. Something about the eyebrows struck a chord, too. He'd seen them recently . . . in his own office.

"John . . . John Preshin? Is that you?" She kept her cool, aloof expression, but a trace of fear made her lips tremble just a bit. Just enough for a trained detective to notice.

He beamed at her, guaranteed to lull her into a false sense of security, or so he hoped. In the past, it had seldom failed him. That smile, combined with a twinkling eye, usually put people at ease.

"Bunny Adams . . . Mrs. Roland Evans, now, isn't it? You're lookin' good, Bunny."

Her hand went to the base of her throat, barely touching the pink silk scarf tucked discreetly into the V of her suit jacket. Rather charming, he thought. And practiced.

She looked down, her eyelashes brushing the tops of her model-perfect cheekbones. "How kind of you to say so. But, tell me, why have you stopped the elevator between floors and left me stranded without my bodyguard?" A note of steel crept into her soft, cultured voice. She moved against the railing in the back of the small space.

He tried his best Jimmy Stewart humble. "I just wanted to talk to you without all those people around. I'm not after any political favors and I'm certainly not out to cause you any harm." He stepped back, putting his hands behind him.

Bunny's eyes narrowed ever so slightly, then once again the expression disappeared behind the cloak of non-emotion she must be used to displaying at all times.

"Pretty soon my bodyguard will get this thing going and you'll be in big trouble with him, John, so you'd better talk fast." A certain haughtiness colored this, but he'd expected it.

Spreading his hands open in front of him, he smiled again, toned down somewhat. This wasn't a joke to him any more, but he knew her prediction to be correct.

"All I wanted to ask you was if the date February 12, 1987, meant anything to you." He waited for a sign, any reaction on her part.

She didn't let him down. The color drained from her face, though he had to give her credit for not revealing anything more than a palsied tic in her right cheek. Immediately her hand went up to hide it. Her eyes, however, remained fixed on him and, like magic, went blank.

"Lincoln's birthday?" If she thought she could get

away with apparent disinterest, she was wrong. Though her tone remained cool and unflustered, her color heightened and the tic jerked the side of her face faster than before.

He shook his head slowly. "No, Bunny. Not Lincoln's, but somebody's. A sixteen-year-old girl with blue eyes and white blond hair, raised in the convent at St. Hedwig's by a bunch of old nuns."

She sniffed at how much this did not concern her, but her eyes refused to meet John's.

Bingo!

He pressed on, fixing her with an intent stare. "Come on, Bunny. You must remember that date. It must be burned into your conscience, if you have one, which I am beginning to doubt."

She turned on him, her face suffused with blood, her eyes snapping with anger intended to hide the guilt she had to be feeling. "Nice. Nice! How dare you suggest . . . whatever it is you think I've done. . . . You're wrong. Very, very wrong."

"And why would that make you so upset, Bunny? Why won't you give me a straight answer? The truth must be in there somewhere. Tell me something . . . anything to put my curious mind and my nasty suppositions to rest."

Putting her hand on one hip, her expression defensive, she snarled, "One night with me a long time ago in another life doesn't entitle you to anything—do you hear? Not a damn thing."

Holy Christ!

She got him. She got him, all right. Reached into him and raked his soul. But he fought against this blow as he'd fought so many other things in his life. Weak-kneed, he let it slide over him, just as careful as Bunny Adams to hide his reaction.

With a brief blink, he took one small step closer to her in what had become a very tiny space. There was

a clunk and a hum and the elevator started moving.
He'd run out of time.

"She's beautiful, you know. Kid hired me to find her
father. She thinks her mother is dead, but she's determined to find her father. But that wouldn't interest
you, Mrs. Evans, would it?"

With a slight bounce the elevator settled to a stop.
John pressed the closed door button, knowing it
wouldn't last long.

Bunny's chin went up. "You're right, Mr. Preshin. It
doesn't interest me in the least. Now, step aside and
let me out of here. I'll tell Bruno not to kill you if you
open the door immediately."

He pulled away from the door as it opened. He
barely saw the arm reach in and grab his jacket, but
he felt the fist as it made contact with his jaw.

Bunny exited, unharmed, while John slammed
against the steel railing and slid into unconsciousness.

Mr. Savelli droned on about solving the problem
she'd finished fifteen minutes ago. His voice had a
soporific effect on her, lulling her into a contented
daze. Somebody walking down the aisle bumped into
her desk, rousing her from the stupor. Some girl.
Somebody she didn't know. Big deal. If the teacher
didn't move on to another problem soon, Carly knew
she'd fall asleep in class—something she'd never
done in her entire life.

"Miss Williams, can you come up here and help out
this poor soul at the blackboard?" Mr. Savelli tapped
a piece of chalk against his palm.

A different girl sauntered up the aisle, then did the
most outrageous thing . . . she flew through the air,
right alongside Carly's desk . . . and landed with a
ferocious splat on the floor.

She turned, her expression savage, and screamed,

"Look what you made me do! Can't you keep your backpack behind your desk?"

Mr. Savelli, face paled more than likely with fear of a lawsuit, rushed over to the girl and helped her to stand. Not daring to brush her off, he moved away, the words, "Are you all right, Miss Williams?" barely out of his mouth when there was another scream, this time a few notes shriller and plenty of decibels louder.

"A knife! She's got a knife!"

Carly joined the others in the class, looking for someone with a knife in her hand. Then the screamer pointed to the floor and everyone, including Mr. Savelli, gathered close and saw the blade of a hunting knife sticking out of the zippered pocket of Carly's black backpack.

"Stand back!" Mr. Savelli ordered. No one moved. The girl continued to wail. He came toward Carly who, mystified, couldn't imagine how the knife had gotten where it was.

Mr. Savelli motioned for her to get up from her seat. "This is a zero tolerance school, Miss Snow. I don't know about Philadelphia, but we have rules at Mary Immaculate. You others, step away from the backpack. I have to call the office."

He bent to retrieve the knife. Her mind racing, panic rising in her throat, Carly shouted, "Don't touch it! Mr. Savelli, please don't put your fingers on it."

"It's not your place to tell me what to do, young lady!"

Carly hung her head then put her hand out to stop the teacher from bending down. "Fingerprints, Mr. Savelli. The knife isn't mine. I've never touched it." Fear of losing everything gripped her, forcing her to think quickly. "Call in the cops, have them dust for prints. You'll find I'm telling the truth."

Shaking his head, the teacher bent once more. His fingers nearly grasped the blade of the knife when he stopped.

"We'll do just that, Miss Snow," he said as he straightened. Class essentially over for the day, the other students moved away from Carly and her incriminating backpack.

Her heart pounding in her chest, she looked around, hoping to find sympathetic faces. There were none. After all, she was the new girl. She'd only made one friend. Her accuser, on the other hand, stood encircled by three other girls, including the one who had bumped into her desk minutes ago.

Carly knew exactly what had happened.

As much as she might deny it, until the cops came, her butt was grass. This was Catholic School. The students were used to discipline and following rules. Carly had apparently broken a big one. No one would come to her aid. No one cared about her.

If she hadn't been before, she had become a pariah.

Closing her eyes, she prayed for the cops to come.

One good thing about being slugged in the jaw by a ham-fisted bodyguard, a hospital was nearby. He regained consciousness quickly when the emergency room doctor shone a penlight in his eye and snapped open one of those vials of ammonium carbonate under his nose.

"Jesus!" he swore as he pushed the doctor's hand away.

"Lie back, please." The doctor, a woman, pushed against John's chest none too gently.

He struggled up again. "I'm okay. Just let me out of here."

The doctor squared her shoulders, displaying a full bosom beneath the starched white jacket. Her nametag read Dr. Janet Laffin, but from the jaundiced look in her eye, she was not amused.

John thought of asking her what was up, but stopped

himself as he felt along his jaw and into his scalp. A lump the size of a small chicken egg graced the back of his head. He remembered the punch in the jaw only. Where had the egg come from?

As if she'd read his mind, the doctor told him, "You hit the railing in the elevator after your unfortunate contact with Mrs. Evans' bodyguard."

He moved his jaw. He'd been hit harder in his life, he decided. Funny, that tooth that had been bothering him when he woke up didn't hurt any more.

"I'm okay," he declared, anxious to get out of the emergency room. "Where do I pay?"

The doctor didn't move to allow him to get off the gurney. She kept staring at him, probably checking his pupils or something, he figured.

"Really, doc, I'm fine," he vowed.

The woman flipped her light brown hair and fiddled with the stethoscope around her neck. All the while her eyes bored into John's. "You don't remember me, do you?" she asked finally, her voice rough and edgy, bordering on impatience and hardcore resentment.

John looked at her, really looked at her while putting her face through the rolling file in his dulled brain. "Uh, I've never been in this hospital before. Do you know me from somewhere?"

Fire shot through her eyes and her hand struck out with the speed of a cobra. It made contact with his cheek, the one without the burning bruise, and stung like all hell.

"Get him outta here," the doctor called behind her as she left the curtained cubicle.

Oh, man. Another victim of his misogynistic amnesia.

His wallet sixty some bucks lighter, John eased himself into his Jeep, fished out his keys and started it up. Rubbing at his jaw, he felt warmth under the bruise, and stubble already. He had two stitches in his scalp and butterfly bandages on the broken skin under his bottom lip. Flipping up the visor to get a load of himself in the mirror, he determined that he looked rough enough to shoot over to Atlantic City. Looked like a shiner on the way.

But, his morning hadn't been a complete bust.

He headed the Jeep east, in search of the last name on the kid's list.

Chapter 24

"Mr. DeAngelo will see you, Mr. Preshin, but he has a very busy schedule today, so he cannot possibly give you more than five minutes."

John jolted out of the semi-doze at the sound of the secretary's low, sexy voice. He'd been waiting thirty minutes in DeAngelo's reception area, cooling his heels and trying to shake off his vicious headache. Thirty minutes sitting on the red plush banquette that reminded him more of something he'd see in a whorehouse than the office of a vice president of an Atlantic City casino.

DeAngelo's taste was in his mouth.

John fought queasiness as he stood and walked into the big man's office.

Pasquale "Pat" DeAngelo flipped shut his cell phone as John entered. It had been over six years since they'd seen each other. His suit fit him well, but not well enough. The hair of his brows needed trimming. If he'd been trying to look slick, he'd failed. At one time, they had been cursory friends. He gave no indication of any remembered fond feelings now.

He didn't stand, nor did he offer John his hand. In John's book, they weren't off to a good start. The cell blipped out the opening strains of "O Sole Mio" but Pat ignored it.

"What can I do for you, Preshin?" DeAngelo shifted in his black leather ergonomic desk chair.

"Hello to you, too, Pat. Long time, no see." John parked himself in the small chair in front of the massive black lacquer desk. He noted there was nothing on it but the tiny telephone.

Pasquale rounded his shoulders in a shrug. A bead of sweat ran down his forehead, making John suspect the man had something uncomfortable on his mind.

"You still with the FBI?"

Ah-hah. He thought John was there to give him federal trouble. Maybe he hadn't been such a good boy lately.

"No, I resigned six years ago, after Dutch. . . ." The scar on his shoulder tugged and smoldered underneath his shirt. "I have my own business now." With that, he flipped his business card across the desktop.

"Private dick?" Pat's one eyebrow raised slightly.

John watched that drop of sweat trickle under the man's collar.

"Yeah, I went private. In fact, I'm here regarding a client." When he reached into the breast pocket of his jacket, DeAngelo pushed away from the desk, his head ducking toward the floor.

"Shit," he muttered when John slid the photograph across the expanse of the desk. "What's this?"

"Do you remember either of those women?"

Pat picked up the photograph, perused it quickly and let it drop out of his hand. "Yeah. Those babes were at the beach house that summer. I remember them. Good lays."

Inwardly, John cursed. Yet another potential father for Carly.

"Did you do both of them?" he managed to keep his tone neutral.

Pat smirked. The jackass smirked a shitty smile that set John's teeth on edge. The nausea returned.

"Yeah, oh, yeah. Regularly. They couldn't get enough of me. Why do you ask?"

Something snapped in his brain. He had avoided mentioning Carly to the other men. For some reason, he wanted to shock DeAngelo with the knowledge there was a kid. Some insane devil prodded him.

"One of 'em had a kid. The kid asked me to find her father. Your name was on the list she had with her."

Pasquale pushed away from his desk, stood and unbuttoned the lone button on his slick gray suit. Coming around to the side of the desk, he sat on the edge and absently shot his cuffs. Gold glittered at his wrists, meant to impress.

It meant nothing to John.

"So." He paused, bringing his chin up, stretching his neck against his shirt collar. "So, you think I got a kid? Prove it."

John sat back in the chair and crossed one leg over his knee. He flicked an imaginary bit of lint from his trouser leg. "There are tests. They take a bit of dead cells from the inside of your. . . ."

"Hey, wait a minute. I am not going to be tested for anything." Pat's face reddened and he hopped off the desk.

"I should think you'd want to know if you had a daughter. She's a good kid, but she's had it hard. Raised in what passed for an orphanage by a bunch of nuns. She deserves a break."

The other man leaned forward. "What's she look like? I mean, does she look anything like me?"

John considered this a moment, absorbing the thinning black hair, the pampered tight tan flesh and the beady dark eyes then said, "She looks like her mother."

A wicked gleam sparkled in Pat's eyes. "Well, now.

That puts a whole different light on things. I'm always looking for talent, if you know what I mean. What say you bring her around and I take a look at the goods?"

John uncrossed his legs and stood. "What if she's your kid?"

Pat shrugged slowly and gestured with his palms up. "Makes no difference to me. A cunt is a cunt."

The crudeness sickened his soul. John turned to leave, but something tugged him back to face DeAngelo. His fist connected with DeAngelo's face, the power behind it sending the other man careening off the desk.

"What the fuck'd you do that for? Get the fuck outta here! I'm calling security, you stupid shit."

John wiped his knuckles. "You're a pig, DeAngelo. Some things never change. Go ahead and call security. I know most of your guys. I doubt they'd do anything to me. You, on the other hand, you they could take down easily if I told them what a scumbag you are. Then there's the gaming commission. Don't press your luck."

He strolled out of the office, past the secretary who was more interested in repainting her nails than seeing him to the door.

Before he left the building, however, he found the men's room, went inside and puked.

As he splashed his face with cold water, he felt his cell phone vibrate in his pocket—ordinarily not an unpleasant feeling.

He didn't recognize the caller's number, but this was his private line. Very few people other than current clients knew how to reach him this way.

Stepping out of the lavatory, he exited the casino doors before taking the call. He felt like hell, his head throbbed, his jaw ached and his entire upper digestive tract burned. His battered knuckles wanted to bleed.

"Yeah. Preshin."

"Mr. Preshin? This is Sister Rosemary, vice principal at Mary Immaculate."

The usual shudder caused by parochial school memories coursed down his spine. In reflex, he stood up straighter.

Carly. Something to do with Carly. Was she hurt?

"What can I do for you, Sister?" His voice sounded more self-controlled than he felt at the moment. "Is Carly all right?"

After a long pause, no doubt as the good sister tried to think of a way to break the bad news gently, she said, "There's a bit of a situation here involving your ward. We must insist that you come to Mary Immaculate as soon as possible."

Just come out and tell me what the hell is wrong. John moved the phone to the other ear as he fished in his pocket for his keys. "I'm about an hour away, Sister, depending on traffic. Can't you tell me what's happening?"

Again a long pause. "I think you'd better hear it from Carly herself."

Hellfire. "She's all right, not bleeding or anything? Nothing broken?" An unfamiliar feeling clawed its way up his throat as he started the Jeep and pulled out of the casino parking lot.

"I'd rather not discuss it over the telephone, Mr. Preshin."

Shaking himself, trying to dispel the feeling of dread and aching knuckles, John sped along the AC Expressway to the Parkway. Troopers lurked everywhere . . . he spied them behind every shrub and cluster of scrub pine. Why hadn't the nun told him what was up? He searched his memory for all the tricks he'd ever known them to employ and came up with one of the sisters' favorites—divide and conquer.

It went like this: Something happened. Two people or more were involved. The nuns would not let the miscreants get their stories straight by letting them all stay together. Divide and conquer. If you didn't know what your friend had said, you might possibly be the one to trip up on the facts and blam! Both of you were nailed.

He fought a smile thinking how large the crucifix loomed on the wall one had to face while waiting to be interrogated by the vice principal or, worse yet, Sister Jean Baptiste, the principal. It served as a promise of how you'd end up if you'd done something wrong. Just like Jesus, you'd be nailed.

He'd only seen that particular crucifix once or twice in his eight years before high school.

The image of the poor, suffering Jesus hanging on that cross would probably never, ever leave his mind.

Did nuns still employ such gruesome psychological methods of finding the truth?

He'd soon find out.

An hour and a half later, thanks to being stopped by a statie for speeding, John pulled the Jeep into the school parking lot. Girding his loins for battle, having gone two rounds already today, he entered the main office.

A secretary started, actually jumping back at the sight of him. Bandages on his head, the black and blue blossoming on his jaw and eye, he must look like a demon from hell to deserve that kind of reaction. Perhaps, he thought, the rough, unkempt look was a bit too much for Catholic school.

"Sister Rosemary, please?" He felt the weight of all his sins descend upon his shoulders then, with relief, he remembered he wasn't the one in trouble. Yet.

Jesus agonized on the cross directly above where John had been directed to sit. He didn't have to wait long before a short, lean, dowdy woman wearing half a veil over her graying hair motioned him into her office.

"I'm Sister Rosemary, Mr. Preshin. Glad you could

get here so quickly. I hope you didn't exceed the speed limit."

He stood, hands dangling at his side, in front of her desk until she gestured to the chair. Sitting, he still took up more space in the small office than the nun, but she looked him in the eye and silently dared him to get out of line. Yeah, like he would.

"What seems to be the problem, Sister?"

"I'll get right to the point. Your ward, Carly Snow, seems to have brought a knife to school with her."

John's backbone went rigid. "I'd like to see her, please."

The nun glowered at him and his defiance. "You must realize that this is a serious offense. It is cause for expulsion. Now, I know that Carly is new to the school, that she came here from Philadelphia and things can be pretty rough in the city, but we cannot tolerate the carrying of any kind of weapon in Mary Immaculate."

"Let me see Carly *now*, please."

Sister Rosemary was not used to having her own methods used against her and showed it in the firm set of her lips. If he'd learned anything in his years of parochial schooling, it was how nuns acted and reacted. All he had to do was maintain his composure. As long as he didn't crack, he could best her. He was an adult now. And the crucifix on her wall wasn't nearly as big as the one in the main office.

Carly entered the room. He expected her to be staring at her shoes. Instead, she looked at him and pleaded with those luminous blue eyes to believe her. He asked what had happened, Carly told him—all of it, including how she had asked for the knife to be fingerprinted.

John had to hand it to the kid as an odd sense of pride washed through him. She thought on her feet.

"Did you bother with the fingerprinting, Sister?" he asked when the tale was done.

The little nun drummed her fingers on the desktop. "We don't usually like to call in the police."

John stood, his full six foot two filling the room. His beard shadowing the lower part of his face, the worn leather jacket open enough to show his chest hair above the vee of his sweater, that lock of hair a comma on his forehead, he knew he looked like a dusty, battered Indiana Jones. Sister Rosemary didn't back down, but she did stand.

Turning to Carly, he asked, "Kid, is it your knife?"

Carly shook her head. "No."

To Sister Rosemary he said, "It isn't her knife. But let's get something straight. I don't want this incident shadowing her in your or anybody else's mind. I want it clear that the knife wasn't hers, and I want you to find out who put it in her backpack. If that requires her to be fingerprinted then so be it. But I want Carly's name cleared completely."

"But . . . ," the little nun sputtered.

"Sister," John said, relaxing slightly to show his faith in Carly, "I'm a retired FBI agent. I know how these things work. I also know Carly. Somebody put that knife in her backpack. If you want, I can call in the local police right now and get their fingerprint guy over here."

"Do that." The nun's face remained devoid of emotion. John hadn't managed to intimidate her in the least. But he'd gotten what he wanted.

He stayed with Carly throughout the fingerprint process. The local detective dusted the knife first, getting a clear thumb and middle finger. After taking Carly's thumbprint, he held up the print sheet.

"Not a match, Sister. You don't have to be an expert to tell. If you look here, you'll see that big swirl on the print from the knife. You will note that it does not appear on Miss Snow's print. She couldn't have left it. Unless she had rubber gloves, which would have smeared the prints, or used a technology far beyond what any sixteen-year-old kid could obtain, she did not touch that knife.

"Would you like me to determine who did?"

Sister Rosemary had to know the consequences of having the entire school fingerprinted for she shook her head. "I don't think that's necessary, Detective. Carly, I am convinced the knife isn't yours. I guess we'll have to leave it at that."

"Wait a minute, Sister," John interrupted. "You accused Carly of bringing a knife to school. You hauled me in here all the way from an investigation in Atlantic City. I got a speeding ticket trying to get here as soon as possible. Carly had to undergo the humiliation of fingerprinting to prove her innocence and you want to leave it at that?

"I don't think so. I want the culprit located and punished as Carly would have been punished."

"No . . . no!" Carly stepped forward, putting her hand on his sleeve for just a second then removing it. "It's over. Just let me go to class."

The detective put away his gear, listening to the conversation with interest. Detective Rosenberg knew little of parochial school nuns.

John put his hand on Carly's shoulder. "Look, Carly, somebody framed you. Don't you want the guilty party to be punished?"

He looked into her eyes and saw the trouble in them. She knew who had done it, or thought she knew. Her light colored hair wisped across her forehead and once again John thought of the woman who had to be her mother.

Carly shook her head. "There's been enough hassle. As long as Sister Rosemary is convinced the knife isn't mine and I don't know how it got in my backpack, that's enough."

He recognized the stubborn set of her chin and gave in.

"Sister, if you would kindly walk Carly back to class, that will be proof enough that you do not doubt her word."

He waited for some crack in the old nun's façade. They were so used to always being right, it must hurt them to admit being mistaken. Seconds passed in absolute silence and the sister gave no indication of relenting.

John urged her with his guaranteed-to-make-glaciers-melt smile.

The merest hint of a quiver touched the woman's lips.

"All right. You're correct, Mr. Preshin. It is not your ward's knife and I will bring her back to her next class personally."

Pushing his luck, he looked down on the little woman and suggested, "You'll bring her to her class and smile at her to let everyone know she's innocent?"

Sister Rosemary pursed her lips. "You went to Catholic school, didn't you, Mr. Preshin?"

"All the way through college."

She let a small smile sneak over her mouth. "It shows."

"I'll take that as a compliment, Sister."

Chapter 25

Liz watched her grandmother sashay back and forth behind the marble-topped counter, serving soup to hungry road workers who used to be regular customers of the luncheonette. She'd heard a few squawks about no hamburgers, but as they sipped their hearty minestrone and dipped pinches of fresh French bread into the bowls, the old favorites were apparently forgotten.

Big burly road workers might miss their burgers, but the delicious soup warmed them and filled their bellies. The atmosphere of the luncheonette, though changed in décor with a slightly more elegant look, remained friendly and upbeat. She noted that no one left unsmiling after paying their bills.

And tips proved to be quite generous.

Outside, standing in the cool March wind, two men, dressed much better than those who returned to their jobs repairing the road, contemplated the new menu displayed on the Soup Bar window.

When the stools emptied, the new customers made their way in and seated themselves at the counter.

Liz tensed. These customers could do a great deal for the Soup Bar. Recommendations from them could bring in business from the city and elsewhere. She smoothed her apron and approached them.

"Good afternoon, gentlemen."

"Oooh, look at this menu, Gary. Marvelous. Simply marvelous." Turning from his friend, the speaker returned the greeting then asked, "What would you recommend, my dear?"

Smiling, Liz rattled off the specials, carefully planned by Flo and Carly as the best of the proposed menu for this, the first day of the new business.

Lance introduced himself and Gary. "I'll have the grilled Portobello with, let me see, I think the Italian bride soup. There isn't any barley in it, is there? I'm afraid I can't take barley."

"No, sir. No barley, just pearl pasta and simple vegetables in clear broth."

"Gary? What will you have?" He turned to his friend and gazed with affection at the tall, spare man with close-cropped hair and wire-rimmed glasses over dark brown eyes.

Gary clearly did not know what to choose. "Oh, I'll have the same soup, but do you have a sandwich with beef? I'm simply not in the mood for fungi."

"You'll enjoy the Hunter, then. Finely sliced roasted beef on a hearty whole grain roll, served with a dash of horseradish sauce."

Thinking it over, Gary nodded. "Not too much horseradish, please."

Liz, feeling especially agreeable, offered to serve it on the side. Both men seemed pleased with their choices. As she made her way into the kitchen, she overheard them exclaiming over the menu.

Carly knew her stuff. Sprinkling Italian and French in the selection names added something, all right. They could up the prices.

More customers drifted in, a mixed crowd of old

regulars and an entirely new group, all eager to give the Soup Bar a try.

About two thirty, the place was empty. Liz and Flo cleaned up, Flo started the soup bases for tomorrow's menu and Liz took stock of the refrigerator.

"We'll need to get in some more mushrooms, Gram. And parsley and some tomatoes. I hope Danny can find some more of the vine-ripened ones for us. They were noted by some of our more discriminating customers today."

Wiping her hands on her soiled apron, Flo wrote down the list and put in a call to their supplier while Liz took one more look at the counter.

She saw movement at the door and was about to call out that they were closed when John Preshin wandered in.

With his broad shoulders slumped and his head bowed, he looked like a man with a problem. Liz sighed as her heart did a little blip inside her chest. She could shoo him away, back upstairs to his lair and let him suffer whatever it was that had brought him to this condition.

Or, something she did not relish, she could ask him what was wrong. Either way, somehow she knew she would regret his reply. Unless, that is, he refused to answer.

"Tough day?"

He lifted his head, the blueness of his eyes startling her. Had she never noticed the intense color before? Or had she? Had she tried to forget the haunting depth of them or the way they scored her soul when he looked at her just that way? And dare she ask about the shiner?

She felt a little uncomfortable being alone with him right now. Something about those eyes showed her a side of the detective she'd never suspected.

"Yeah. You might say that," John supplied.

Rubbing her hand on the apron front, she asked if he was hungry, avoiding any mention of his battered face.

"Nah. You're cleaning up. It's after closing." He turned up his gaze, a small smile taunting her, forcing her to say it wouldn't be any trouble at all, what would he like?

Manipulative bastard, she thought. *He sure knows how to play me.* "I haven't erased the menu yet. We have a little left of everything, but not much."

John parked himself on one of the newly reupholstered stools at the counter. He spun on the stool and focused on the menu board.

"Kinda fancy."

Liz bridled at his tone. "If you don't like it, you can go somewhere else. . . ."

"Now, Lizzie," he added quickly, "I wasn't complaining. It was merely an observation. Do you have any of that French onion soup left? I'm not in the mood for brides right now."

Letting the comment slide, Liz disappeared out back and called out to her grandmother that John had stopped in. As she fixed the soup, floating the crouton of stale bread atop the steaming onions and tossing a handful of Gruyere on top of that, she wondered what had put their tenant in such a sedate—no, make that thoughtful—mood. What had happened to the other guy? If she asked, though, would he even tell her?

She didn't know him, not really. Well, she *knew* him, but she doubted that allowed her to delve into his thoughts. Eventually, she knew she'd ask him. It would just slip out and she regretted it already. His troubles had nothing to do with her.

Removing the bowl of soup and cheese from the salamander, Liz carried it out to him. She noticed that the towel she was using had stains on it and as soon as she set the bowl down in front of John, she tossed the towel in with the other soiled towels to be picked up by the laundry tomorrow morning.

"Everything okay?" she asked before turning to leave for the apartment.

Her customer sighed. "Soup's great. Really great."

The sigh undid her.

She came around the counter and stood by the empty stool next to him. "I know I'm going to regret this, but what's the matter, John?" Without thinking, her hand went up to smooth his hair. Horrified at what she'd done, she put it behind her back, hoping he hadn't noticed.

He stopped the spoon in mid-air and set it down. "I got called to Mary Immaculate just before eleven."

Concern for Carly rose in Liz's throat. "What happened? Is Carly all right?"

John resumed eating, speaking in between spoonfuls of soup and onion and gooey cheese. "Somebody put a huge hunting knife in her backpack, setting her up for expulsion from school."

Surprised he didn't act even *more* distressed, Liz leaned her forearm on the counter, bringing her closer to him, getting into his face. "How could that happen?"

John put down the spoon and blotted his lips with a paper napkin. "I'm not exactly sure, but the kid handled it like a pro. She refused to touch the thing and demanded to have the knife fingerprinted."

"Like father, like daughter," murmured Liz.

John started. "What did you say?"

Liz shook her head. "Forget it. Just tell me the rest of the story."

John's eyes narrowed, then apparently dismissing the thought, he continued. "Carly wouldn't tell me who did it, if she even knows, but I have a feeling she knows damn well who framed her. The vice principal was ready to kick the kid out of school, I think. At least it seemed that way when I first talked with her. But she wasn't going to check, wasn't going to call in the cops. Carly and I insisted . . . I even called them in myself. One of the detectives came in and dusted the knife for prints then took Carly's prints and it was plain as day they didn't match."

Liz sat back with relief. "And? Come on, John, finish the story."

John swallowed. A look of pain crossed his face for a second then vanished. "And Carly and the nun thought that was enough, but I didn't. I wanted it made clear to everyone that the nun believed that Carly had nothing to do with the knife and that it wasn't hers."

Liz nodded in understanding. "I see what you mean. You wanted the kid exonerated. It wouldn't do to have her peers suspect her for the rest of her time in high school."

"Suspicion can be an ugly thing, with or without proof," John observed.

Tears burned Liz's eyes. Suspicion could be more than an ugly thing. It could destroy a person.

Carly bounded down the street feeling exultant. She passed Curtis at the newsstand and gave him a smile and a wave. He grinned back at her and called out, "Looks like somebody had a good day!"

Skidding to a stop, she leaned her two hands on the counter and looked the elderly man in the eye. "Actually, this had the potential to be one of the very worst days of my entire life, but it isn't. No, it certainly is not."

He slipped her a chocolate bar, gave her a wink and waved good-bye as she took off toward home.

"Watch those cars!" he shouted at her back.

Carly laughed and slowed down before dashing across the street. The lights were still on inside the

Soup Bar. Funny, she thought they'd agreed to close up after three. It was nearly four o'clock.

Coming to a complete stop, she peered inside the window. Liz sat beside John on the stool near the cash register. They both looked wary. In fact, it looked as if Liz had been crying, but they were talking and they weren't shouting at each other, which was good. She watched them awhile, until Liz looked out at the street. Carly made faces behind the glass.

Laughing, Liz waved Carly around to the side door.

Banging her backpack against the interior walls and hitting her hip into the worktop, Carly entered the luncheonette with her own unique fanfare.

"Hi, everybody!" she called out.

"Hi, yourself," Liz shot back. "Before you get started, let me tell you that everything went well today."

Carly leaned against one of the small tables and digested this news.

"Great! That's wonderful, Liz. How was the crowd? Did anybody complain about the new menu? How bad was the rush?"

"Big. Not really. Pretty good after noon, slow around one forty-five and over by two-thirty, as you predicted."

Feeling a part of the apparent success, Carly allowed herself a small I-told-you-so grin before sobering. She had to say something to John who was just sitting there. Had to. Maybe it would be easier to say it in front of Liz. Or maybe not. He was watching her, but hadn't said anything yet.

"Uh, Mr. Preshin . . ." she began, her voice reflecting none of the joy she'd felt earlier.

He pushed away his soup bowl and swung around on the stool. Waiting. Waiting for her to say something more, she just knew it. She had to do something, had to cross that invisible, impassable line she'd drawn between them from the beginning. He'd saved her. He'd come to her rescue like a knight on his charger. *Move Carly. Go over to him.*

Still he said nothing. But his eyes were alive. He waited for her to. . . .

Carly flung herself at him, wrapping her arms around his neck and hugging as hard as she could.

John let out a surprised grunt then put his hands around her waist and gave her a tight squeeze.

That did it. Carly started crying. As tears streamed down her cheeks, she tried to tell him how grateful she was, how he was the best, how he'd saved her life, how he'd faced down Sister Rosemary and actually made her acknowledge that she'd been wrong. He was the best. The absolute best. More than great. Cool beyond belief.

Liz stepped into the kitchen as the tops of John's cheeks reddened.

"Hey! Wow!" John pulled away and looked into Carly's eyes. "I did what I had to."

Wiping away a tear and sniffling, Carly tried to regain control of herself. He dug around in the pocket of his jacket, then plucked some napkins from the dispenser in front of him.

Carly hiccoughed and started to wipe her sleeve across her nose, but accepted the proffered paper napkins instead.

"Honest, Carly. I did what was right." He looked away, no longer scrutinizing her. Carly dabbed at her tears.

"You don't understand. Nobody ever stuck up for me in my entire life. Nobody. Not until you." Her voice, a mere whisper, sounded shaky.

John leaned closer to hear her. More tears came and, without saying another word, John put his hand on the back of Carly's head and drew her into an awkward embrace. She buried her face into the soft leather of his jacket.

And snarfled.

John didn't push her away.

Viewing this from the kitchen door, Liz heaved a sigh and turned back to the unpleasant task of gathering up the day's dirty laundry.

Carly sucked in her breath. An e-mail from Choochie. What could this be about? He'd only written to her six or seven times in the past month, each time only after she'd inquired about him through Frankie. Her heart pounded as she moved the cursor to his name and clicked.

Her eyes scanned the note, her stomach tightening with each syllable. *Oh, no. Oh, wow. Oh, man. What can I do?*

Hey, Carly, how's it going? Nothing much here, but it's always dead here. "So much for small talk."

I was wondering if your school has a prom and if it does, would you consider going with me?

"Oh, would I! The girls would throw themselves at his feet if I brought him to Mary Immaculate. He is so hot!"

Our school has a prom only for juniors. The seniors had a senior ball, but that was in November and I didn't know you then. "That's because I was in Philly!" *I know this is pretty late and all, but I think you're really okay.*

So, if you have a prom and you need a date and would like to go with me, let me know so I can clean out my car.
—Jason

Carly sucked in air. Her heart felt all fluttery and her mouth felt as if she'd swallowed dryer lint.

Too many thoughts rushed around inside her head. Prom bids cost a hundred bucks. He lived about an hour away. He'd need a tux. Oh, God! She'd need a dress! Where was she going to get the money for a dress?

She couldn't ask John. She owed him more than the hundred dollars she'd paid him to find her father. Besides, he'd spent all that money on clothes for her already. Grabbing her backpack, she dug around to find her wallet which contained her entire life savings.

When she upended it, the bills spilled out onto the desk, floating over the keyboard. Everything she'd earned from working at the luncheonette was there. All the bills, mostly singles and fives with a couple twenties and tens, she gathered up and put into piles by denomination.

Ninety two bucks and a ton of change.

Ninety dollars.

She couldn't get anything decent to wear for that.

Maybe she could make some more money cleaning up again for Liz and Flo. She'd had to stop most nights when she had so much catch-up homework to do. Then the luncheonette had been closed for awhile so it could be fixed up for the new business. She'd worked, but it had sorta been like she'd been helping friends, not something to be paid for. Besides, she ate most of her meals with Flo and Liz. She couldn't ask to be paid. Not while mooching food off them.

She couldn't go.

Everything went cold inside her.

She'd hold off writing back to Choochie, though, because just for a little while, until she told him she couldn't go, she wanted to feel special.

Chapter 26

John left the soup bar and headed toward the beach, shoulders bowed by the weight of realization.

No matter how he looked at it, not one of the men on Carly's little list was good enough to be her father. Discounting the one who was dead and the one who was a priest, the pickings didn't leave much of anything even remotely human, much less father material for a teenage girl like Carly.

Mike, well, he was completely out of the question, now, wasn't he? Leaving the priesthood would probably kill him or kill something inside him. John had no doubt that Mike would do that if he had to, but that wasn't the way. Mike's parents were still alive, by some miracle after having all those kids. But they had to be close to eighty. Mike had been their last kid. No way could they start all over again, though he didn't doubt that they would try. He did doubt that they were healthy enough to take on the task. And the shame. That would kill them outright. Their beloved priest son with an illegitimate kid?

Mrs. Ryan would clutch her heart and expire, but not until after spouting assorted Irish curses and exhorting several obscure saints and the Virgin.

The image brought a tight smile to his lips.

Dutch was completely out of it. He couldn't imagine Barb entertaining the idea of raising her dead husband's bastard kid. And that was precisely the word the shrew would use. No. Not Barbara.

Georgie Hahn. How had he faded into the shadow of what he'd been only a few years ago? Three daughters and a sweet wife. Working at the refinery and living in Linden his entire adult life . . . John wondered whether the very air had damaged his old friend, leaving him a shell of his former self. Could steeping in fumes and hydrocarbons for almost forty years do that much damage to a human being?

Jesus. He couldn't even think of Stu. What the hell had happened to him? What was with those piercings and the tattoos? He'd turned into a sideshow freak. A bald one at that. And his wife? How would a dominatrix handle a sweet young girl like Carly?

Those footsteps were not what Carly deserved to follow in. Jesus, no.

Oh, yeah, that left Pat. Pasquale DeAngelo. Now that was something else.

Rubbing his knuckles, John felt the urge to beat the hell out of that son of a bitch. Lowlife scum.

Passing by Tillie's idiotic grin, he looked up at the bizarre face and noted that even more paint had peeled away. The green background of the building had mildew or something in the creases and cracks.

Asbury Park.

It looked as bad as he felt.

That was some consolation, now, wasn't it? John shoved his hands into his pockets. No need to hunch over as the lowering sun, though weak, added a touch of warmth to the early March day. It would set soon and the misery of the old shore resort would settle in around him.

Asbury Park—his shell.

He ought to get drunk.

Deep in his belly the memory of oblivion called to him with her siren song. There was a bottle in his desk, but the kid was there. He could walk over to Dank's. He didn't think he'd been banned from there, yet, but it was about a mile away in the worst part of town. What was he doing? He hadn't taken a drink in years. What good had it ever done him? It hadn't wiped out the shooting, hadn't made anything better ever before.

He'd been up since four thirty or so and his legs stung as he walked toward the ocean. What he should do was go to sleep, but, not with this problem on his mind.

It wouldn't happen. Not without anesthesia.

And the kid was there.

Nobody ever stuck up for me before in my entire life. Not until you.

She'd tangled herself into his brain almost as much as that blasted redhead. The redhead he could understand being there, but the kid . . . when had she become so important?

Could he choose which name on the list was her old man?

The kid deserved a righteous, upstanding old man.

Nobody until you. John stopped on the sand colored sidewalk and rubbed his face with his hands.

His old man. His old man was all right.

His old man was better than that. He was one of the good guys. His family meant everything to him. Still did. Stan Preshin loved his daughters and grandkids and wife with a quiet ferocity John had never thought about before. But it had always been there.

He'd never thought about his father and how hard he'd worked at being what everybody needed him to be. And how he hadn't hidden behind a bottle of bourbon or a wall of self-pity, either.

The old casino shuddered before him, casting an eerie shadow amidst the deepening dusk. Too beautiful to tear down, too broken to be used, it sprawled along the beach, looking over its shoulder toward the dying Tillie. The ocean pounded the beach beyond, giving a heartbeat to the decrepit buildings. A wave of longing swept over John.

Leaning against the glass door that once contained Asbury's famous carousel, John pulled out his cell phone and called home.

"Liz, can I talk to you a minute?"

Liz jumped in surprise. With her hand on her stomach, she spun around to find Carly standing in the small chintz-filled living room of her grandmother's apartment.

"Hey, jeepers. You scared me." Liz sucked in two breaths and tried to calm herself.

The kid shifted feet, some panic crossing her expression despite her effort to hide it from Liz.

"Sure, kiddo. Come on in and have a seat."

Liz slid into an armchair and leaned her head back, closing her eyes for just a second.

Carly hesitated. "I'm sorry. I can see you're tired. I'll go upstairs. It can wait."

Opening one eye, Liz assessed the situation. "You need someone to talk to. I'm here. As long as it isn't about nuclear physics or Egypt, I can listen."

Carly's face scrunched. "Egypt? Mummies?" Her voice went up softly and Liz had to laugh.

"I don't like 'em. Outside of that, and the aforementioned nuclear subject of which I know nothing, I'm fairly knowledgeable about all things."

A small smile crossed Carly's lips. "Aw, shucks. I needed help with my model pyramid."

Liz let out a tired laugh. "Sorry. Anything else on your mind?"

She plopped into the other armchair and put one leg over the curled arm. "Well, yes."

"Spill it."

Carly cleared her throat.

"I got asked to the prom."

"Oh, honey! That's great! Who's the lucky guy?"

Carly tossed her hair with a shake of her head. "Jason. You know, I talked about him after I went to dinner at John's parents' house. He's a friend of Frankie's."

"Ah, now I remember. The one with the silly nickname and the great shoulders and nice brown eyes."

Flo stepped into the room, her ginger hair sticking out in tufts from the pink plastic rollers and paisley scarf. "And the cute smile. That Jason."

Carly blushed. "Yeah, that Jason. His nickname is Choochie."

Flo laughed on her way to her favorite seat. "You do know that means 'jackass' in Italian, don't you?"

A look of horror flashed across Carly's fair features. "No! Why would anyone call him that?"

"Probably because they heard someone use the word and didn't know what it meant but decided it sounded cool. I knew a guy in college from around here who answered to that name. He was a real doll, too." Liz drifted off slightly remembering the kind-hearted Chooch of her past.

"Well, I call him Jason," Carly stated with conviction. "That's a great name for a guy."

"Yes, it is," Flo demurred. "Manly."

"So, Carly, what's the problem and how can we help?"

"I need a dress."

Liz left Carly and Flo going over options. She could tell her grandmother was working angles, which was good, because Carly would learn something about how the world worked and she'd end up with the dress, too. They needed help in the luncheonette or whatever it was they were going to call it. But they didn't want to be open Sundays during the spring.

When the ice cream parlor opened for the summer, then they'd need serious help. But the prom would be over before they got rolling.

So, however Flo decided to go with this, Carly would get her prom dress and it would be perfect, but she'd earn it.

Liz dug through the laundry basket, feeling apron pockets for bills and toothpicks and tip money. The service didn't check and often wads of wet paper were pressed into the aprons and towels. Disgusting. So she felt around, glad she wasn't actually looking at the stains. But John Preshin's intense, battered face kept creeping back into her mind.

She'd seen John head upstairs after leaving them. Then she thought she'd heard the outside door hiss closed. Not that she was spying or really interested or anything. She just had exceptional hearing. And she always felt John's presence like a thrum in her chest. Odd, that.

Her hand brushed against some thick paper in one of the apron pockets. Pulling it out, she unfolded an unopened letter. California postmark. Her lawyer's address in the corner.

Liz's brain evaporated and knees gave out as a wave of dizziness swept over her. She grabbed the edge of the stainless steel countertop and leaned her hips against its solidity.

Breathe! Breathe, you idiot! She chided herself when the world started going black.

With her eyes closed, she forced herself to inhale and exhale with some sort of rhythm. Gradually her heart rate slowed and feeling returned to her legs and face.

It might be a check, she considered. *A rebate!* Fat chance of that happening, but she'd never know what was inside if she didn't open it.

This took courage Liz wasn't sure she had, but she reached for one of the paring knives on the holder and slit open the back of the envelope then shook out the contents.

Two smaller envelopes hit the counter weighted by a sticky note.

Liz saw her hand shaking as she picked up the first and opened it.

She read it carefully then folded it up and stuck it back in the envelope before reading the note. "Thought you'd like to see this, Liz. Of course, we'll fight it." That's all. Nothing else. Nothing other than what she'd learned from the paper. But that was enough to send her into shrieks of laughter.

Tearing off her apron, Liz turned left and right, searching for the way out of the confines of the small kitchen. Panic and hysteria seized her as she bolted through the door, down the short hallway to the side door and out into the looming dusk.

Heedless of the chill, the evening damp and lazy traffic, she ran toward the ocean with a scream fighting its way out of her throat.

John found her huddled against one of the pilings of the ancient pier by following the dying sound of her scream.

One look at her tear-streaked face and he knew he was in trouble. He knew he shouldn't get involved. He wouldn't know what to do or say anyway. Maybe she hadn't seen him and he could still turn his back on her. Yeah, right.

"Ah, Lizzie," he said as he folded his arms around her quaking shoulders, "hush, now. Hush. Tell John what's wrong, baby. Tell me what's wrong."

Liz pushed at him, pounded her hand against the

leather of his jacket, whimpered and touched her forehead to his chest before calming into a series of deep
inhalations and hiccoughs. His hand softly caressing her
hair caused another set of short, pitiful sobs before sub-
siding into wavering breaths as she refused to look at him,
turning away from his probing stare.

"Ah, darlin'," he said as he held her. "Another shit
day, I suppose."

One hand moved up to clutch at his shoulder. The
crushed envelope it held grazed his cheek.

"What's this?"

John eased it from her fingers though she tried for
a moment to withhold it from him. Keeping one arm
around her, he took his time reading the document
by the light of the security lamp a few feet away.

"Sweet Jesus."

Liz's sobs returned with a vengeance and John held
her close and rocked with her.

"Shhh . . . shh," he crooned. Liz inhaled sharply
and John felt her struggling for control as her body
trembled against his. Not the way he would have
wanted, but he forced that unholy thought away.

Liz, having won part of the battle, stepped away
from John who kindly loosened his grip on her.

"May I have it back?" she asked, some of her assurance
returning, but not all for her voice wavered at the end.

John shrugged. "Sure. Do you want to fill in the blanks?"

Liz shook her head and looked away, her head
moving in the direction toward the street, then back
to the foaming low tide as it eddied on the beach.

Why did this always happen to him? A damsel in
distress . . . and the only way he could think to ease her
pain was to ease himself inside her? Sex in this case might
not be the answer she needed. He'd watched enough
afternoon television to know that even though she said
she didn't want to talk, what she really wanted to do was
talk. But to him?

Did he care enough to ask?

She'd felt too good in his arms. So strong yet soft, so womanly. Her hair smelled great, too, even after a day serving in the café. Her perfume, a faint floral beneath the enticing fragrance of cheese and beef and subtler edible scents, caught his unconscious attention. If she hadn't broken away, she'd have felt how sincere he was about comforting her soon enough.

"Look, Liz, I'm not real good at this stuff, but I know there's more to this letter and I know it left you wrecked, standing out in the cold, on the ugly beach of Asbury Park, New Jersey. Can't get much more desolate than that. Why don't we go someplace and talk?"

She shivered and, with more gallantry than he knew he possessed, John doffed his jacket and put it around her shoulders. With a grateful, watery smile, Liz tugged it tighter.

"Now you'll be cold. Let's go someplace . . . any place with a lot of people in it maybe, and maybe we can just hang out together."

Jesus! Now what?

"Okay. I don't suppose you're hungry, but there's an old diner in Neptune City. It's never really empty. Would that do?"

Liz nodded. "Anywhere but back home. Not just now. I can't face my grandmother now. Just for a little while."

Somehow satisfied, feeling slightly elevated in humor now that she agreed to go someplace with him to talk, he guided her back the two blocks to where he'd parked the Jeep. Liz kept to herself, but that was okay.

He didn't know what he'd say when she did open up.

Chapter 27

John fiddled with the heater control on the dashboard of the Jeep, hoping the small space would warm before they got to the diner. Manly as he pretended to be, the cold March night seeped into his bones. Liz looked nice and toasty in his leather jacket.

He shivered as the temperature plummeted outside. Without something warm in him or around him, he felt the cold as he never had before.

But he was doing a good deed.

If it came down to being a son of a bitch or having this one good deed on the books when he met his demise, he'd rather go down with something on the pro side to help balance out the cons.

He no longer thought he believed in sin.

"Do you believe in retribution, John?"

Liz's question, out of the blue, rattled him. Suspicion of mind readers was high on his list of qualities he'd cultivated in the Bureau.

He kept his eyes on the road even if he had traveled it hundreds of times before. "Yes."

She turned toward him, her eyes capturing his face in the glare of the headlights. "Good. That's good. So few people are willing to admit it, even if they carry the 'eye for an eye' business in their black little hearts."

He laughed. "So, now I have a black heart?"

"No, that's not what I meant. I meant the people who admit they want an eye for an eye at least are open about it while the bleeding hearts seem to want it but never admit to their feelings."

"Uh-huh. Now I get you. No, I'm a big believer in retribution and vengeance, too, when it comes right down to it."

"Hmm. I never would have guessed."

"You do know that I was in the FBI, don't you?"

"Mmm, Gram mentioned it. But you aren't any more. She didn't know exactly why."

Pulling into the diner parking lot, John refrained from answering until he helped Liz out of the battered Jeep and into the steamy warmth of the eatery.

The waitress standing at the end of the counter pushed aside her older counterpart in her hurry to reach their booth. Flipping the heavy laminated menus to the latest arrivals, the waitress cracked her gum and waited. John studied the menu and ignored the waitress.

After a swipe at her eyes with her hand, Liz buried herself behind the plastic menu.

The waitress, gum snapping, asked, "What will it be?"

John looked over his menu to Liz. "Anything? Pie, coffee? Burger?"

"No food," Liz said softly. "A cup of coffee . . . no, tea if you have it, please."

The waitress stabbed her pad with her pencil and turned to John, smiles and warmth she had not offered to Liz pulsing from her. "And you, sir?"

He looked up at her and gifted her with a smile, the one he practiced on women from Maine to Louisiana with great results. "Apple pie and coffee, darlin'."

His charm worked once again. The woman preened

and after a quick adjustment to her tight uniform skirt, wiggled away to fill the order.

"Do you always do that?"

"What?"

"Have that effect on women."

"Apparently." He kept a straight face, though it was difficult. "It doesn't always work, though. It hasn't worked on you."

Liz laughed, a good low sound that went straight to his most reactive parts. Could she be jealous?

"Never mind the waitress. Tell me about the letter. Or better yet, start at the beginning of the story so I know how it concerns you."

The waitress set a small teapot in front of Liz, along with a cup. She arranged the coffee and pie in front of John with great lingering care. He smiled, this time turning down the wattage and with a disappointed frown, the woman left.

"You have women fawning over you wherever you go, don't you?" Liz shook with laughter.

"Sometimes it has its advantages, sometimes it's just a pain in the butt. But . . . continue with your story." He smiled around the rim of the coffee cup. Liz's reaction warmed him more than the drink.

"Okay. Remember that last awful day?"

He smiled then sobered, saying in a low, sexy voice, "Parts of it."

Liz blushed, but resumed her tale. "Yeah, well, I'd gotten a letter forwarded by my lawyer in California regarding my ex?"

John nodded, still hesitant to sip his drink.

"I was upset because my ex had had another child and named him after *our* son."

"That was cruel. You said your son had died."

Liz breathed back tears before continuing. "What I didn't tell you was that my husband blamed me for it."

John put down the cup, nestling it in the little

depression of the saucer carefully, thinking of what to say. "How could he?"

Liz fiddled with the used teabag. "I believe with all my heart the baby died from SIDS. I didn't kill him and he was perfectly healthy. But SIDS strikes for no apparent reason . . . I read a great deal about it. But I was home with the baby when it happened. I thought my husband had come home early to play with him, maybe be with us, you know, do some family things I'd wanted us to do together."

"If you don't mind me sayin', this guy sounds like a real jerk-off." John reached out to tap her hand, urging her to keep going.

"We'd argued the night before about that. He was never home. He had no time for the baby or me, for that matter, because he was making money to support us, he said. Working night and day, it seemed. I never really knew what his job was because he worked for his father in the family business. He did come home that night, though, and I thought I'd gotten through to him. He was the one who found Jesse. Keith went in to check on the baby. And came out shouting. He was out of control, shouting to call 911, which I did."

"What happened?" John focused on Liz, only Liz as she spoke.

"The baby didn't move. He just lay there. Not breathing." Her voice caught while her eyes filled with tears. She wiped her hand across them.

"I couldn't wake him up. I tried mouth to mouth, but it didn't work. When the firemen came, they tried, but it was too late. Jesse was dead."

He felt pressure in his lungs and tried to shake away the deep sense of loss he felt for Liz and her child.

"Long story short, my husband, my dear husband, turned around and accused me of smothering the baby."

His hand fisting, John tried to understand what this meant to his companion. "There was a trial?"

Liz played with the tab on the teabag, not looking at John. "No, not a real one. It would never have come to that. No publicity to ruin the family name! The family doctor took care of me by keeping me so heavily sedated I missed my own child's funeral. There was talk of putting me away—you know, in a nut house— but the family and the doctor just kept me heavily medicated, alone in my room. All I really remember was agreeing to a divorce.

"My baby was dead . . . my sweet baby boy. In the end, I was to be provided for, but divorced. And my ex husband wasted no time at all remarrying and starting all over again."

"How long ago did all this happen?"

"Two years, give or take a few months." Liz closed her eyes and rubbed her fingers over her forehead."

John could almost feel her pain. He spoke softly now, hoping to calm her. "So the letter—what gives?"

"He has decided to go to court to stop paying me alimony. Because I left the state, he feels he can cut me off. That's fine, I don't need his money. I have a trust fund of my own he never got. And then there's the soup bar and all, so I'm okay without his money. But this is really pretty low."

She didn't cry. Her emotions must have been spent, he figured, to tell him this so calmly. He knew, however, that if her ex were in Jersey somewhere, he personally would pay him a little visit. "Is that all of it?"

Liz cleared her throat.

"There is something else. I've never seen Jesse's grave. Never even saw his body after the doctor took him from my arms. I've hired a detective to locate it, but so far he's been unable to get on the family estate. That's where my baby is buried."

"Are you going to fight this thing?"

She pursed her lips, thinking it over. "I just might. He owes me something."

John knew she meant what she said. That bastard didn't stand a chance. Not this time.

He felt the corner of his mouth go up in only half a smile because he applauded Liz's attitude but couldn't think of a way to say it. Determined silence enveloped them as they sipped their hot drinks. When John finally met her eyes, he saw more in them than he expected. He could never claim to be able to read more than "yes" on a woman's face; what he saw in Liz went beyond the usual.

She wanted him. She wanted to lose herself in him. Now.

Reaching across the table, he covered her hands with his and pulled her arms toward him. Why did Liz bring out these feelings of protectiveness when no other woman ever had? Why did he suddenly know how he had to react, and know that bedding her was not the right response even when she silently begged for it?

She didn't need him. Not that way.

Not now.

Liz studied John as she sipped her tea. His dark hair curled over the collar of his shirt and that one lock fell over his forehead just like Superman's. No wrinkles in his forehead anymore, but they'd been there the whole time she'd told her story.

Those bruises! He needed a shave. He always looked as if he could make inroads with a blade, but she'd never seen him without the shadow. It gave him a tired yet wary look that only left when he flashed his killer smile.

What was it with him? He could be such an arrogant jackass one minute then turn around and be so kind. How did the kid put up with her father's moodiness without wanting to pick up and leave?

She knew she shouldn't judge. He'd listened to her tonight and offered comfort when she really needed it. She owed him.

Despite what she'd said to him after that infamous morning, she couldn't forget their night together. Maybe he could. Maybe it wasn't that memorable.

She could stand being with him tonight. She wouldn't mind feeling those strong arms around her again. His warm body could do wonders for the chill in her heart.

One more time.

It wasn't as if she could get addicted to him.

Nobody was that good.

Nobody but John Preshin. Bourbon John.

Chapter 28

On the drive back to Asbury Park, Liz nearly fell off the seat when John asked whether she'd like to go to the movies with him the next night.

"Nothing special," he added, "but a buddy of mine offers a film course at the community college. He's managed to obtain an original print of *Casablanca*, he said, with the second ending."

"Second ending?" She liked movies, but had never heard anything about another ending to *Casablanca*.

"Oh, ho!" John laughed with such wickedness she turned to face him directly. "This is great. Evidently, two different endings to the movie were shot. The one they kept is the one you've seen for years. But there was a second ending, one that was completely different. Happily ever after. I've never heard of anybody ever actually seeing the second version. I don't know how this friend got hold of it, but he says it's worth seeing."

"I don't know," she hesitated. *Would this be a date? Is he asking me on a date?*

The charm turned on. She could actually feel him turn up the heat of his smile on her. *Is this how it affected other women? Hmm. Did she dare?*

"Sure."

She watched him, watched his expression very carefully to see whether he really hadn't wanted her to say yes. The smile heated up a notch.

"Great! I'll be out most of the day, but the show starts at seven and it will take about an hour to get there that time of day. So, can you be ready by six?"

Why not?

"Sure," she replied.

"It'll be fun," he assured her as they pulled up to the curb alongside the luncheonette.

As soon as she got into her room, avoiding John's courteous offer of seeing her in for fear he might try to kiss her, giddiness overtook her already frazzled emotions.

"Get hold of yourself," she whispered as she readied herself for bed. It was just a movie. Not a real date, not really. Or was it? Off the cuff. Spur of the moment more or less. He was going, asked her to join him. Was that a date?

Oh God, what would she wear?

"That was the funniest, the absolute funniest thing I have ever seen." Liz wiped tears from her eyes, laughing again to the point where she could barely breathe.

John appeared to be having trouble breathing and walking as well. Between guffaws that rocked him, he staggered, his arm draped casually over Liz's shoulders, back to the Jeep.

Her sides hurt.

"I hope that student got an A for that film."

John stopped and clutched his sides. "If he didn't, it will be a loss to the world. I've seen worse parodies, but using vegetables," here he stopped and laughed so loud it echoed across the parking lot between the brick buildings, "especially Bogart as celery! Oh, man. What a warped sense of humor. I'd love to meet this kid."

"Whoever he is, he's a genius. Wait," she held out her hand. "I've got to catch my breath."

John sat in the driver's seat, his eyes focused on her, scanning her face so intently she blushed.

"What? Is something wrong?" Something about the seriousness of his expression alarmed her.

He started up the engine. "Nah. It's just good to see you smile for a change."

Brought back to the previous night, Liz sobered, then the memory of the elegant eggplant that portrayed the Ingrid Bergman role made her giggle. "I can't stop laughing now."

"Good. What say we stop off at the diner for some dessert? That pie last night was tasty."

"Are you always hungry? Practically every time I see you, you're eating."

He switched on the charm thing again. Liz felt heat rush up her chest.

"What can I say, I'm a growing boy. It's on the way, and it's early enough. What do you say?"

Liz settled back in the seat. "Sure, why not? I think I've laughed enough to deserve some pie myself."

Sporadic laughter punctuated the short drive to the diner.

John pulled into a parking slot and shut off the engine. He didn't get out, instead he turned and looked at her. It made her uneasy. Did she look awful? Her hand reached up to her hair, feeling the curls that had escaped the clip she'd used to pull them back from her face.

In a soft, seductively low voice, John said, "Don't worry. You're beautiful. Even more so when you laugh."

She spun around in her seat so fast she got a stitch in her side. "What did you say?"

He chuckled. "I give the woman a compliment and

she doesn't hear me. Or do you want me to say it again? Okay. You're beautiful, Liz. And when you laugh, the frown lines disappear and you're even more beautiful."

"Uh. Oh." The blush started rising on her neck. Good thing is was dark in the parking lot. "I . . . well, thank you, John."

He didn't laugh at her awkward response, instead he left the Jeep and opened the door for her, then, with his hand on her back, he guided her safely inside the diner.

Rather than waiting to be seated, John led her to the booth they'd shared the previous evening. Liz noticed a different waitress from last night push her way from the counter in an obvious hurry to get to their table. Was that a look of barely disguised fury on the waitress's face?

Flipping the heavy menus in front of them, the waitress kept her eyes on John, while he didn't even look up at her. Liz sensed there was something going on behind the other woman's watery blue eyes that gave her the distinct impression that the waitress knew John.

He looked over the menu and asked Liz if she'd like some breakfast. Pancakes? French toast? All the while, the waitress tapped her pen against her pad.

John remained oblivious to the woman's pique.

"What will it be?"

Again John asked Liz, "Something special? Sandwich? Salad? Pie?"

"I'll have some rice pudding. And tea with lemon, please."

The gum snapped. Liz could feel the tension even if John didn't.

The waitress marked her pad then turned to John. "You?"

He looked up at her and gifted her with a smile, the

one he always used on waitresses with great results. "Apple pie and coffee . . . make that a la mode, please, darlin'."

Through slitted eyelids, the waitress stared at him. "Darlin'?"

He grimaced ever so slightly. "Oh, no, please. I forget sometimes. That's no longer politically correct, isn't it? Well, I can't read your nametag from the little froufrou on your handkerchief, miss. Sorry. I'd still like the pie a la mode, though."

That heart melting smile upped in intensity, apparently to no effect because the woman spun on her heel and strutted away, muttering as she went.

Liz stared after her, sheer astonishment at what she'd just witnessed bringing on more laughter. "What was that all about?"

John reached for a sugar packet to play with. "Dunno."

"Old friend?" Curiosity bubbled in her chest. This byplay was almost as funny as cabbage gendarmes.

"Damned if I know," he shot back, although it appeared to Liz that he was giving the matter some consideration from the furrow in his brow. "I haven't been here in weeks before last night with you. Maybe she waited on me before, but I can't place her."

Liz looked over to where the woman behind the counter shot coffee into a cup. Her hands shook as she flipped the spout shut.

"I hope she doesn't pour that coffee in your lap, John."

"Uh, oh," he whispered. "Here she comes."

Liz got her pudding and her tea with the bag still in the cup. The waitress set John's drink in front of him with such a crack Liz thought she'd break the saucer. A customer at the counter called the woman away and she left.

John's pie would apparently have to wait.

"The woman is upset with you, John," Liz ventured.

He picked up the cup. "All women eventually get

upset with me, Liz. I'm growing used to it. Wow," he added. "This is boiling hot."

Shifting in her seat, Liz thought back to a scene in the movie and laughed a little. "I have to thank you for taking me with you tonight. I honestly can't remember the last time I laughed this hard, John."

His sensuous lips curled in a tight smile. "I'm glad. You really should smile more often."

Before Liz could respond, he broke eye contact with her and looked at the waitress who stood behind the counter. The look goaded the other woman into action.

She wondered whether John noticed the woman's lower lip, how if it stuck out any further, she'd need to Botox the other one, just to even things out, but she kept the thought to herself.

The waitress jerked up her head then unhurriedly went to the plastic pie safe and cut the prescribed size slice, plated it and walked hip-swingingly slowly to their table, her eyes, Liz noted, were still slitted and fixed on John.

Finally she spoke. "I've been waitin', Bourbon John. All this while for you to remember me."

How she managed to say this through teeth clamped so tightly made Liz marvel. At least she now knew why they'd been given such cold treatment.

Liz leaned back against the booth and watched them both, hoping against hope the inevitable face slap would not happen, for John's sake.

John looked up slowly before fastening his gaze on the woman. Liz hid her smile behind her hand.

"I'm sorry . . . miss. I haven't been here in awhile. Did you wait on me?"

His face was too blank to be faked. Liz knew he had absolutely no idea who this woman was. It seemed to be a common occurrence with him.

The telltale flush spread up the other woman's face.

Liz felt the sparks shooting off her, but John remained clueless. Oh, oh, here it comes!

"We spent the night together. We boinked like rabbits and you fell asleep, but you said, 'good night, Terry' to me."

Apparently nothing was ringing a bell with John because his expression remained as blank as ever. It didn't even look like he was trying to remember. *This should be cute*, Liz thought.

"Ah, then, you're Terry. Sorry." But he had the decency to look chagrined.

The poor waitress snapped. Liz could tell the exact second the woman lost it. With a quick flip of her hand, the plateful of pie and ice cream landed on John's chest.

"My name is not *Terry*! Not *Terry*, you jackass! It doesn't even start with a T! I thought I made that perfectly clear with the tape!"

Realization came slowly to John's face. Though Liz wasn't exactly sure what the livid woman meant about . . . oh, the duct tape! She found herself eager to hear more as she leaned closer to the action.

"Zelda? Zoe?"

The hapless man struggled so, she could almost smell wood burning as he tried to come up with a name.

The waitress, purple-faced and puffed with indignation, struck out at his cheek with a resounding slap that made all the other diners swivel in their seats.

"Nora, you sonovabitch! My name is N-O-R-A!"

With that, the woman spun on her heel and headed behind the counter while the cook shouted at her in Greek, so no one understood what was going on.

Liz forced herself to remain stone-faced while John, recapturing his aplomb, picked pieces of pie from his shirt and placed them on the table. With a shake of his head, he said simply, "Well, that's one mystery solved."

Then burst out laughing.

Liz joined him.

He did not leave a tip.

She tried hard to ignore the stain on his shirt as he walked her to their building. She tried hard to laugh only to herself and not spoil the moments they'd had between them. They were precious, though, and his kindness had managed to seep beneath the hardened shell around her heart.

Perhaps he'd been this way with all these other women, she thought. Maybe that was why they were always so offended that he didn't remember their names.

As she and John stood at the outside door, the little tingle of anticipation filled her. She'd stood here like this before, back in another lifetime. Would it end the same way tonight? Would he want to kiss her and should she let him? Oh, sweet Jesus! This wasn't high school. She was a grown. . . .

John took away any further thought by stepping close, putting his arms around her and drawing her to his warm, apple-scented body. She looked up, trying to read his intent in his eyes, suddenly hoping he would kiss her the way he'd done when she ripped off Nora's handiwork.

He didn't let her down.

Softly at first, his lips touched hers just the way she wanted. A minute spark, static electricity from the dry air and their clothing maybe or she was thinking too much because it was more tender, more wonderful than that previous stolen kiss. But the spark had happened. They both felt it, pulled away at the surprise and looked at each other through half-closed eyelids.

And once again he met her lips and continued a long, slow kiss. Liz's toes curled in her shoes as she raised her hands to encircle his neck and pull herself closer to his heat. This time, when his tongue traced the seam of her mouth, she let him plunder. Giving in to this man was easy. So easy.

Before she lost herself completely, she broke the kiss, but rested her forehead against the softness of his jacket. What was she doing? What was going on?

He held her close for a few seconds more then whispered, "Good night, Lizzie. Sweet dreams."

Was she imagining it, or did his voice sound as shaky as she felt? Another thought to ponder as she lay awake in her lonely bed.

Chapter 29

He'd been sitting at his desk, fiddling with a paper clip and thinking about last night with Liz and how much he wanted her again when Curtis walked into the office. Curtis only ventured out of the newsstand during the day if he was on fire. The grave expression on his worn, dark face warned John before the man even spoke a word. The time had come.

They didn't waste words on formalities.

"She said the old lady got admitted on the night shift, John."

Curtis slowly shook his head while John sat up straight and dropped the paper clip with a loud ping.

"Thank you, Curtis. You know how long I've waited to hear this. I appreciate you coming over here to tell me."

"Yeah, well, this was the first time I could get away from the newsstand, but I figured you'd need to know."

John loosed a tight laugh.

"Yeah, it's been quite awhile. This gives me time to prepare, though. How bad did Lucille say the lady was?"

"Real bad. Her daughters were all there at her bedside, if that means anything. Lucille said she'd look at the old lady's chart next shift, but from what she could tell, it didn't look as if she had much longer on this earth before God called her home."

"Curtis, I don't know if God will want her anywhere around."

After a long pause, Curtis spoke in a hushed, serious tone. "Now, don't say that, Bourbon. Just because her son is no good, doesn't mean she's not in the Maker's hands."

"I guess she can't help the fact that her son is a murderer, Curtis. Right. You're right."

Another long pause. "Well, John, don't you do anything to soil your immortal soul. The Lord wants us to turn the other cheek always."

With vehemence, John replied, "Not this time, Curtis. I cannot turn the other cheek. That little shit killed my partner, ambushed us when we thought he was going to make a deal. He deserves to die, Curtis. And I swore to Dutch he would."

Carly stood outside the office door, paralyzed as she eavesdropped on the two men.

"Oh, God, please, no . . . don't let this be happening," she whispered. *What? What can I do? Blessed Mother, what can I do?*

"There has to be another way. Call in the FBI . . . they're the ones who can bring him to justice. You're not the Lone Ranger, Bourbon."

She heard a terse laugh.

"There's where you're wrong Curtis."

"I ain't wrong. It's up to the Lord to send an avenging angel. Last time I looked, Bourbon, you weren't an angel."

The desk chair scuffed back against the wooden floor. "You're right, Curtis. I'm no angel. But I made a vow that night and I will keep it."

"All I ask is that you think about it, Bourbon. Think

about that sweet little girl of yours. What's gonna happen to her if you're in jail or dead?"

Carly caught her breath. His little girl? What did that mean?

"I have that all figured out, Curtis. Rest assured, I have everything under control."

More movement, foot-shuffling, coming closer to the door. Carly ducked back behind a corner of the hall, well out of sight. *Oh, God, oh, God, oh, God!*

The door opened. "You be careful, Bourbon. Think over what I said. You're a young man still, you got a lot to live for. No use wasting your life for revenge."

Curtis left without an answer from John.

Terror held Carly in the shadows for a long time. What was going on? She needed a plan, a darn good plan. She had to act as if she hadn't heard a thing, yet she had to find out what Curtis had meant. What it all meant for her, too.

John sorted through three days' worth of mail stacked neatly on his desk by Carly, he assumed, and added what had come in today without even looking at it. She was a good kid. A real good kid. Sharp as a tack and with a wonderful future ahead of her. He planned on making sure all his finances were in order so he could leave her with enough funds to make it through college, at least.

He had money he'd received when he'd gotten shot . . . compensation from the Bureau. He'd never touched a cent. That was stashed in a locker at the bus station. Not very bright of him, but safe as anywhere else. And he had insurance money he'd changed over to her name instead of his parents. They'd be okay. They'd never use it to take a trip to Europe even if he bought them tickets, so it was best for Carly to have, in case he should be killed instead of just sent to prison.

He shook off that thought.

Liz.

Carly would be set, but how would Liz handle this? He scrubbed at his face, the memory of Liz's warm body against his overriding his senses, fogging his determination around the edges. This complication he'd never guessed, never planned to happen.

He dreamed about Liz. He caught himself thinking about the texture of her hair, the sweet fragrance of her perfume. Her gruff act, pretending not to like him when he knew damn well she did. That fire in her eyes drew him like no other woman ever had.

He was falling in love with her.

He'd never dreamed his life could have gotten so complicated; he'd avoided distractions and attachments so easily for the past seven years, and now this.

Somehow, he'd have to settle things with Liz, too. Hell. It wasn't going to be easy. It was going to hurt, but he'd take care of it the only way he knew how.

The time for *if only* had run out.

Consulting the list he'd made right after Curtis had left, he ticked off several other things he'd been able to handle by phone.

One item remained that he could attend to tonight.

John went to church.

Mike was hearing confessions.

John decided he couldn't wait for him to finish so he entered the vacant confessional.

He'd forgotten how cramped the confessional was, how tight the fit as he knelt inside and considered what he had to tell Mike. There was no air . . . that much he remembered from his childhood. And a discomfort stumbled through his body while he waited, feeling all the short hairs he possessed tugging at his skin, especially around his balls.

That much he remembered, too. All the sins he ever had committed or made up because he lacked enough wrong-doing to be believed by those ancient priests came stealing back into his mind. What he would confess today would top them all, and he knew there would be no Hail Marys or Our Fathers to cover his planned transgression. He mouthed out an Act of Contrition, just to make sure he remembered the words.

Wood slid over worn wood and the dim outline of the priest shone through the screen. John fought ancient fears before speaking.

"Bless me, Father, for I have sinned."

Silence.

He wondered whether Mike had heard him.

"Father? Mike?"

"Jesus! Is that you, John?"

He felt the corners of his mouth turn up. "Yeah, it's me, Mike."

He heard the priest turn in his chair. "What are you doing here? Are you drunk?"

John hung his head. "No, I'm regrettably sober and have been for years."

"What do you want?"

"I have to talk to you."

He sensed Mike leaning closer to the screen. "Couldn't it wait? I'm sure I'm almost done here. Nobody really comes to confession anymore, and I've been here over an hour."

"Well, I needed to talk to you right away and I figured this was as good a place as any."

"Were you serious about confession?"

John exhaled as he thought. "Yeah. I'm serious, Mike. I have a lot on my shoulders right now and I need to make sure you understand what I have to do and why. And I need you to take care of Carly, to make sure you bring her up to my parents' house. There's money in a locker—the money I got when I was shot.

It's enough to see her through these last years of high school and probably, since she's smart, enough to get her through college, providing she doesn't blow it. I need you to handle this."

"Wait," Mike said, no longer whispering. "What are you going to do, John? This sounds terminal. What's going on?"

"It's time. The old lady is dying. Her son will be coming to Jersey from Sicily to see her buried and you know what I swore to do. I intend to do it."

He pictured Mike rubbing his big hand over his broad Irish face. "Don't do this, John. You're under no obligation to Dutch. You made that vow when you were nearly out of your mind with pain and guilt. Turn away from it. Dutch wouldn't want you sacrificing your life this way. Not for him."

"Why not, Mike? He sacrificed his life for mine when he pushed me out of the way."

"You'd already been hit! You were probably falling down anyway! Jesus, John! Think, man! Is this what you really want?"

Silence.

"And what about Carly? What's going to happen to her?"

"I told you. I've taken care of that. But I need you to take her to my parents' house. Maybe explain to her. I'll either be dead or in jail."

Silence, this time drawn out considerably.

"Is she your daughter?"

John rubbed his face, feeling sweat on his fingertips. He had to swallow hard. "I'm not sure, but I think so. At first, I thought I was out of the picture. But then I found her mother, Mike. She didn't admit to it, but it wasn't the other one, so it had to be her. And she told me we had spent one night together. So, along with everybody else, I could be her father.

"What about the others?"

His knees ached from kneeling. "They're all bums. Unbelievable. If I had time, I'd tell you about them, but it's a long story, so I'll just say that of the others, you and I are the prizes and you, my friend, don't suck the jelly out of the doughnut first."

Mike said nothing. John guessed he was too stunned to speak.

"I'm not going to hand her over to any one of them. Since I could be her father, and I like the kid . . . I really do, I'm just going to say I am so she has a family."

Mike made a funny noise, either a laugh or a cough or some indefinable sound in his throat.

"No test?"

John shook his head. "No tests because I don't want a test. She's my kid because I want her to be."

"Then don't you want to stick around to be a father to her?"

Long pause. "I'm going to do the best I can. I've seen to her welfare. She'll have my parents and my sisters and brothers-in-law and all my nieces and nephews and cousins. More family than she's ever had before. She'll be okay."

"John, think about this . . . think about what you're going to be throwing away."

"I have, Mike. I've thought about little else for the past seven years."

Mike's voice, low and slow, came through the screen. "I won't grant you absolution."

John sighed. "I didn't think you would. I just wanted you to know what was going down. You're my friend and I need your help. Give me that much, Mike." Not a plea, but a bargain, that's what he wanted.

"What else can I do for you, John? I want to save your soul."

John rose. "Save it for Carly. She's gonna need you. As a friend of her father's, you can help without any questions."

"Aw, hell, John. This stinks."

Before he left the confessional, John had to agree. "Yeah, it surely does. Thanks, Mike."

He thought about lighting a candle and saying a prayer, but in the end, he just left.

Carly felt like a thief, sneaking into her home. No, scratch that, the place she slept and kept her clothes, but had no right to be in without John Preshin's good graces.

She could smell the faint traces of aftershave that lingered most of the day. Here it was evening already and the heady scent tickled her nose.

Putting her backpack on the floor, she decided to take a look at the papers on John's desk. Perhaps there was a clue as to what was going on. She'd become an expert at reading opened mail, she thought. And her routine stacking of it accounted for the fingerprints.

Not that John would look. He knew that she knew. . . .

Ah. Her fingers caressed a large tan unopened envelope. When she flipped it over, her stomach fluttered. The envelope bore her name.

Fingers turned to claws as she ripped the flap to irreparable shreds.

Inside, a sheaf of papers—legal looking things with letterhead and seals and a sticky note in Mother Superior's spidery hand. "These are yours. Hope they help."

"Big deal," she muttered while her impatience flared.

Some sort of formal looking paper bore the title of non-identifying information. Hmm. This looked promising. Parking herself in John's swivel chair, she read. Her insides turned to water at the information it contained. All sorts of things from the height of her mother to the fact that no father was named slapped at her sensibilities. No known birth defects in family. No heart disease known. Mother's grandparents living at time of her birth. Mother did not need glasses. Hair—light blond. Eyes—blue.

Carly sat back, feeling gut-punched. Her mother had blond hair and blue eyes. Just like her. Somewhere out there, somewhere on the planet was a woman about thirty seven years old with blond hair and blue eyes who was her mother. If she was still alive. If she hadn't dyed her hair or shaved it all off.

God! Somewhere out there, along with a father she couldn't find, might be a mother. If only. If only she could . . . could what? Search everywhere?

Letting those papers fall from her shaking hand, she picked up the one with the letterhead. Hmm, lawyers from Philly. All with the same last name, Coleridge. Very big bucks, oooh. *What did they have to say?*

Blah, blah, blah, "cease and desist from searching for birth mother."

Cease and desist searching for birth mother? She wasn't looking for her. She was supposed to be dead!

Was she?

Carly closed her eyes as the tears squeezed out. Mother Superior thought this would help?

Wait. She looked at the date on the letter from the lawyers. A week ago. It had come to the convent seven days ago. That meant that someone had poked his nose into her life and twisted somebody's knickers.

It also meant her mother was alive and knew he'd been looking.

Had Mother Superior ratted her out somehow?

Lawyers wouldn't send a letter to protect a dead woman.

John Preshin.

Carly reached for a tissue, found the box on the desk empty and threw it across the room. Wiping her eyes with her uniform sleeve, she bawled like a baby until no more tears would come.

Her mother never wanted to hear from her. Threw

her away and never, ever wanted to know whether she lived or died.

Rot in hell, lady.

John knew something was wrong the second he turned the doorknob to his office home. A quick check of his watch told him it was only a little after five. The kid ought to be inside, doing her homework at his desk.

She was. But with her face tear-stained and reddened, the emotions blazed through her blue eyes and in turn, ripped through John.

"Carly. What's the matter?"

With the inevitable future on his mind, he shook it off, clearing his head as much as possible.

"You're finally back. I need to talk to you."

He took her anger as if it were a gift.

"I had a bad day. A real bad day."

It was easy to share this. After all, he was her father.

"Have you had anything to eat yet? I'm starved."

She looked toward the small kitchen area. "Flo brought up some leftovers. There's lasagna and salad, but I'm not hungry."

Going over to the kitchen, he began pulling containers out of the refrigerator. "Well, I am. If I'm hungry, you're probably hungry and just don't know it. Let's stuff our faces and then talk. I always think better on a full stomach."

The kid slanted a look his way. "I hired you to find my father. I need to know if you've been looking for him."

He paused in his quest for dinner for a second then continued opening containers and making up plates for the microwave while he thought.

What to tell her? How to tell her?

"Here," Carly said, pushing him out of the way as he

dumped salad greens into a large bowl. "You're messing up the counter with that."

He had allowed two pieces of curly lettuce to escape. "Sorry."

Hands on hips, she came closer to him, red-rimmed eyes looking up into his own with a mixture of anger and sorrow over a wall of disdain.

"Sit down and I'll tell you."

Evidently surprised by his response, the kid pulled out one of the two chairs at the tiny table and sat.

"You know that list you had for me when you arrived on my doorstep?"

"Yeah. The six names."

John juggled plates out of the microwave and set them on the table one at a time, feeling the heat in his fingers, smelling the fragrant tomato and cheese, hoping he knew what he was doing. "I knew all those names. I shared a beach house with those guys the summer before you were born."

The fork stopped halfway to Carly's mouth. "You *know* all of them?"

John sat down across from Carly. "Yeah. I know all of them. So it wasn't hard to locate them."

Carly stopped eating, but John motioned for her to continue. "I'll only talk if you eat." He liked giving orders and having them followed, especially since it gave him time to think of the right words.

"As I was saying, I looked for the guys and found them. I went to see them and questioned them. All of them had had relations with many women over that summer. You do know what I mean by that, don't you?"

"Duh," she replied from the edge of her seat.

John gestured for her to put the fork into her mouth. "Okay. One man is dead. One runs a rather unsavory club for sickos. One is a pathetic, worn out individual who will probably be dead in a few years from the kind of work he does. Another guy is a complete scumbucket who thinks he's a gangster. One is so completely out of the question it doesn't matter. And then there's me."

Carly dropped the fork. "What do you mean by that?"

John ran his fingers through his hair and looked away from her. "It means that of all those guys who could be your father . . . I am really the top of the list."

"How . . . how do you know? Do you know who my mother is?" Her voice broke and the waterworks started.

Now came the hard part. John hadn't been able to figure out how to handle it all afternoon and in his own kitchen, it wasn't any easier.

"Carly, here's the thing. There were two blond women who more or less stayed at the summer house with us. I didn't know them very well, in fact, I didn't remember their names if I ever knew them, but some of the other guys did. I followed the surest lead and found one of them."

"My . . . mother?"

John felt a stab inside his chest as he looked at the kid and saw pieces of her mother there. "No. This woman wasn't your mother. She had been in an accident that summer and couldn't have had a child."

Carly's face fell. "Oh."

"So, by process of elimination, the other woman had to be your mother."

"The sisters told me my mother was dead."

"Yeah. They told me that too." *Oh, please let me stop here.*

"But," Carly stood and went to retrieve the papers from his desk, "you and I know that isn't true, don't we? My mother is alive somewhere. She'd have to be to send me this."

She threw the papers at his chest. Deftly he caught them and gave them a quick look-over. *Oh, man.*

"Ah. When did you get this? Today?"

Carly's eyes were almost even with his . . . blue and so full of hurt. He wished he could take it away. But he was just getting to the hardest part of the story. "Look, let me finish this. I know I'm not doing a very good job of it, but let me tell you what happened."

Anger flashed, but she sat once again.

He sucked in a deep breath. "I found the other woman. She denied having a child. She wouldn't say much to me, but she did let me know we had . . . we had been together. I have to take her word for it, Carly. I swear to God, I don't remember. . . ."

"You don't remember making a baby?" Carly spat.

John steadied himself and looked directly into her eyes again. "Yes. That's right. I barely remembered the two blondes. I could have sworn I hadn't . . . been with either one of them, but this one, the one I think is your mother even though she denies it, said we had."

He watched as Carly digested this news. "So, you don't even remember being with her, but you think you're my father."

Her tone was dead. After all his earlier soul-searching, he had hoped she'd be a little happier about it. "Do you want me to be?"

Silence overtook them as John waited for an answer. Carly sat so still, he couldn't even see whether she breathed.

"I know I'm not much. No real prize. You've seen the kind of life I lead, but I'm not that bad . . . am I?"

"Those other guys. Did they look like me?"

Shaking his head, he tried to smile. "Not in the least."

"Do I look like my mother?" Her voice wavered as she trembled now, fighting to hold back emotions.

"You're more beautiful than she ever was."

Carly felt the involuntary shaking and could do nothing to stop it. Her mother was alive. This was the mother she'd thought dead for her entire life. This was the woman she dreamed had held her and loved her as her life ebbed away and the nuns had pried the baby from her dead arms.

Or, she hadn't really died and this was the woman who was going to go on Oprah and send out a call to find her daughter and they'd be reunited, maybe even on television, and everything would be wonderful. The woman would be rich and famous and have spent the last sixteen years searching everywhere for her daughter.

That hadn't played too well with her, but, heck, it had crept into her brain every time she'd watched Montel or Oprah or John Walsh reunite kids with their long lost parents. She'd seen kids who talked about how their parents had given them up but were all rock stars or basketball players and would suddenly remember they existed and come for them. There were plenty of shows on television about that kind of thing.

She'd never ever dreamed of a father, though. Only her mother. A father hadn't occurred to her until she'd taken that list from Mother Superior's office.

On that long scary walk to the Parkway, she'd thought that maybe her father the musician or football player would have this huge mansion and limos and tons of money. He'd be movie-star handsome, too. Well, realistically, she hadn't thought about it that much, but the thought had crossed her mind.

And she'd found her father and he was not exactly an ideal specimen of manhood and worse yet, he had some kind of secret thing going on that sounded pretty bad.

Deadly, in fact.

And yet, he sat in front of her, stabbing at the cooling lasagna and looking kinda worried.

"Would this make your parents my grandparents?" John choked softly then swallowed. "Yes, it would."

Carly stood up so fast the chair tumbled to the floor. "I gotta get out of here," she said. "I . . . this is too. . . ."

John came to her side, put his hand on her shoulder and tried to turn her to face him. "This is a lot to take in, I know. Imagine how I feel—learning I have a beautiful daughter who's smart and honest and everything a parent could want in this world. Out of the blue. Let me tell you, it sure surprised me. But," here he paused and a small smile turned up the corners of his mouth, "I'm getting used to the idea. In fact, I think it's pretty cool."

Carly turned away from his searching look. "I can't . . . I don't know. Look. Let me think about this. You've been great to me, all this time, letting me hang around here and treating me really well. But that was what you did for me because I hired you." Her heart felt as cold as the lasagna she'd messed around on her plate.

"This is all different now," she whispered.

John put his hand on her halo of hair. "I think I know how you feel, but it's late. Maybe you shouldn't go outside to think. How about I leave you alone for a couple of hours and come back here and we'll talk some more if you want to?"

She wrenched away from his gentle hand and looked him square in the eye. "What's gonna happen to me if you're dead or in jail?"

John stepped back. "What? Where did that come from?"

Carly swiped her forearm across her nose. "I overheard Curtis and you talking when I came up from school. I heard something that sounded like you were going to be killed or something."

John shook his head. "You weren't supposed to hear any of that conversation."

Carly spun around and pointed her finger in his face. "Oh, no. You tell me you're my father and break all this heavy news on me and I'm all mixed up and trying to figure out what to do because I heard you say something like that. Are you? Are you going to do something that will put you in jail? Are you going to die?"

John tried to pull her into his arms but she wouldn't let him.

"Something that has nothing to do with you, some unfinished business that happened a long time ago, has to be finished. I made a vow and I have to keep it. I may have to go away for a long time, but I've made provisions for you, Carly. You'll be fine. I promise."

She felt her chin rise in defiance. "Oh, yeah. You never made a vow to *me* and certainly not to my *mother*, so it doesn't count. I don't count. In fact, I probably came along at just the wrong time. That's me, all right. Wrong-time Snow. Oh, wait . . ." she tossed back her hair and gave her most regal look. "My name is really Preshin. Carly Preshin. I have a legitimate last name now, don't I? Well, not really legitimate."

Tears filled her eyes but she didn't care to wipe them away. "And of all the men who could have been my father, the one I wind up with might end up in prison or, worse yet, dead. Well, that certainly is an improvement in my life. Whoopee."

Chapter 30

Carly saw him shrug, try once more to hug her, but she turned her back on him and prayed he'd go away. Not far, but away. She needed time to think about all this. She needed to work all this information around her brain and see if she liked it or not.

She heard the door shut softly as John left, as she'd asked him to do. Christ, where would he go?

Running to the door, she threw it open and yelled out after him, "Don't get run over by a bus!"

His deep laugh rumbled from the stairwell, but he didn't promise not to.

Yeah, some father.

With the door shut, Carly sank to the floor and hugged her knees. What was she supposed to do now?

She allowed herself fifteen minutes of wallowing in self-pity before getting up, clearing up the mess in the kitchen and standing there with her hands dangling at her sides.

She thought of going online to get in touch with her friends. She could call Bridget, but this latest earth-shattering event was a little too personal to unload on a brand new friend. Besides, if John had found her father and he'd been the rich, handsome celebrity, it would have been different. But John Preshin was something else altogether.

He was okay looking enough for an old guy, even Bridget had thought so. But to tell someone that some old guy she thought was cute actually was your own father, well . . . that wouldn't be cool.

"Carly? Are you in there?"

She turned at the voice coming from the hallway. "Yes, Flo. I'm here. Hang on. I'll get the door."

Flo stood there, wearing a large flowered apron over a loose housedress. She'd tied up her hair with an ancient scarf, but bits of gingered gray poked out from underneath the silk.

"You okay, sweetie? You look kinda peaked."

Nothing got past this sharp old lady.

"I'm okay. Just trying to sort out my life, you know. Teenage stuff."

Flo gave her a crooked smile. "Do you think you could help me sort out some of *my* stuff at the same time? I need strong young arms."

Carly had to smile. End of pity party. "Sure, Flo. I just happen to have 'em. What's going on?"

"I've got this great idea, kiddo," she began. "The luncheonette is all spiffed up, but it doesn't have any theme. You know, like ferns in hanging pots or antique dressers or old pictures."

"So?"

Flo led her out into the hall, explaining as she went.

"All my old trunks are up in the attic. They're full of costumes and programs and all sorts of show-biz bits and pieces. I thought maybe we could salvage some of it to hang on the walls downstairs, kind of decorate the place. And I thought of a name, too. A real name. S.R.O. Do you know what that means?"

"Nope. I do not."

Flo scowled and rubbed at her temples. "Standing

room only. Box office . . . they'd sell tickets so you could stand in the aisles if the house was full."

Carly saw her sway slightly. "What's wrong, Flo? Are you okay?"

The older woman stopped scowling and pursed her lips. "Headache just came on. It's a doozy."

"Maybe we should stop and you lie down or something."

Flo dismissed the suggestion with an impatient wave of the hand. "I got this idea and I want to see it through. Leastways, if I show you where the stuff is, you can look through it tomorrow or over the weekend and bring it all down to Liz. Maybe we can get John to help us with the decorating."

"Okay, let's find the trunks so you can get off your feet."

"Now, that's more like it," Liz looked at her reflection in the salon mirror. Her hair tamed finally, sleeked and smooth, the fiery color glowing with subtle highlights, she knew she had something better to work with at last. Oh, yeah. This was hot stuff. Sssss!

Three hours for an instant makeover. Not bad, she decided. Not bad at all.

Hello, New Jersey! Look out, Preshin. Liz Atwater is back.

Her cell phone buzzed in her purse.

"Where's my grandmother?" Liz demanded through clenched teeth.

John and Carly perched at the edge of the plastic seats in the waiting room.

John stood and attempted to put his arms around her while she pushed him away. "Calm down"

"Bullshit! Where's my grandmother?" she asked, barely able to control her temper.

"She's in with the doctors. She's had a CT scan and she's comfortable. They won't tell us much more because we're not close relatives." He softened his expression but Liz couldn't be mollified. The terror clawed and snarled in her belly, goading her to scream to let it out.

"What happened? What was she doing? Whose fault is this?"

"Hey, now, wait a minute, Liz. First of all, it's nobody's fault. Flo was going up into the attic with Carly. I don't know exactly why, but Carly came down when she realized Flo hadn't followed her up. She immediately called 911 and I arrived just a few minutes after that. The ambulance came, picked Flo up and I followed. Carly called to say she'd finally reached you, so I went home to bring her back with me."

Liz sucked in a deep breath and held it, trying to calm down. Silently she berated herself for leaving the apartment to waste time at the beauty salon. For what?

"I shouldn't have left her alone. I just wanted to get out of the restaurant and the apartment. I knew what she wanted in the attic, but I didn't want to run up there and get it for her."

John tilted her head up and looked into her eyes. "You know your grandmother. You also know that nothing can stop a stroke if it's going to happen."

Liz's knees gave out on her. "A stroke?"

John guided her to an empty chair. "That's my guess."

"Is that what the doctor said it was? A stroke? Oh, God! Oh, God!" She put her hands up to her face and started to shake.

John turned to Carly. "Looks like it's going to be a long night. Maybe I'd better take you home. We probably won't know anything for hours."

Carly protested. "No, I want to stay! Please . . . I want to stay."

John shook his head. "It's after ten already. You're

dead on your feet. You did what you could do for Flo, Carly. You've done all you can. I'll take you home and we'll let you know if anything happens."

"But," she objected.

"No buts," John said softly. "I'll get you home and tomorrow is Friday and we'll know more in the morning."

"But Liz," she said.

"I'm coming back to stay with Liz."

She turned to the other woman and waited. In her distraction, Liz didn't answer right away. She felt rather than saw Carly standing at her shoulder, a look of concern etching deep furrows in her forehead.

"Oh, Carly, honey, thank you for helping Gram. Thank you for getting her help when she needed it." She stopped, took a deep breath before continuing, letting her brain instead of her heart do the talking. "But there's nothing you can do for her now. I'll be okay. No use you staying when you have school tomorrow."

"She's a tough lady, you know that. I want to be just like her when I grow up." Carly hesitated, then bent over Liz and put her arms around her shoulders. "I love her, too."

That brought a smile to Liz's pale face. "She's in good hands, thanks to you, sweetie. You go now and as soon as I know what's what, I'll call."

She watched John's broad back as he left, his arm around Carly's shoulders and held back the urge to call out to him, to beg him to stay with her. She didn't need him, she was used to facing tough things on her own. But it would be nice to have someone to put his arm around her. She wouldn't have objected to that.

The long terrifying night loomed ahead of her.

She hadn't felt this empty since the night baby Jesse died.

Closing her eyes, she tried desperately to put the dark thoughts out of her mind. All around her the hospital hummed. Disembodied voices sang out over the P.A. system.

Liz attempted to pray, but she hadn't had much use for God in the past couple of years.

A big hand on her shoulder startled her out of a meditative sleep.

"Any word while I was gone?" John's deep baritone voice caressed her with the kindness behind it.

Liz shook off her lethargy. "No. Nothing. I guess I fell asleep sitting here," she admitted as color tinted her cheeks. "Nobody disturbed me. What time is it? How long ago did you leave?"

John checked his watch. "I got Carly home and convinced her I'd find out what I could about an hour ago. Here," he said, thrusting a white paper bag into her hands. "I stopped and got you something to eat. I figured you hadn't had time to get anything for yourself. I know for a fact that the food here is lousy and I know you've been too worried to eat. You need something in your stomach and this is guaranteed comfort food."

Her half-hearted smile didn't seem to deter him. The man definitely wanted, no *expected* her to eat.

"I'm not hungry," she stated.

"Yes, you are, you just aren't aware of it. Here. Take a bite of this." He held out a plump hamburger wrapped in waxed paper. She saw cheese dripping down the side and smelled grilled onions. Then her stomach began rumbling and she took the burger from him.

One bite and she remembered she hadn't eaten since breakfast.

Second bite and she remembered that maybe she'd only had coffee for lunch.

Third bite and she forgot she wasn't hungry.

She finished it and accepted the soft drink he offered her. "Thanks. I guess you were right."

He gave her a quirky smile. "I usually am. And I like your hair."

A caustic retort formed in her head but remained there as a doctor approached them. Liz slid forward on the chair.

"Ms. Atwater? I'm Doctor Patel. Let me tell you first that your grandmother is resting comfortably and you may see her for one minute—one minute only."

Liz wanted to cry. "What happened, Doctor?"

"She suffered a small stroke. The CT scan showed that it was caused by a blockage in a small artery and she was given medication immediately. We have found that in this type of stroke, these medications given within three hours can actually reverse the damage done to the brain. In this case, we were lucky. Your grandmother arrived here in less than one hour.

"I cannot promise you this, but in most cases that I have seen, there is a very good chance of complete recovery. Of course, she must be monitored and there will be medication and some physical therapy may be needed, but we are hopeful for a full recovery. With luck, your grandmother will be her old self in no time."

"When can we take her home?" John asked the very question she couldn't get out of her throat.

"Oh, we will have to see about that," the doctor wavered. "I don't want to give you a definite day, but I will say that I hope it won't be very long." He smiled, looked from John to Liz and then his watch. "I'm afraid I must be going. You may stop in to see her, but she's got to rest and she may even be asleep, so I do not want you disturbing her. Tomorrow will be time enough to talk, I should think."

John stood and brought Liz up with him. She felt herself shaking but couldn't stop it. "Thank you, Doctor," he said for her. She managed a tight nod as tears trickled down her cheeks.

"Can you walk?"

She gathered her wits and ordered her muscles to work. "I think so. Let me see her. I have to see her."

With a gentle squeeze, John put his arm around her and held her as they walked to the curtained off area behind the swinging doors. A nurse told them where Flo was. John went with her but allowed Liz to peek through the curtains at Flo by herself.

She let out a small cry. Her grandmother looked so tiny and pale in the harsh hospital light. Tubes in her arms. Oxygen apparatus distorting her delicate nose. Hospital bracelet hanging in dreadful fluorescent orange around her thin wrist. Liz watched her chest rise and fall but said nothing to her.

Flo would have a fit if she could see herself this way, but blame it on poor stage lighting and makeup.

"Take me home, please. I don't think I can drive."

"Sure," he said, gathering her to his side and giving her a hug. "Let's get you home."

Chapter 31

He watched his daughter as she slept on the sofa bed, her light hair spread out on the pillow as a slash of streetlight seeped through the window shade. Her thumb rested on the end of her bottom lip as usual and he tried to picture how she had looked as a baby.

No one had memories of her that way. No photographs existed. No tender "first bath" to embarrass her. No first steps—who saw them? The nuns? Did they clap for her the way he had clapped for his nephews and nieces? Did they hug her close and shower her with kisses? Or did the day workers in the social services home do anything more than change her diaper and feed her?

All this first stuff was too late for him to share with his daughter. And he'd only just found her.

His thoughts turned to Liz. She'd had all her baby's firsts, but he realized that it hadn't been enough. Would never be enough for her. She deserved another chance. Maybe a little red-haired baby girl this time around, for her to love and cherish. He could almost picture it, a little Liz clone, toddling around, riding on his shoulders, teaching her how to blow spit bubbles, playing patty-cake and those stupid baby games. All the stuff he'd missed with Carly.

If he had more time, if the sexy redhead had only come along a few years earlier, maybe he and she could have. . . .

Nah.

This was no time to get sentimental.

Curtis had called. The old lady would be dead before morning and her son had made his deathbed visit without pretense of disguise.

The bastard figured he was safe from capture and prosecution.

There was no statute of limitations on murder.

Now he had a few days before the funeral. John knew that was where he'd be able to take out the sonovabitch.

He looked again at his daughter. She would be killer beautiful in a few more years.

Carly opened her eyes and slowly levered herself up. "How's Flo?"

John felt the weight of the world descend on his shoulders once more. "It looks good for her. The doctor came out and told us that, thanks to you, they were able to get the newest medicines into her and everything looked promising. She'll be rocky for a few more weeks, but she'll be back at the restaurant and carrying on in no time."

She stifled a yawn with her hand. "That's great."

"Why don't you go back to sleep? You've got school tomorrow." He shook his head when she sat up straighter.

"I think we ought to talk."

"Not now, kiddo. I'm beat."

Carly put her pillow behind her head and crossed her arms over her chest. "We need to talk."

He gave up. "Okay. What's on your mind, little girl?"

She flinched at the words at first, then smiled.

"Plenty. We ought to talk about this father-daughter thing. We ought to tell each other stuff. I have stuff to tell you."

John shook his head, realizing that she was right, even though it was after midnight and they both should be asleep.

"Okay. Go ahead. I'm here for you."

Carly raised one delicate eyebrow. "I got invited to the prom. I'm working for the dress money, so you don't have to worry about that."

This was news. "Do I know your date? You do have a date, don't you? I mean, you're not going stag . . . I think that's stupid."

"Yes, I have a date."

Fatherhood flared in his gut. "Do I know this guy?"

She stifled a yawn. "Yeah. It's Frankie's friend Choochie—I mean Jason."

He'd watched the kid grow up with his nephew and knew his parents. They were okay. "That's good. Jason's a nice kid. He's responsible and a good base-ball player."

She beamed. "Yeah, I know. He's sweet."

John couldn't believe he was having this talk with his own daughter in the middle of the night after a day like today had been, but he found he enjoyed the intimacy.

"So, what else? No more trouble at school?"

"Nope. I handled it."

"Good."

"If it's okay, I'm going to sleep over at Bridget's to-morrow night."

His eyebrows went down. "No boys?"

She recoiled in mock horror. "Of course not. Brid-get's parents will be there an' all. No boys."

"This is where I say 'okay'?"

"Yeah."

He found himself grinning. "Okay, you can go."

"So, what's with you?"

John shook off his weariness with great difficulty. "Not much."

Carly looked up at him, her eyes rounded with fear. He felt this tightness in his chest get even tighter as if someone were ratcheting a load binder. "Please," she whispered, "please don't go through with it."

Refusing to answer, he rose and made his way to his room. "Good night, Carly."

Sleep tight, little girl.

Liz called the hospital four times before breakfast.

Nothing had changed. Flo was sleeping comfortably. The doctor had not seen her yet, probably not till ten.

"That means probably not until after lunch." She understood that the nurses couldn't tell her much, but she longed to hear the truth.

She might as well open the soup bar. What was Flo going to call it? S.R.O. Yeah. And fix it up with old posters and costumes. It really wasn't such a bad idea. Sort of a theme. Fine for the soup bar, but would it hold the same allure when they switched over to soda fountain?

What the hell . . . she'd look over those old trunks and see if there would be something to make a theme that would cover both aspects of the restaurant. Soup bar. Soda fountain. Luncheonette. Whatever this place was . . . it was all hers for awhile.

Hers to build or ruin.

She hastened up the stairs, attic key in hand. Just in time to see Carly gently pulling the door to John's office shut.

"Hey, sweetie."

Carly hurried over, backpack slamming against her thighs. "Hear anything about Flo?"

Liz shook her head. "Nah, they just tell me she's resting comfortably. I'm going to go down there right after lunch is over, but I'll try calling around ten or so. That's when the nurse said the doctor would be coming around."

Carly's face grew solemn. "Look, if you need any help, I can stay and help you. . . ."

Liz smiled, despite the real need for her help. "I've got everything under control. She has enough soup base stored in the freezer to last about a week and if we run out, you can come down over the weekend and help me make more. I expect you to help out Saturday. You didn't forget, did you?"

"I'll be there for lunch. I'm staying with Bridget overnight, though. We're going to have pizza and talk about boys and she said she wanted to try out hairstyles for the prom . . . she says she's good with hair."

Liz laughed, remembering all her friends who were good with hair. "Just don't let her strip it for you. A friend of mine once ended up with white hair that had the ugliest black roots you can imagine. She looked like a cartoon. But you'd better get a move on it or you'll miss the bus."

Already in motion, Carly called over her shoulder, "It's still not too late for me to stay. Call me back any time before I hit the stairs."

"Go to school!" Liz shouted at her then waited for the sound of Carly's footsteps down the stairs and out the door. Turning, she made her way toward the attic door and realized that there were two other offices, small, to be sure, but probably big enough for two rooms apiece in this front part of the building. Why hadn't her grandmother rented them? Surely she could always use the income. Hmm. Something else to consider since it looked as if she'd be staying in Asbury Park for some time.

Now, up to the attic to see what treasures, if any, awaited her.

John heard someone thumping around overhead and woke with a start. Sliding from his bed, he stepped into a pair of jeans then padded silently to his closet. Removing his gun safe, he took out his Sig and slinked into the outer office and the hallway on cat's feet.

He waited by the attic door, weapon held at the ready close to his cheek.

Arms full of delicate, faded costumes, Liz turned on the landing to find herself looking into the barrel of John's Sig Sauer.

"Stop right there," he growled at her.

"Christ Jesus!" she squeaked.

Seconds expanded into elastic time as he looked down the length of the gun which was aimed directly at Liz's heart.

All the color washed from Liz's face and Flo's precious old garments fell to the floor.

John pulled up the gun, checked the safety, and stuck it into his waistband. "Sorry," he murmured as he bent to help Liz pick up the clothes.

"Sorry," she seethed. "You nearly scared me to death! I've lost at least ten years—no, make that twenty years of my life over that little 'sorry.'"

John grinned at her, leaning with indolent leisure against the door jamb. "Would 'oops' be any better?"

He could see her trying to hold back her smile as her lips twitched before finally giving in. "You jerk!" She shoved some lacy skirts into his arms. "Help me get these downstairs."

John deposited the weapon back in his office, tossed on an FBI sweatshirt, then went down to the kitchen where he accepted the cup of coffee from Liz. "I guess I woke you up."

He saw the dark circles under her eyes, the general weariness that enveloped her, even turning her bright coppery hair dull. "You didn't sleep much," he observed.

She sighed. "It just didn't happen until about four, I think. Leastways, that's the last time I looked at the clock."

"I know what you mean."

"Want some breakfast?" The corners of her mouth quirked up but the smile didn't reach her eyes.

John shook his head. "Tell you what, since you or your grandmother has made my breakfast for the past couple of years, how 'bout I make some for you?"

At her protest, he held up his hand. "In case you're wondering, I know how to cook *some* things. You've had my steak and baked potatoes and I didn't hear you complain about the meal."

Liz had the decency to blush. "Okay. The grill is all yours. Know how it works?"

"Do I know how it works, she asks. I should be insulted," he said as he set to work, "but considering your condition, I will overlook it. In fact, I will even offer to help you out with the lunch crowd."

Liz sputtered a protest but he would have none of it. "I know what to do. Just say 'thank you' and that will be fine."

Looking at him over her shoulder as he demonstrated his proficiency, she demurred. "Thank you, John. You're not half as bad as you make yourself out to be."

He raised his eyebrow. "Oh, no? I thought I was downright badass."

With a shake of her head, she boomed out a laugh. "You? Badass? You're a pussycat, John Preshin. Just a pussycat."

Knowing better, John didn't respond. The rock in his gut, having temporarily been forgotten, made itself known once more. Not a pussycat.

Lunch was frantic. Word about Flo had passed through the street and many of the locals stopped in for soup and take-out sandwiches. Even the construction workers who had taken to the restaurant expressed their concern to Liz. Her grandmother would be delighted to know so many people held her in such high esteem.

She'd made three calls to the hospital during slow periods with John manning the counter. Nothing new to report except that Flo had eaten and complained about the food but appeared chipper and without anything discernibly debilitating other than weakness in her left arm. They were going to get her out of bed later and Liz wanted to be there.

During one of his breaks, John expressed the desire to drive her to the hospital. "You'll thank me for the ride," he told her and Liz knew she'd be grateful, she just didn't want to grow too dependent on his kindness. She knew damn well how easy it would be to fall in love with him, except for the fact that he scared her. Kind, always kind. But mysterious all the same, except for that one night.

But she'd been drunk and he'd probably forgotten all about it.

She just wished she could.

Flo had looked surprisingly good for an old lady who'd suffered a slight stroke. John and Liz were not allowed to stay long, however, so they left after half an hour.

"Shouldn't Carly be home by now?" Liz asked as they entered the luncheonette.

"She's staying with Bridget tonight. They're going to do girl stuff, she told me earlier. Getting ready for prom stuff."

Liz slowly nodded her head in understanding. "Oh, yeah, I heard all about that. She and my grandmother worked something out. She's supposed to help out to-morrow and help with the prep on Sunday."

"She'll do it. I'll make sure she does."

Liz stopped walking and faced John. "Your daughter is a great kid. She's been a super help, you know."

John looked down into Liz's face. "How did you know? I haven't told anybody."

Liz frowned. "Told anybody what? That she's a hard worker?"

"No."

"Then what?"

John looked away briefly, then fastened his eyes on Liz's. "That she's my daughter."

Liz walked into the restaurant and carefully locked the door behind John. The air still smelled like cream of broccoli soup with toasted parmesan bread. "What do you mean? Of course she's your kid. She has your eyes, your dimples, the way you carry yourself . . . she's your kid. Isn't she?"

John parked himself on one of the stools and ran his hand through his hair. "Yeah, well, I just realized she was mine two days ago."

Liz plunked herself down next to him. "You're joking, right?"

"No. I never even knew she existed until a few weeks ago when she showed up at my door. Did you know she *hired* me to find her father? The kid had a list she'd taken from her file at some convent in Philly with the names of six men on it."

Liz backed away. "Do you mean she's been living upstairs with you all this time and you didn't know she was your kid?"

"Whoa, wait a minute," he said. "I kept her safe and off the streets. I didn't realize I could have been her father until after I'd done some investigating. I looked up the men on the list and none of them could possibly have been responsible for her."

"And, like, what? Her mother? Did you forget her the way you seem to have forgotten all these mysterious women who come up to you on the street or in stores and slap your face?"

John felt the heat rise in his cheeks. "If you want the truth . . . yeah. I didn't remember sleeping with her mother. But I found her mother, even though the woman denies Carly is her daughter, and she told me we had slept together. It must not have been . . . never mind. But I realized I could be the kid's father and after meeting those other men, I knew I *had* to be her father."

"So," Liz tried to get a handle on this, "you didn't know you'd fathered a child?"

John squirmed to hear it put that way. "No, I hadn't a clue. If I had known, things would have been different. Believe me. The woman, or her lawyers, took care of disposing of the baby, but they were careful to make sure she would not be adopted. The nuns kept her with them all these years. Poor kid," he added. "No one will admit to anything and we can't force the issue in any way whatsoever."

"But you never noticed the family resemblance?"

He had, all along, felt some kind of bond with Carly, but he'd denied it. "Not really. Except for one thing."

Liz put her hands on the counter. "And that was?"

John leaned back and laughed. "Remember that morning when you held me at knifepoint?"

His interrogator blushed again. He liked the way her eyelashes fanned against her fine cheekbones. "Well, I brought up some jelly doughnuts for her. Damndest thing, the kid sucked the jelly end first, just like I do. I guess I should have known from that."

Liz threw back her head and laughed until she almost fell off the stool. When she sobered, she looked at John and gave him a rueful grin. "And you missed that big a clue? What kind of private dick are you?"

John stood, pulled Liz from the stool and wrapped his arms around her. Before she could protest, he lowered his lips to hers and lost himself in a deep, probing kiss.

"Want to find out?" he whispered into her ear.

"Yes."

He almost stopped himself. He almost kissed her hand, put it to his heart and explained that it wouldn't be right for him to lose himself in her. It would be crass and unfeeling of him to take his pleasure knowing that he'd be in prison in two days' time, or dead. It didn't matter how much he liked her or wanted to be with her, he'd be leaving her. It wouldn't be fair to let her think that there might be something between them, something that meant something, and could grow and possibly flower.

He couldn't give her the family she'd lost and wanted so badly to replace with him behind bars. And that would be if he was lucky enough not to get the death penalty.

At least he was leaving Carly with a family. He'd leave Liz with nothing more than shame.

He couldn't do that.

Even in the dark he knew Liz watched his eyes. And wise woman that she was, rather than wasting time asking questions, she put her hand on his fly and squeezed gently at first, then more insistently.

John knew better than to be cruel at this moment—first of all, she had his dick in her hands, secondly, she'd been able to forget their first encounter, so perhaps she could brush this one off, should it happen.

Yeah, that was logical. Not.

Besides, it was too late since she already had her

hand at the waistband of his jeans and yanked open the fastener. He heard the rasp of the metal zipper—then he was free.

Her breath hitched softly.

That small sound undid him.

It tore away any good intentions he might have entertained, the last bit of honor in his soul toward women in general and his respect for Liz in particular.

"I want you," she whispered, her hand gently tugging at him, her heavy-lidded eyes beckoning him. . . .

Then she wet her lips and it was all John could do not to come then and there.

"If you don't stop doing that, I'll shame myself," he said, his voice a low, seductive exhalation directly into her ear. She shivered in response.

Liz was clearly enjoying herself. Though the store was dark, there were huge windows and people passing by on the sidewalk. She was not on display, but he was. He could tell she wouldn't mind if he took her right there on the stool. But he knew she'd never be able to enter the luncheonette again without thinking of what they'd done on the stool, or the counter, or behind the counter or covered with chocolate syrup, so he stayed her hand and led her up the back stairs to his place.

The thought of licking chocolate syrup from her belly stayed with him through the first frenetic mating, dulled during the second, more tender and sensual connection, but returned after midnight when he went downstairs and helped himself to a cupful of liquid chocolate.

Hot fudge would never mean the same for John.

Chapter 32

Liz awoke with a start in the strange bed. Not strange, as her brain clicked in. John's. The bedside clock read six. More than enough time to get downstairs, shower and get started for the day. But despite the stickiness clinging to her torso, she didn't want to leave the rumpled bed just yet.

John stood in naked splendor just outside the door, reading a newspaper. His brow, arched low and menacing, matched the scowl on his sensuous lips, the lips that had given her so much delight just hours ago. Longing brought goose bumps to her skin and pebbled her nipples.

God, he was beautiful! What a splendid creature! Just looking at him made her wet. Snuggling deeper into the blanket, she thought about everything they'd done together. Warmth spread throughout her body, but the realization that daybreak had come and the endless thrills were not likely to be repeated made her eyes sting.

But night would come again. Maybe many nights, strung together in a glistening chain of incredible lovemaking. The prospect brought with it a satisfied quiver.

She ran her hand over one breast then the other to make sure she still had sensation in them, considering what they'd been through.

John stood in the open doorway, looking at her. She stared right back.

"Like what you see?" he inquired.

Liz propped herself up on one elbow and let the blanket fall. "Do you?"

He moved over to the bed, the set of his shoulders, the near strut to his stride being sheer animal arrogance on display. Liz allowed her eyes to rove, settling for more than a brief glance on his glorious body.

He laughed as he joined her on the bed, diving under the blanket to bring her to explosive climax one more time.

God, how happy I could be with this man.

He pulled himself up from the depths of the covers, his wickedness reflected in his teeth-baring grin. Liz thought she ought to say something. Or do something, yet when she reached for him, he grabbed her hand and held it.

The joy disappeared from his face.

Liz's brain caught fire. *No, he's not going to do it! He's not going to say "It's been fun, kid, but it doesn't mean anything"! Oh, no, oh, no! Don't let him brush me off, dear God. Don't let him do this to me!*

John pulled her captive hand to his lips and kissed her knuckles, then tenderly bit the muscle beneath her thumb.

Oh, no! This is the part where he tells me it's not me, it's him. She shook with the fear and rage building inside her.

"Liz, we have to talk."

She fell back on the pillow. Her free hand went up to push the hair from her forehead. If there was going to be anything more than what she expected to hear, she had to be able to see all his expressions at once.

"You talk. I'll listen."

He moved alongside her, his long warm body touching hers wherever possible. "I . . . you know the scar . . . this one here on my shoulder?"

She nodded, mute for once.

"The man who shot me, the man who killed my partner, is back in town."

Liz moved her arm so she could cover the ugly puckered scar with her fingers. She wanted to convey to him how it disturbed her, how she wished it had never happened, but didn't think words would be appreciated now.

John's head turned away briefly then his attention went back to her. "I have a job to do. I may be gone for a long time. Carly's going to live with my parents if I can't make it back here. But you . . . I don't know what to do about you."

What did he mean? Go away? Why? And send Carly away? Liz didn't need much more to reach a conclusion.

"So, you're leaving. You've taken care of Carly . . . that's fine. She's your daughter and you owe her something."

He nipped her shoulder. "Yes, I owe her a lifetime, but I can't give it to her."

Her stomach turned liquid. "But you have to do the right thing! You're not running away from her, are you?"

John shook his head. "That's the last thing I want to do. But what I want and what I have to do are two different things."

"What's going on? Are you ill? You sound as if you're going to die."

He shrugged but traced his finger along the line of her jaw. This subtle lovemaking didn't quite go with the words he managed to get out.

"Don't try to make me shut up, Johnny."

One side of his mouth went up ever so slightly, showing one deep dimple. "I'm not trying to. I just enjoy touching you, Liz." He kissed her fingertips next and Liz tried to deny the sensation that ran straight to the core of her being. Distracting as it was, she wanted him to finish his thoughts.

"So? There's more, Johnny. Out with it."

John worked his hand to her breast and tweaked her swollen nipple, letting his fingers rest there, massaging and forcing Liz to squirm despite her desire to make him finish his little speech.

"Okay. I don't want you to think I don't care about you, Liz. I don't want you to think this night, or the other one, meant nothing to me, because they did. But I don't know if there can ever be anything more to it. Not because I don't want there to be . . . you get to me, Liz. You really do. With me it's always been f . . . fornicate and forget. But not with you. You've stayed in my brain. But my future is . . . I don't know if I even have a future here. Or anywhere. And I just wanted you to know that, whatever happens . . . I care for you. I care what you feel, what you think. I care about what lies ahead of you, but I do know that I won't be around for you."

His words rolled over, not settling into her brain, not fully understood, but not because she didn't want to hear him. Little by little her mind wrapped around his meaning.

She brought her head up and looked him right in the eye. So that was his game. "Brush off, with explanation. Squirrelly explanation, but brush off, all the same."

Heat rushed through her entire body as she swung her legs off the bed.

She'd Jersey herself out of this.

Grabbing the discarded sheet, she held it to her breast and faced John who, not yet wary, lazed on the mess of blankets.

"I didn't come upstairs with you for anything other than a good screw, Preshin. I needed it. You evidently needed it. And I guess that's all. Well, good-bye. It's been nice knowin' ya. See ya around . . . maybe."

A pained look crossed his face, but he said nothing.

Liz stomped around the room, gathering up the clothing she'd discarded. Every single second of her evening replayed in her mind as she remembered how each garment came off.

And later on, lying in his arms feeling well loved and splendidly naked, she'd been on the verge of telling him how she felt about him! Thank God she hadn't told him she loved him.

But her blood was up now and rational thought receded from her brain.

She could only find one shoe. Frustrated, she searched a bit, then as the anger boiled over, she threw the shoe at the reclining man and headed for the door.

"I'll leave the sheet on the stairs. Cleaned."

One last look, one last sight of him in that bed, that dark brown curl on his forehead, the blue beard beginning to tinge his jaw. For one brief moment, she thought she read regret in his eyes, but it was gone in a flash. Had she really seen it?

Or was it wishful thinking?

She'd bet on the latter.

A different crowd filled the soup bar Saturday. The early spring sunshine brought out more of the newer wave of inhabitants of Asbury Park. Liz had pulled out all the stops, preparing some of the more elaborate soups Flo had made and frozen in advance. Exotics like winter melon with mint and coriander, something heartier, a beef ragout to be eaten with bruschette, and cream of wild mushroom set tongues wagging with approval.

True to her word, Carly had appeared at ten and

started right to work. Liz watched her when she got the chance, wondering if the kid knew what her father had in store for her or if Carly knew more about John's situation than he'd told her last night.

"Hey, Liz, some of the guys asked me when the fountain was going to open." Carly wiped her hands on a clean towel and sipped at a soda during a lull in the rush.

Liz stopped what she was doing, pushed away from the sink and blew the hair out of her eyes. Leaning against the clean prep table, she said, "Tell them it will open after Flo is back on her feet."

Carly wrinkled her nose. "That's kinda vague."

"Tough shit," Liz snapped. One look at Carly's face and Liz broke down. "Oh, Carly, I didn't mean that, honey. I'm just so . . . so not ready for making decisions without Flo. I'm . . . I . . . I just want to sit down and get myself together and I . . . we haven't had a break all day."

Concern creased Carly's face. "Do you want to close early?"

Liz shook her head. "No. I just need to get off my feet. It's almost closing time, anyway, and the crowd has thinned out. I can make it another hour."

Inhaling sharply, Liz pushed away from the table. "Is John upstairs?"

Shaking her head, Carly told her no, she thought he said he had to go to the post office and the bank. Liz accepted this. She just wanted to make sure John was gone.

Carly looked as if she wanted to say more, but someone called for her so she left Liz to take the man's money and gather up his generous tip. She smiled and the old guy winked at her and told her he'd be back.

Carly slipped the five buck tip into her apron pocket.

* * *

Mike genuflected in front of the altar and made the sign of the cross. He turned to find John standing in front of the altar rail.

"Hey, John."

John dug his hands into his pockets. "Hey, yourself."

Coming down the two steps, Mike didn't smile. John knew how their last discussion had disturbed the priest. But he felt he owed it to the man to bring him up to date and remind him of his promise.

"I told her, Mike."

The priest nodded. "And how did it go over with her?"

John had to fish for words. "Okay, I guess. She was shocked, I think. And upset and asked questions, which I answered. But I didn't give her too much information because it seems as if her mother's lawyers threatened us with a cease and desist, more or less. The kid figured out that her mother must be alive and that I'd been snooping around and I must have found her. I think that bothered her more than finding out I was her father."

Mike nodded in understanding. "What else did you tell her?"

John turned away from the crucifix behind the altar, the grisly body of Christ looking over Mike's shoulder at him with sorrow etched deeply into His face. "I didn't tell her much of anything, but the kid overheard a discussion I had with Curtis."

The priest's eyes went cold. "What did she overhear, John? Your whole asshole plan?"

John jerked up his head. His friend's slip of the tongue while in the church surprised him.

"Let's get out of here," he suggested.

"I can't have a beer before mass," Mike reminded him softly, "no matter how badly I'm going to need one."

The men went into the rectory kitchen at John's request. Today the air smelled of cabbage.

"Want anything?" Mike asked.

"Just need to remind you of your promise."

"I saw the obituary. I was asked to participate in the funeral mass over at Sacred Blood, but I had to decline. They already roped in four other priests for the old lady. Besides, I made arrangements to be over at Mary Immaculate Monday morning. That way, I can take Carly away . . . Jesus, John! Think what you're doing to that kid! She just gets a father and she's going to lose him? How can you do this to her? To yourself? Think, man. You have your whole life ahead of you."

John leveled his gaze of Mike's flushed face. He knew how much he was hurting his friend, and Carly, but he had to keep his word.

Rising, he answered the priest, "Yeah, I do, but Dutch doesn't."

"Where are we going?"

John adjusted the rearview mirror. "I thought maybe we could do something together. Get to know each other. Since you can't do any of my favorite things, I thought maybe we could do some of your favorite things."

"Huh?" Carly flashed him a look of pure skepticism.

"I mean, we could actually do something together. Not me taking you someplace where you could do something and I wait for you to finish and then I take you back. Something where we walk together, sit together, laugh together."

"Key word being 'together,' right?"

John gave an exaggerated nod. "Right."

She sat with her lips pursed, her eyebrows joined in deep thought mode. "I think maybe it's time we went to the mall."

His groan lost emphasis after he sighed. "I thought you reserved that pleasure for Liz or Bridget."

Carly shot him a look so intense it made John's neck prickle. "I told you I got asked to the prom and that I'm earning the money to buy a dress, but as yet I haven't actually looked for one. Bridgey and I looked in some fashion magazines, but all those dresses were skanky looking. I do not want to look like a skank."

Ah. Skank. Now what does that mean?

John rotated his shoulders. The leather of his jacket squeaked pleasantly and he relaxed.

"Okay. We'll go to the big mall in Woodbridge. There ought to be enough places there for you to find a dress. I thought girls wore gowns to the prom. My sisters did. Are you going to look for a dress or a gown?"

She laughed out loud, making no attempt to make him think she didn't think that was a stupid question. "Oh, man!" she murmured over and over.

Pretending to be affronted, John turned the Jeep onto Route 9 and stepped on the brake while waiting for an opening in the heavy line of cars. "Okay, laugh at the old guy."

Sobering, Carly stifled a giggle. "I will know what I want when I see it. Depends."

"Depends? On what?"

She turned in her seat. "Depends on if it is the right color. Right length. Right size—they don't always have the dress you want in your size, but I guess you wouldn't know about that. Guys' clothes are always the right size. And they're either black or blue, so what does it matter?"

"You have a low opinion of men for one so young."

She giggled and the sound lightened John's heart. "Not really. I don't know many men. I just know that clothes are something very particular for women while for men they don't mean too much. Any guy who really cares about fashion—well, let's just say I served lunch to a bunch of them yesterday and I doubt they'll be going to the prom. But I bet they know what I should wear to it."

They both laughed. John weaved the Jeep in and out of traffic, swearing and gesturing to less intelligent drivers. Carly grabbed the door handle once or twice to keep upright. He slowed the vehicle, turned into the mall drive and began looking for a parking space.

"There's one!" Carly shouted, pointing to a space near the main entrance. John slid the Jeep into it and put it in park.

He tried hard to be a good sport. The kid went into every boutique on the ground floor and tried on at least a hundred dresses and/or gowns. They blurred into a rainbow. Carly preferred vivid colors and John noticed that her hair color tended to wash out. At the first shop on the second level, he went through the rack himself while she was in the dressing room and found a gown that caught his eye.

"You have excellent taste, sir. That cerulean shade can't be worn by just anyone. With her coloring, it's perfect. Your daughter will make heads turn at the prom, that's for sure."

The saleswoman, a chic young thing with achingly high stiletto heels and a skin tight black outfit that barely covered her private parts seemed impressed at his choice and delivered it to Carly in the dressing room.

"Try this one, kiddo," he called back to her.

"Why?" Carly bit out the word. He pictured her wrinkling her nose, just because it was not her choice.

"Do me a favor, will ya?"

Her "okay" was muffled.

Five minutes later, Carly stepped from the dressing room, a vision in the shiny blue dress. John felt a lump form in his throat and to his surprise, his eyes misted.

"Wow."

Carly turned, catching her reflection in the three way mirror. "It's so. . . ."

John's heart swelled in his chest. This was his *daughter*. She was a knockout.

"Beautiful. It's absolutely beautiful," he said, his voice hushed, almost reverent. "You are magnificent, k . . . Carly."

She spun on her heel, catching every angle she could in the mirror. The saleswoman beamed. John figured she was on commission.

"Wrap it up," he said.

Carly protested. "I don't have enough money for this." Nothing in the world could have prevented him from buying her that dress. Nothing. If this was what being a father had going for it, he knew he was hooked.

They went to a movie together. The ticket seller looked at them askance, but at his age, he'd have looked askance at some old dude with a young chick, too. If anybody thought there was something wrong with the two of them being together, he'd proudly proclaim Carly as his daughter. No one asked, no one suggested. The kid in the ticket window was probably wondering why two sane people would want to watch Johnny Depp suffer in yet another movie.

She liked nachos, without the jalapenos, and devoured half a tub of popcorn, a hot dog with yellow mustard, half a box of chocolate covered peanuts and downed a mega soda.

"We could go to a restaurant for supper," he whispered during the final scene of the movie, but she didn't hear him. Before leaving the theater, she ran to the ladies room and came out some time later, looking a bit green.

"I'm not hungry," she croaked. "Remind me never to do this again."

He paused to look at her. "What, go with me to the movies?"

"No. Eat junk and puke my guts out."

"Ah. Lesson learned, then."

Still slightly green, Carly groaned, "Oh, yeah."

He'd learned one too. He couldn't spoil her in one day, even though he'd tried.

Chapter 33

Why did Catholic funerals take place first thing in the morning? Who would it hurt to start at eleven? Nobody. John watched the mourners pile out of the three limos outside Sacred Blood RC Church. There were two flower cars. He'd seen more black Mercedes and Cadillacs parked in the lot than he'd seen in his entire life. Someone had thoughtfully provided a long black limo for the five priests who'd no doubt sing the praises of Guiseppina Montebroccochetti, deceased.

From his vantage point directly outside the front of the church, John waited. He'd seen Alfonso "Dumb Al" Montebroccochetti enter the church surrounded by his five older and somewhat larger sisters instead of bodyguards. After the *disgrazia*, Alfonso had become *persona non grata* with the mob, so he probably didn't deserve a personal bodyguard any more. Setting up agents and not killing them both evidently was shameful to the family. The fact that John lived to tell the whole story, in which he was positive Alfonso was going to turn states' evidence, should have gotten Dumb Al cement flippers. That it did not meant something else was going on. Something bigger?

Maybe his mama had something on the *capo*.

Who knew?

All those black cars were full of wise guys with their
wives, however. It was thought erroneously by them
that the feds wouldn't bother them with their families.
John knew this to be true, but mostly the feds stayed
away from funerals, or remained only within tele-
photo lens distance.

Dumb Al had put on weight. All that good living in
Sicily, he figured. All that excellent pasta. He'd tried
to grow a moustache, too, but John had to admit the
sisters all had Al beat in that department.

The center doors swung out. Members of the family
lined the steps, heads down, hankies in hand, as the
gurney bearing the tiny coffin with Guiseppina hopefully
inside was placed in the back of the hearse. One of the
sisters collapsed. The drama passed quickly as someone
lifted her back upright and fussed over her. The other
sisters stoically made their way to the limo followed by
Alfonso. They allowed him to ride up front.

Deferring to the male. Made John want to retch.

Assorted elderly persons entered the other limo,
probably brothers of the deceased or brothers in law.
The Montebroccochettis were pretty small potatoes in
the family; nevertheless, if the agency hadn't been
alerted to the funeral, John doubted anyone would be
there taking pictures.

He'd spotted a white laundry delivery van outside
Wong's Pizzeria and thought it might be full of FBI,
but things could have changed in seven years. Maybe
they didn't give a rat's butt about Alfonso Montebroccochetti any longer.

He did.

His shoulder ached. The weight of the harness
pulled against the scar. He gritted his teeth and bore
the pain. It was his crown of thorns, but would soon
be relieved.

As the procession began to move, John pulled the

Jeep into the line and went along for the ride, past the old family home on the beachfront in Belmar. He wondered why funeral directors still practiced this. It wasn't as if the old lady could say good-bye or anything. The limos paused in front of a sweet little stucco with tiled roof, probably built in the '20s. It would have been nice growing up so close to the ocean, but he knew Alfonso used dirty money to buy this place for his mother only five years ago. Blood money.

Shit.

The procession speeded up on the way to the cemetery. With this crew, probably thoughts of the repast made the drivers use some lead on the accelerator. It would be at Luigi's in Neptune and the food would be incredible.

Too bad Alfonso wouldn't get to eat any of it.

Parking far away from the cortège of black cars, John got out of the Jeep into the weak spring morning light. Rain clouds hovered overhead, pushed by a strong salt breeze from the ocean. Already a fine mist dampened his face. He shoved his right hand into the pocket of his jacket to keep it dry.

There they stood. Out in the open, some of the biggest Mafia names in Jersey, surrounded by their bodyguards and their well-kept wives. Oddly enough, there were no children present. John knew Guiseppina had fifteen grandchildren.

Somebody had some smarts, after all. Somebody suspected something might happen and had wisely kept the kids at home.

As he approached the mourners, he noted that the sisters had their faces veiled now. Dressed in unrelieved black, the women wore mourning veils to cover their tear-swollen faces. Most of the Montebroccochetti family were large women, linebacker large. One

smaller female, maybe placekicker size, turned back
from the open grave as he looked in their direction.

Lots of movement, people shifting for better position. Suits and skirts, even the priests moved about.
Perhaps there was a specific plan like stage blocking,
who got to stand where, who deserved the best view of
the box. Without a word to anyone he moved behind
Alfonso and waited, head reverently bowed, hands
clasped at his waist.

He said an Act of Contrition, more out of habit
than hope of forgiveness.

The priest spoke Italian as if everyone gathered at
the graveside understood. Maybe they did, but most
probably only knew enough of the language to read a
menu at Luigi's.

John's shoulder ached in the damp, pinched by the
holster and heavy gun. Once again, he wore no vest.

The priest made the sign of the cross and tossed a
bit of dirt onto the coffin. Family members clustered
around the funeral director who handed long stemmed
red roses to them. One by one they turned to the coffin,
crossed themselves and placed their roses on the box.
John's hand moved to his holster.

From the recesses of his brain, his daughter's face
flashed before him followed by a soft voice that
sounded in his ear, sweet and sultry, full of heat and
promise . . . Liz urging him to do the right thing.

He hesitated.

"Alfonso!"

The shout came from the other side of the coffin.
His eyes now riveted on the sisters, John saw a woman
rip off her hat and veil, exposing her face. Jesus!

Barbara Van Horne stood with a gun in her hand!

As Alfonso looked up, she fired.

John pushed at Dumb Al, knocking him to the side,
but the ugly sound of the bullet exploding into flesh
rent the air, followed by a chorus of screams.

Alfonso's sisters encircled Barbara with clawed hands and shrieks. The suits reached into their jackets but were stopped by the inpouring of men and women dressed in the dark utilitarian suits favored by Feds.

Someone yelled for help as Alfonso's bleeding carcass poured his life into the dead grass.

Pushed away by strangers, John melted into the milling crowd.

Carly's brain went into overdrive when Father Mike offered her a ride home. She'd seen him hanging around the school all day, but never made eye contact with him. He was at Mary Immaculate for a reason and she thought she knew why. Going through her classes like a zombie, she kept waiting to be called down to the office. The day dragged on and Carly's nerves stretched tighter than a rubber band, ready to slingshot her into hysteria.

Once in Father Mike's beat up Chevy Lumina, Carly bit her lip until it bled. Her hands shook as she cast furtive glances over at the priest.

"He did it, didn't he? He killed that man, didn't he? Like he said to Curtis, he couldn't just walk away. Oh, God!" She bit down harder to hold in the scream she felt growing inside.

Mike shook his head. "I don't know what's happened, Carly. There hasn't been anything on the news that I could tell. I don't know how much you know about all this, or why he felt he had to do what he had to do. But I want you to know, I've prayed for God to give him the wisdom to see that it was wrong."

Carly wondered why he prayed rather than tie her father up and keep him away from that funeral. She wanted to rage at the priest, but what good would that do? Her own pleas had fallen on deaf ears. If his own daughter couldn't prevent him from killing a man, what would a priest do to stop him?

It seemed pretty obvious that John Preshin couldn't be moved by reason or tears or fear of God.

Father Mike interrupted her thoughts. "Do you believe in miracles, Carly?"

She sniffled. "Not really. Not in my life, anyway. Maybe I believe more in the crapshoot approach God takes to our lives. Good or bad, right or wrong, it's chance that decides whether things go the way we want them to or just the opposite. Then there's the stuff that makes absolutely no sense at all . . . the kind of things that happen without logic. Like if you were shooting dice and one rolled and landed on edge, or fell in the sewer or somebody came and picked it up before you could read it."

"There is that. But until we know otherwise, we can hope for a miracle." His voice sounded hollow, telling Carly that even he didn't believe what he was saying.

The Chevy turned off the main street and slowed at the side of the luncheonette.

John's Jeep sat at the curb.

"Sweet Mother of Jesus!" whispered Mike.

"Holy crap!" Carly bit out. "Holy crap, holy crap, ho-ly crap!" She was out of the car before Mike had even put it in park, running to the door and up the stairs.

John sat at his desk, tapping two envelopes against the oak, listening to the sharp sound they made. Sort of like gunshots.

He'd broken his promise to Dutch. Dutch was dead because of Alfonso Montebroccochetti. Now Dumb Al was dead, but not by John's hand.

Who would have thought Barbara?

Thank God the people from the agency had been there.

His hand went up to his face and rubbed, as he tried to wipe away the scene that kept unfolding in slow motion in his mind.

He ought to wash Alfonso's blood from his slacks and jacket. Damn, the bastard had bled like a pig before he went down.

If she hadn't used the hollow nose bullets, Alfonso would only be in the hospital now instead of the morgue.

He could hear her shouting at him, too, in his mind, as she told the entire world that she knew he didn't have the balls to avenge Dutch.

She was wrong.

He'd decided to avenge Dutch the right way.

Sharp joyful shouts sounded from the stairwell. Ahh.

Carly must be home.

A small smile quirked his lips. He stood and walked to the door. Mike's ponderous footsteps followed Carly's.

Opening the door, he was unprepared for the screech and leap that landed Carly in his arms.

"Oh, God, oh, God, oh, God!" she said. "You're okay. You didn't do it, did you? You're okay and everything is okay. Oh, God."

Tears streamed down her face. John picked her up and carried her into the office. Mike followed.

"I'm here, and I'm okay, kiddo," he said softly into her hair.

"And you're not going anywhere, you're not going to leave me?" She looked into his eyes, her own filled with relief and fear.

"Nope," he said and gestured to Mike to have a seat.

"I'll be going," the priest said. "I just wanted to see if you were all right. The letter . . . ?"

"Don't need it. Don't worry about it. You'll see what

happened on the news, maybe. It was ugly, but it's over and Dutch is avenged."

Mike left. Carly stopped sobbing. John brought her over to the couch where she curled against him.

"I was so afraid you'd leave me."

Her words tugged at his heart.

"I prayed for you."

"You did? You prayed for me?"

Carly sniffled. "I know it doesn't always work. I know you probably don't deserve miracles, but maybe this is one of those crapshoot things and I got lucky and won. There's a first time for everything."

He didn't quite understand her, but he was touched that she'd prayed for him. "Did you think I would leave you after just finding you? You're my daughter! Don't you know how much you mean to me?"

She pulled away, her tear-filled eyes boring into his own. "How did I know? How could I know? Your word, you gave your word to your partner. I didn't know if I meant the teeniest bit more to you than he did."

"Sweet baby," he said as he hugged her to his chest. "There were enough Bureau people there to arrest the entire funeral party. They were looking out for me, I guess, but no one thought someone else was out for revenge. I was just going to nail the son of a bitch and bring him to the cops. Somehow the FBI had the same idea."

"Good," she stated, firmness in her voice that hadn't been there before. "They believed me."

"What? Carly, what do you mean by that last bit?"

"What I mean is, I called the Asbury cops and the FBI and anybody I could think of and told them about the funeral and how this guy was going to be there. I overheard plenty and Curtis told me everything else I needed to know. He's my buddy, Curtis, and he didn't want anything to happen to you."

Typical. Everybody looking out for him, even when he didn't care about himself.

"Remind me to thank Curtis for his help," he muttered. Then, he laughed. Carly pushed away from him, her eyebrows lowered in unspoken question.

"That's what friends are for," she whispered.

"Come on, kid," John said as he rose from the sofa. "I have work to do. And I'm getting hungry. Aren't you supposed to be helping Liz or something?"

"Yeah, I'm supposed to scrub pots. Part of my job to pay for the prom dress. But hey, since you bought it for me. . . ."

"Don't get any ideas. You still need shoes to go with it. And I'm tapped out until I get a check. Soon, I hope.

Carly walked behind the desk, her eyes sparkling with triumph. She saw the two envelopes John had been handling. "Since I'm going downstairs, I can take this to Liz."

He moved quickly and took it from her hand. "No. No need. In fact, I'm going to tear it up. Watch me."

"What was in it?"

"Nothing I can't tell her myself," he said. "Nothing at all."

The three of them watched the news that night, sitting in Flo's crowded living room.

The newscaster droned, "Thanks to an anonymous tip. . . ."

Carly snickered at the words. "Hey, that was me! I gave my name and all."

"Yeah, if they gave your name, little girl, you might have half the Jersey mob after you. Did you ever think of that?" John tugged at his daughter's hair with mock seriousness.

"Um, no." Worry creased her brow.

"Best to be anonymous then, sweetie," said Liz as she stood and stretched.

John caught her eye and motioned for her to join him in the darkened kitchen. She hesitated, then followed him out the door.

He stood, arms dangling, fingers twitching. "Lizzie, now that this whole thing is over, those things I said the other day—well—I still mean them. Most of them. How I feel about you, how I care. Except that now maybe I can be around for you. I want to. If you want me to be."

Sweat trickled down his neck. "I'm not doing too well here, am I."

"Look, John," Liz interrupted, putting her hand on his chest lightly and feeling the quickening beat of his heart, "you've just become a father. I've just started this business and Gram's going to need my help more than ever. Neither of us is in any real shape for anything serious right now."

John shuffled his feet and looked into her eyes. "Not now, but eventually."

"Yeah, eventually," she agreed, her heart thundering inside her. "How about we go nice and. . . ."

"Slow?" He grinned that infectious, guaranteed-to-melt-her smile.

Liz felt a tingle of hope she hadn't felt in a very long time. "Yeah. Nice and slow. Sounds good to me."

John pulled her against him and squeezed. "Nice and slow. I'd like that."

Epilogue

June 11, 2004

Perfect day for the Mary Immaculate of the Grotto high school junior prom. Perfect day for the much anticipated removal of the wall of Palace Casino where Tillie's bizarre yet familiar face leered out at the public. John and Carly and Liz and Flo watched as workmen cut through the brick and freed Asbury Park's most famous landmark from over fifty years in its place.

"Tough seeing him go," Flo sighed.

"Gram, are you okay? Do you want to go back?" Liz asked, her voice full of concern.

"Yeah, pack me into the Jeep and let's go. I think we might have a crowd for lunch."

"Unh! You and that restaurant! We should have closed today. After all, Carly's got the. . . ."

"I know damn well what's happening. There will be people coming in and then there's a little something Rose and I planned for later. We've got to get movin'."

Carly looked from Liz to Flo to John.

He shrugged. "Don't ask me. I know nothing about anything around here."

They drove back to S.R.O., chatting about the big event

to come that evening. Carly danced her way down the broken sidewalk then stopped to peer into the window. Even John who cared little for decoration, had to admit the theater props and costumes really classed up the place. It still had the best coffee and jelly doughnuts in Asbury Park. Perhaps all of New Jersey.

Two hours before the limo was to arrive to pick up Carly, the ladies of the Preshin clan together with the ladies downstairs were abuzz with excitement and fussing over Carly.

"Sheesh, you'd think nobody ever went to the prom before," she observed. "All this for me?"

John stood with his shoulder to the jamb of the door to Flo's apartment. "It's all about you, baby. Your relatives are so happy. I couldn't drive them away. Besides, your grandmother would pitch a fit if I'd told her she couldn't come."

"I'm not getting married or anything. I'm just going to the prom. Geez, what will Choo . . . Jason think when he sees Frankie and all the others? It's like being on display or something. Like a sideshow."

John stood away from the door frame. "You'll get used to it. My grandmothers were both still alive when I took Cheryl Kuchinski to my prom. God, they must have taken a thousand pictures. When I close my eyes, I can still see a big white spot."

"You're lyin'."

"Yes, I am, sweetheart. But it made you smile, didn't it?"

Preshins crowded along the sidewalk outside S.R.O., cameras pressed to their faces, as the stretch limo pulled up, disgorging dark haired Jason, tall and handsome in a jet black tuxedo. John gave him the once over, then a look of warning that would have frightened a lesser man. Good, the kid had balls enough to stand his ground. But he knew who was in control, and it was definitely the girl's father.

Carly carefully minced down the flight of stairs while her cousin Frankie held open the door. A collective sigh passed through the assemblage. John thought he saw a tear in Strap's eye while Curtis and his wife nodded in approval.

Carly Preshin was beautiful. No doubt about it. John's breath caught as he watched her shyly take the flowers from her date and look around for help with them.

John's mother slipped them on Carly's wrist then patted her on the cheek. Whatever she whispered in her granddaughter's ear was strictly between the two of them.

Liz came up behind John, slid her arm around him and asked, "Why do you keep looking up and down the street? Any relatives you didn't invite?"

Twirling her into his embrace, he bent to place a kiss on her soft, ripe lips. Someone in the collected crowd of relatives clapped while others hooted approval. Reluctantly, he broke away. Liz ducked her head and laughed.

"In a way, yes," he said. "Let's see the couple off first, then I'll tell you all about it."

Jason helped Carly into the limousine, handing over her clutch bag and stuffing in the long cerulean skirt of her gown. Carly looked at John and mouthed, "Thanks, Dad."

That was a first! He grinned like a crocodile, startling Jason. But the boy had guts.

With one more guarded look at John, he joined his date inside the limo. A final wave and they were off.

Though the street was lined with familiar cars, John looked up toward the beach once more before tucking Liz under his arm. Man, she smelled good.

From the corner of his eye, he saw the big black Navigator drive away. "What say you and I go someplace and split a jelly doughnut?"

By Best-selling Author
Fern Michaels

Weekend Warriors	0-8217-7589-8	$6.99US/$9.99CAN
Listen to Your Heart	0-8217-7463-8	$6.99US/$9.99CAN
The Future Scrolls	0-8217-7586-3	$6.99US/$9.99CAN
About Face	0-8217-7020-9	$7.99US/$10.99CAN
Kentucky Sunrise	0-8217-7462-X	$7.99US/$10.99CAN
Kentucky Rich	0-8217-7234-1	$7.99US/$10.99CAN
Kentucky Heat	0-8217-7368-2	$7.99US/$10.99CAN
Plain Jane	0-8217-6927-8	$7.99US/$10.99CAN
Wish List	0-8217-7363-1	$7.50US/$10.50CAN
Yesterday	0-8217-6785-2	$7.50US/$10.50CAN
The Guest List	0-8217-6657-0	$7.50US/$10.50CAN
Finders Keepers	0-8217-7364-X	$7.50US/$10.50CAN
Annie's Rainbow	0-8217-7366-6	$7.50US/$10.50CAN
Dear Emily	0-8217-7316-X	$7.50US/$10.50CAN
Sara's Song	0-8217-7480-8	$7.50US/$10.50CAN
Celebration	0-8217-7434-4	$7.50US/$10.50CAN
Vegas Heat	0-8217-7207-4	$7.50US/$10.50CAN
Vegas Rich	0-8217-7206-6	$7.50US/$10.50CAN
Vegas Sunrise	0-8217-7208-2	$7.50US/$10.50CAN
What You Wish For	0-8217-6828-X	$7.99US/$10.99CAN
Charming Lily	0-8217-7019-5	$7.99US/$10.99CAN

Available Wherever Books Are Sold!

From the Queen of Romance
Cassie Edwards

__**Enchanted Enemy**
   0-8217-7216-4 $5.99US/$7.99CAN

__**Elusive Ecstacy**
   0-8217-6597-3 $5.99US/$7.99CAN

__**Portrait of Desire**
   0-8217-5862-4 $5.99US/$7.50CAN

__**Rapture's Rendezvous**
   0-8217-6115-3 $5.99US/$7.50CAN

Available Wherever Books Are Sold!

Visit our website at www.kensingtonbooks.com.

Contemporary Romance By
Kasey Michaels

__Can't Take My Eyes Off of You
   0-8217-6522-1   **$6.50**US/**$8.50**CAN

__Too Good to Be True
   0-8217-6774-7   **$6.50**US/**$8.50**CAN

__Love to Love You Baby
   0-8217-6844-1   **$6.99**US/**$8.99**CAN

__Be My Baby Tonight
   0-8217-7117-5   **$6.99**US/**$9.99**CAN

__This Must Be Love
   0-8217-7118-3   **$6.99**US/**$9.99**CAN

__This Can't Be Love
   0-8217-7119-1   **$6.99**US/**$9.99**CAN

Available Wherever Books Are Sold!

Visit our website at **www.kensingtonbooks.com**.